NIGIRO
RISING

A novel

PATRICIA HOPKINS

NIGIRO RISING (nee-jhee-row)

(The sequel to OUT OF NIGIRO)

Visit my website at http://www.patriciarhopkins.com

Published in the United States by Wanderlust Books LLC

Original Cover Art: Anthony C. Kaczka; IG @ AK_Highflyer2
Cover Design: Kamaldeen Tope; fiverr.com/pro_design190
and Zachary J. Kaczka

ISBN-13: 978-0-9914491-5-6 (Paperback)

ISBN-13: 978-0-9914491-6-3 (eBook)

THIS NOVEL IS DEDICATED TO YOU!

...I AM YOU

YOU ARE ME

WE ARE ONE

~~~ NOVELS ~~~

OUT OF NIGIRO

LOST IN THE OFFBEAT

LOVING IN THE OFFBEAT

LIVING IN THE OFFBEAT

MORE THAN A NOTION

~~~ SHORT STORIES COLLECTION ~~~

I AM THE SHADOWMAN (AND OTHER
SUPERNATURAL TALES)

OLD GRACIOLA YOUNG

INVASION OF THE GLOBOTS

Karma
Whispering Clichés

It is, what it is.
Ya-know-what-I-mean?
For there is nothing new under the Sun.
What once was, is once again,
As everything old becomes new.
The left hand does not know what the right does;
So left becomes right and right becomes wrong
Thus wrong becomes right.
When the light of day morphs into darkness
We will all get what we deserve
Because...
At the end of the day
What goes around, comes around.
C'est la vie!

~ ~ ~ **Patricia R. Hopkins**

NIGIRO RISING
(The Present: The Gift)

Introduction

The sands of time swept over the southeastern region of the United States, courtesy of high-level winds traveling across the Atlantic Ocean from the Saharan Desert in Africa, taking a similar path carved out by numerous destructive hurricanes, to spread tiny particles of dust over North America. The storm that weather forecasters had dubbed 'Godzilla' also "coincidentally" followed the route made infamous by the Trans-Atlantic Slave Trade centuries earlier. Environmentalists and scientists alike predicted the low-level dust cloud formation would be extremely hazardous to those with sensitive respiratory systems, cautioning all to avoid outdoor activities. As a gust of warm wind passed by, I was unfazed by their warnings. I ignored the possibility of triggering my seasonal allergies and deeply inhaled those fine particles of African soil—delicately scenting the air with tropical fragrances of tangy limes, fresh coconuts, ripe mangoes, and all manners of blossoming flowers—not caring if it caused my eyes to itch, my nose to run, or my throat to scratch. I desired to experience the physical presence of the ancestral land; wanting those minuscule particles to become part of me. I wanted to understand what the old folks meant when they used to say the rich soil—from Mississippi or whichever southern state their families had originated—ran through their veins.

I exhaled, trying to dislodge a memory struggling to free itself from behind a mental wall created from living in this world. My spirit momentarily took a nosedive with the realization that after all those years of promising our child we'd take her on a trip to Africa, I now realized that trip would never happen. On the bright side, I was ecstatic because Mother Nature had brought the Motherland here. To me. On the wings of heavenly angels soaring high above the currents of wind. All the way to the United States of America.

Chapter One

My name is Carmen Williams, although I prefer to be addressed by my self-chosen nickname, 'Zumira'. My husband, Gerald, and I moved from St. Louis to Oklahoma City over three years ago, in an attempt to escape the pain we experienced every time we passed by our daughter's empty bedroom. Kenya's abduction had changed me—aged my heart emotionally and my body physically, several times over. Her disappearance almost devastated Gerald. He became wracked with guilt and blamed himself for not doing more to protect his baby girl. With each passing day, Kenya's absence threatened to tear us further apart. We started to avoid one another thinking it would ease the pain. Sadly, it only seemed to magnify it.

The realtor was busy taking photos to emphasize our home's curb appeal. I headed to the mailbox for the last time, stumbling on a crack in the sidewalk with aggressive dandelions pushing through. We had always planned to replace that concrete slab, but never got around to it. My eyes lingered on the "For Sale" sign hammered in the exact spot where I wanted to plant a coconut palm tree, just to see if it would grow in this climate.

We did not want to move again; we had to. Gerald and I decided to sell when the excitement over the book *OUT OF NIGIRO* brought unwanted attention to the neighborhood. Things had gotten so far out of hand that some residents couldn't leave their driveways due to the crowds camped out to capture a glimpse of Oklahoma City's newest celebrity author.

I could tell it was going to be a gorgeous day. I marveled at the multitudes of varietal flowers we planted in the flower bed last fall that had only now begun to sprout. I was very particular with choosing just the right combination of bulbs so we'd have a continuous burst of color when the coolness of spring warmed into the hot summer months.

I recalled countless Saturday mornings standing in the yard holding a coffee mug in one hand and a water-hose in the other. Nurturing the small investment we'd spent on landscaping had all been for naught as we would never have the chance to see the flowers in full bloom. Hopefully, another family would tend to the fruits of our labor and not simply allow weeds to thrive under the forecasted drought conditions. The realization hit me like a ton of bricks. We had spent a huge sum of money fixing up a house we would no longer live in. The effort expended adding wood floors, updating the kitchen with new appliances, and landscaping the backyard to resemble a tropical oasis, would never again be enjoyed by us.

I pushed down the emotions enticing me to rip the sign from the yard and toss it into my neighbor's garbage bin. I had to be cool. The house was now nothing more than a business transaction. We weren't overly concerned about the house selling because Oklahoma City was still considered a hot market. We'd already received several offers at prices well above what we were asking even before it was officially listed on the market.

The sound of someone clearing their throat drew my attention. If I had one complaint about living in a cul-de-sac, even if the lots were over an acre each, it was that our house directly faced the one across the street. The neighbors stood in their garage watching the activity inside ours. When the woman spotted me watching her, she began moving about as if she were searching for something. Her husband tipped an amber colored bottle he was sipping on in my direction as if to say, 'hello'. I thought their behavior was a bit odd, because for the entire time we lived there, we rarely shared more than a few words. Instead of engaging in a conversation, I gave a quick wave and returned my attention to the activity happening in my own yard.

While my dear husband talked business with the realtor, I wondered that by taking this leap of faith and fulfilling Kenya's request, if we were doing the right thing. Gratefully, in the same moment as those inklings of doubt dared to reenter my thoughts, the prophetic words my daughter had gifted to me returned with a vengeance to push them away. A miniscule seed had been planted with the story about the glory of our ancestors. I now knew that we were much more than slaves and our history began well before 1619. We were not only born free, but born as God's children.

As the young man went about his business preparing to put our 'dream house' on the market, I realized the emotion stirring inside me was one of relief. I had no regrets about what we were doing. In fact, I was relieved to be free of the thirty-year albatross of a mortgage that was literally weighing us down with worry about keeping up payments after Gerald and I no longer held jobs. Although I felt liberated, Gerald had mixed feelings about us selling the very home where we had invested most of our hard-earned money.

After making a final walk-thru of the house, I disposed of trash that one of the workers had left behind, and flushed a toilet someone had carelessly forgotten to flush. My husband gathered up the remaining debris in the garage and tossed the items into the garbage can. He did not want to leave any unwanted trash for the next owners to deal with. He did this for no other reason than his desire to leave the house in the best possible condition for the next family. After all, that was the right thing to do.

Releasing a sigh heavy with anticipation of what was yet to come, but weary from all we'd gone through since Kenya's return, I went to my husband's side. I found it difficult to believe how quickly our lives had changed since the book's popularity had taken off. Yet still, in moments of quiet reflection, I sometimes wondered if Kenya's story had been but a dream. Had it not been for the magnificent story of the Nigiro, I might still be questioning myself.

As I stood on the sidewalk staring at the magnificent house that was no longer our home, I pondered my very existence in a world dominated by an archaic set of rules specifically put in place to destroy all knowledge of an amazing people. By trying to live up to the so-called 'American Dream', I understood we had fallen victim to the very system that oppressed us. As far as I was concerned 'American Nightmare' would be a better description of how most of us now lived.

Gerald wrapped his arm around my waist as I rested my head on his shoulder. He was casually dressed in shorts, a colorful button-down shirt and *huaraches* sandals. With a summer-weight fedora topping his clean-shaven head, it looked as if we might be heading out for a vacation instead of moving.

"You ready?" he asked.

"Yeah, I guess I am." I climbed into the truck. I had to admit, it hurt a bit to say good-bye to the house we had carefully chosen to spend out the remainder of our years in.

"I love you," he whispered, briefly taking my hand in his.

"I love you, too."

We backed out from the driveway. None of the neighbors had come to wish us well. On the contrary, they were probably happy to see us go. The attention we brought to the neighborhood had upset the delicate balance of their quiet lives. But I couldn't consider their small feelings. The message in the book was too important.

Gerald slowly drove the few streets of the neighborhood to reach the exit of the subdivision. When he signaled to turn left, he visibly relaxed for the first time in months as if the weight of the world was no longer on his shoulders. Or on his mind. While he drove, silently immersed within his own thoughts, I contemplated what the future might bring for us...

My late grandmother, Nana, Kenya's great-grandmother, noticed my child's 'brilliance' early on. She brought it to my attention when she was just a few months old. Although I couldn't see it, she declared that Kenya was an 'old soul', born under the mark of holiness. I didn't know what she meant at the time, but as my child grew, Nana advised me to nurture her burgeoning spiritual abilities. *'Kenya is destined for a life of greatness'*, she often used to say.

For months after her abduction, whenever I happened upon a teenage girl sitting alone on a park bench, or a young woman strolling down the street with her head slightly lowered, I silently prayed when she looked up, it would be my child. Kenya's oldest brother, Malcolm, pounded the pavement every weekend handing out flyers. My youngest, Stokely, started a 'crowd-funding' account and raised over $10,000 which was used to purchase ad space on billboards throughout the city. After school the boys spent countless hours going door-to-door asking if anyone had seen their sister. The perseverance they displayed in searching for Kenya fueled my heart, yet broke it at the same time.

We kept up the search well past the day the police told us there was nothing more they could do. After only six months, the overworked detective assigned to the case explained there were just too many children being trafficked to invest their sparse resources into finding them all. His well-intended advice was to move on with our lives, because the chances of finding our child were basically nil. We made a lukewarm attempt to get over our loss. My husband and I joined a support group for parents of abducted children, but we quickly discovered the group was filled with parents who were mainly looking to console one another's grief instead of expanding the search for their children. We weren't at that point of resignation, so we stopped attending.

Her brothers became furious at the mere suggestion that they relegate their sister to the unfortunate status given to the hundreds of thousands of missing children as 'unsolved'. They questioned why anyone would even suggest that they simply 'move on' with their lives. Unfortunately, after a year of spending outlandish amounts of money with no leads, we reluctantly ended the search. However, although we had stopped actively looking for Kenya, we never stopped praying for her safe return.

When Kenya first brought up the concept of being 'awakened', I was scared. At her young age, she knew much more than I ever did about what was wrong in this world. She even questioned the phrase, *'one nation under God'*—something she was told to profess in school during the *Pledge of Allegiance*—which was a dangerous position to take in this country.

Initially, I thought Kenya just watched too much television, or was trying to get attention, but she often predicted occurrences before they happened. She was convinced that angels spoke to her. *Who was I to say they didn't?* But after that incident in the Dominican Republic, when she told us that spirits of the forgotten enslaved Africans had reached out to her, I was increasingly worried about her state of mind. So was Gerald. However, keeping my grandmother's advice in mind, I refused to take her to doctors. I did not want her to ever be labeled 'crazy' or diagnosed with some mental disorder. I threw up all kinds of roadblocks in my child's path to discourage her from becoming who she was. Sadly, my husband and I knew what happened to children once they were labeled as 'different'. As a young black girl growing up in these divided states of America, she did not need yet another strike against her. Thus, I tried everything within my power to discourage my daughter's spiritual growth.

I will never forget the day my life changed. It was Kenya's sixteenth birthday. We were planning a surprise celebration that was supposed to begin Friday evening and culminate with a barbeque in the park on Sunday afternoon. Kenya didn't know about the surprise party, but she was excited because it was her birthday. I knew something was terribly wrong when she didn't immediately come home after track practice. The last text I received said she was on her way. But as the darkness of night settled upon us, my concern quickly turned to worry when she didn't answer my calls. We gathered the family members together and tasked them and all our friends to initiate a search of the neighborhood before calling 911. Our experience with the police was they did very little to help locate *our* children. Furthermore, everyone in the community understood that once you contacted the local authorities, it was just as good as giving up all hope.

The following morning with no updates from anyone saying they had found my child, I was a nervous wreck. With heavy hearts, we decided to report her missing. However, because of my daughter's age, the police said there was nothing they could do until 48 hours had passed. When we hadn't heard from Kenya on the second day, that is when I finally accepted the fact that she was gone. That is the moment my world came tumbling down. Kenya was missing without a trace. Lost in the world. Not only to me, but to her father, her brothers, and to all those who loved her.

After the allotted time had elapsed, the police issued an amber alert which resulted in hundreds of tips concerning girls who resembled our daughter. Though none of the tips panned out, the sheer number of 'runaway' teenage girls was absolutely shocking. As I scanned the national website for missing and exploited children, filled with thousands of faces—boys and girls of all ages and races—my eyes were opened to the sheer enormity of it all. It broke my heart when I learned that the vast majority were never found.

For months on end, my life—my family's lives—became consumed with trying to find my baby. Ultimately the police filed the missing person report, surmising that Kenya was probably just another runaway. However, no one who knew Kenya believed she would ever just up and leave. So Gerald and I organized search parties, her brothers assigned teams to hand out flyers to every house within a five-mile radius. We tasked her friends to monitor her social media accounts to see if she posted anything. I took a leave of absence from work. I couldn't eat. I rarely slept. Gerald and I barely spoke to one another unless it had something to do with the search. Despite our efforts, they were all in vain. After a while, my boys pretended it didn't bother them as much, but I knew better. We all did.

And then one day, I simply decided to stop looking. Now, I remember why. I was sitting in the kitchen having a cup of coffee, planning yet another search party. The air surrounding me became very warm and I thought I was having another hot flash, so I put the coffee down. A picture on the refrigerator of Kenya looking surprised because she'd lost her first tooth, fluttered freely to the floor from two magnets which somehow remained in place. I felt a presence—like someone was there with me. Then I heard Kenya's voice as clear as my own. Although I was more than a little freaked out at the time, I believe that is the moment I instinctively knew she was still alive.

Today, with everything that has been revealed to me about Kenya, I now know there was nothing I could have done to stop my child from becoming who she was meant to be. My extraordinary daughter was not abducted, she was rescued!

I believe her when she says she is one of God's Chosen. Because, she is. *And* she chose me and her father to help her fulfill her destiny.

Chapter Two

In the wee morning hours after Saturday night ended and Sunday morning began, I lay in bed struggling to fall asleep. The strange events surrounding that missing day played over and over in my mind until it became like a favorite vinyl record that skips the lyrics in the same spot of a beautiful song. I couldn't dismiss that nagging feeling that I was missing something important. Suddenly, I had the sensation of a hypnotist snapping his fingers to awaken me from whatever hypnotic spell I was under. The memories of Kenya's return flooded back...

Though Gerald was rudely awakened from slumber that took its sweet time coming; he was extremely patient—listening as I explained everything that I remembered. I told him that Kenya had given me this 'thing' that looked like a metallic wireless mouse. Because I was so out of it, I must have forgotten that I stashed it in my office desk drawer for safekeeping. So when that memory returned, I ran straight to the office and pulled the thing out of the desk. I didn't know what it was or how it worked. But when I finally figured out how to turn it on, I jumped with joy!

The look on my husband's face when he came into the office was priceless. We both watched as if some unseen hand had selected the 'print' option. The wireless printer kicked into action, automatically spewing out page after page of typewritten text converted from an unknown language into English. When the printing finally stopped, I carefully retrieved the pages from the printer tray and carried the still warm stack into the living room.

Gerald watched me the entire time, but didn't say a word as I placed it on the coffee table. We both stared at the stack of pages. Thankfully, he took the lead and picked up the first page. He read through it twice, and after he was finished, he handed it to me. And sitting on our living room floor, we continued with this process until we read every single word on every single page.

~ ~ ~

"Gerald, do you realize what this means?" I whispered, waiting for his excitement to kick in.

"Honestly, I'm not sure *what* I just read," he replied, incredulously.

"Oh my goodness! Kenya's alive!" I shouted, my hands trembling with excitement as I held the last page.

He looked at me dumbfounded, and quietly said, "Kenya's alive?"

"Not only is Kenya alive, she is doing some amazing things!"

Gerald, struggling to come to terms with how little he actually knew about his child, dropped his chin to his chest, laced his fingers together as if in prayer, and tried his best to contain the plethora of emotions coming at him all at once; relief, love, apprehension, fear. Guilt.

I searched my husband's face. I could tell by the look in his eyes that he did not share my excitement. I was not about to act like this wasn't the best news ever! I told my husband, "She gave me this story to tell us what happened to her! It's a gift!"

"Zumira, we haven't heard a single word about Kenya's whereabouts since she disappeared. Now she just shows up out of the blue?"

"Not literally *out of the blue*, but I know what you mean."

Gerald peered through the window blinds. The last remnants of dawn had given way to the rising of the sun through a thin layer of pink and orange tinted clouds. A few neighbors were out early that Sunday morning, getting a jump on watering their lawns before the intense heat of the day began to build.

"Oh my God!" I gushed as a quiet thought surfaced. "I know what she wants me to do!"

"What?" he asked with a frown. In his eyes, Zumira was getting a little too excited about something she had no idea of.

"I'm supposed to publish her book!"

While Gerald continued to stare out the window, a string of thoughts swirled deeply within. He didn't wish to sound petty or feel envious of Zumira's spiritual connection to their daughter, yet the hurt feelings were still there. Apparently, this connection was something he and his daughter did not share, considering Kenya had not reached out to him. A troubling question tugged at his heart strings, *why hadn't she contacted him? He* loved his little girl. In fact, he cherished the ground she walked on. Kenya was his pride and joy; the child who filled him with delight each and every time he witnessed her beautiful angelic smile. But he had failed to express those feelings to her. On a regular basis, he chastised himself for failing to have those important father-daughter talks, the ones he promised he would get around to, but never did. His only consolation was to maintain a thread of hope that his child knew how much he loved her.

Watching my husband's expression, I believed his skepticism had far less to do with *disbelief* than it did the ache of our daughter not making her first appearance to him. I knew my husband very well. He was trying his best to share in my joy.

He stepped away from the window, stared at me wearily, and lovingly explained, "Sweetheart... Even if this is her story, we can't put this out into the world."

"Why not?" I asked, looking at him sideways. "Look, we just spent entire night reading about what happened to our daughter! I thought you'd be even more excited than me."

Gerald guffawed. He said, "I'm sorry, but the entire story sounds absolutely ridiculous! People are going to think we've lost our minds!"

"Who cares?!" I shouted.

"I do!" he retorted. "And I don't want anyone to think either one of us is crazy!"

"Now why would anybody think that?"

"Several reasons! Who is going to believe that, one—our daughter is flying around in a UFO with a ten-foot-tall black alien?; Two—God's chosen people are *black?*; Three—you want me to believe that we are spiritual beings having an human experience?"

"I know how it sounds, but we cannot be swayed by what other people feel or think. This is *our* baby's truth." I bound the draft together with a large document clip found earlier in my office. "Kenya intentionally gave this to *me* because she knew I would know what to do with it. I can feel it in my soul. She wants me to publish this because of its importance."

Gerald paced the floor, continuing his rant, "...and reason number four—The title... *Out of Nigiro?!* Really?! That word is too close to Negro *and* sounds way too much like 'nigger' for my comfort."

"Take a breath, my love," I felt his growing anxiety from all the way across the room. I explained, "I think the title is *supposed* to be controversial. It's supposed to make us think."

"I still don't like it, Zumira," he grumbled. "It just doesn't make sense."

"It does when you think about it. Nigiro is the word *o-r-i-g-i-n* spelled backwards. The word 'negro' was an old-world reference to a highly-melanated dark-skinned people. When the natives were asked to what tribe they belonged, our people probably said they were 'Nigiro'. Colonizers thought they heard 'Negro' and because of their dark skin... Well, you know the rest."

"Your logic is a stretch," Gerald interrupted, slowly coming around. "Yet somehow it adds up."

"What's *really* on your mind, my love?"

Gerald took a seat in his favorite lounge chair and then picked up *The Holy Bible* from the coffee table where he kept it for easy reference. He leafed through the book given to him by his grandfather when he was but a child himself. The worn pages of scripture contained sacred text that served to comfort him whenever his world turned upside down. Which was more often than not lately.

I watched my husband struggle with processing what amounted to the unfathomable. The topics Kenya covered in what was literally a dissertation: child abductions, pedophilia, human trafficking, slavery and organ harvestings; the government's plan designed to destroy black and brown communities through gentrification and red-lining; our being the original hue-mans—The Lord's chosen ones. My eyes were opened to see a reality beyond what I was taught.

Notwithstanding the story of their child's return, Gerald simply could not wrap his mind around Kenya having anything to do with a UFO. Or that extraterrestrials were plotting to come down to the planet Earth to rescue black and brown people from further bondage. That concept itself was unimaginable to him. Teetering on the verge of being almost Biblical.

"Love, you read what was on those sheets of paper. How can you not want to put this out for others to read?" I stopped speaking when the sound of a helicopter caught my attention. The thought of those two NSA agents returning was fresh in my mind. Thankfully, the whirring lessened with each passing moment until the helicopter was totally out of earshot.

Also hearing the helicopter, Gerald asked, "You think those men who came to the house last night have anything to do with what's going on?"

"I don't know what they wanted. But what I do know is, I'm not gonna allow a couple of feds to scare me away from doing what I know needs to be done."

"I hear you, Zumi. And if this were any other situation, I might tend to agree with you. But this time... I think things are a little different."

"I cannot just sit here and do nothing."

Gerald allowed his mind to become clouded by the injustices he and others who looked like him had faced for centuries. He uttered, "All that talk about white supremacy and the foundation of this country being built on lies. I know they have done some serious harm to us..." Pausing before continuing, he said, "... and you know me; I'm all about getting the truth out. But this... what I read on those pages...."

I stared at my husband praying that he would not fall to pieces. To believe what we read was possible required a tremendous leap of faith. If I couldn't rely upon Gerald to keep me grounded, we were both in big trouble. Because I believed Kenya's story with every fiber of my being.

With his eyes glazed over by fear hiding in the wings, Gerald shouted, "I do not believe in extraterrestrials! Or aliens! Or that there is a race of ancient superior melanated people from a distant galaxy who travelled to Earth in invisible spaceships! This is madness!"

"Why is it so easy for you to believe in a God of whom you cannot see, but you won't even consider the possibility of the existence of extraterrestrials?"

"That's different..." he sighed, struggling for a sensible retort. "I know *He* is real."

"Listen, I am not comparing the existence of The Almighty God to *aliens*. I am just saying that the belief you hold in an entity that you cannot see should open the door to the possibility that there is more to life than what meets the eye. Consider this... We know even less about this world than we think we know."

"Well, I need to have tangible proof for the existence of aliens..."

"...extraterrestrials," I gently corrected him.

"Like I was saying, Zumira. If you actually want me to believe that extraterrestrials exist, I need proof."

"Be careful what you ask for," I cautioned him.

"I'm just saying, show me!" Gerald insisted.

"For the sake of conversation, let's put aside the discussion about aliens and extraterrestrials. Just for just a moment," I insisted. "Consider everything else that was in the book. Way too much of it was historically accurate for all of it not to be."

He relaxed when he spoke about a more familiar topic when he murmured, "Well... One thing Kenya did get right. She made a good point about white people being evil."

"She's not just talking about 'white' people. She's also describing *capitalism*, a diabolical system with a defined set of unwritten rules and laws that were intentionally put in place by a few unimaginably powerful families to enslave us all. Black, brown, red, yellow *and* white."

"You're right. There are some really cool Caucasian brothers and sisters out there. But those white folks who believe they are superior because the color of their skin is pale... those hateful muthafuckas are delusional. They are the ones we need to watch out for."

"My love, we are all victims of this wicked system. And with everything that is going on to destroy this country, the truth about the original people needs to finally be known."

"Mark my words, Zumira. That book is going to change our lives," he said, wondering if the change would be better or worse. He closed the Bible and returned it to the coffee table.

"Sweetheart, our child returned to us! It wasn't in a dream. Nor was it my hallucination. I spoke to Kenya! She took me up in a spaceship high above the earth! I saw the horizon from outer space!"

"Yeah... You believe you were abducted. Then there's that."

"I never said I was *abducted*. I said I went with our daughter in a spaceship, and as much as I want to remember, I keep drawing a blank on what happened between the time I got into that UFO and when you woke me up."

He clasped his hands together and exhaled so forcefully, his breath tickled my nose. "So you really believe Kenya is living on some other planet with ancient elders?"

"Yes, I do. In fact, I saw one of them!" I pushed down the irritation threatening to surface because if I were in his place, I'd probably be even more skeptical.

"Just when life was finally getting back to a semblance of normalcy, this shit happens!" Gerald huffed.

"Look, I know you're nervous, but I didn't ask for any of this."

"You're right, Zumira," he sighed. Then he asked, "So what else do you think is inside that thing?"

"I don't know. Let's find out." I held the precious metallic object that Kenya had given me and pressed it close to my chest, just as I had done the night before. Unfortunately, this time it did not energize.

"What's wrong?" he asked.

I tapped the thing against my hand. Nothing happened. "I can't get it to work."

"Let me see it..." Gerald examined the mouse shaped thing. He too tapped it gently against his hand before giving it a good whack against the table. It remained about as useful as a paperweight.

"Why won't it turn on?" I asked.

"I don't know," he said, frowning. "That thing is the only proof we have about what happened last night."

"Not the only thing," I said referencing the stack of pages.

Gerald's gaze followed mine. He briefly closed his eyes as if this motion would somehow make the situation easier to accept.

"Honey, we need to be really careful with this," I replied, only now beginning to understand the enormity about what I was getting myself into.

"Let's make a copy. Just in case," Gerald offered.

"I think that's a good idea." I handed him the draft and whispered an unnecessary reminder, "Be extra careful."

"Look... I don't know what happened last night or what you experienced, but I know *you* believe you saw Kenya."

"I did see her."

"Fine," he exhaled. "But have you asked yourself, why? Why would she just show up and give you this?"

"I've been asking myself the same thing ever since it happened. I know there has to be more to this than what we're seeing."

"Like what?" he asked.

"Well... for starters, why is the NSA interested in us? Do you think it has anything to do with Kenya and the UFO?"

"I don't know," he said shrugging. "For all we know, maybe their badges were fake."

"You're not making this any better!" I blurted out, searching my husband's eyes, suddenly feeling very tired.

Gerald gasped, "Baby, you want to know what I'm feeling about now? I feel we're getting pranked for some science fiction reality show. "I just wish I knew what was really going on."

Watching my husband search for an impossible answer to an eternal question, I pondered over snippets of the manuscript's storyline filled with aspects of the supernatural, spiritual, metaphysical and science fiction, all woven together into one fascinating tale. *Although many of the historical aspects cited in her book could be backed with factual evidence, in regards to the spiritual aspect of the story, who was I to judge what was the truth when it involved matters of which I had very little understanding?*

Gerald's expression shifted with every conceivable display of disbelief.

"It's all good, my love," I uttered. In most situations, I deferred to my husband. He was the level-headed one in the marriage, the one who tended to not be swayed by emotions. He was my rock; the one I leaned on when times were tough. I knew my husband well. In time, he would come around to face the truth. And when that happened, we would once again be on the same page.

"You're right. We're in this together," Gerald said, tapping the thick draft of pages against his leg.

I sighed my relief at his declaration. Thank goodness! My husband was onboard much quicker than I had hoped.

"Be right back," he said.

The repetitive sound of the copier spitting out page after page almost caused me to falter in my resignation. The first inklings of doubt began to surface. More questions than answers now swirled inside my mind. Had I received the book through nefarious methods from someone intent on destroying us? Was it possible I had been drugged or imagined the entire episode? Did I actually travel with Kenya inside a UFO that night on the way to see Malcolm? And did she really give me that mousey-looking metal thing filled with an account of her abduction and subsequent life? But most importantly, why? For the umpteenth time since I had awoken in my bed fully dressed with dirty feet, upon discovering I had lost an entire day, I wondered, *'Why did this happen to Kenya? And after all this time, why is she now trying to contact me?'*

It would be several minutes before Gerald would return to the living room. In the meantime, we had to eat. The effects of the coffee kicked in giving me a jittery sensation that would only be relieved by digesting solid food. I went through the motions of preparing a healthy breakfast, minus the bacon or sausage thanks to reading Kenya's revelation that she had given up meat, especially pork. I don't know how I could have missed that important detail in my child's life. Yet I had. Just as well though... While the government was working diligently just to get the latest pandemic under control, meat products had become scarce, not to mention extremely expensive. We eat more grain and vegetables than ever now.

As I rinsed the fresh veggies I purchased from my favorite roadside produce stand, the full weight about what I was about to embark upon settled on my shoulders. Though the load was heavy, my determination to fulfill what I said I would do, won out.

Gerald made his way into the kitchen with the original copy in hand. Dark circles underneath his eyes relayed both a lack of sleep and a profound weariness. His neck muscles were tightly tensed, just like they were when we first heard about Kenya.

He exhaled and said, "All done. I placed one copy inside the safe."

"Thank you, my love."

"You know what, Zumira?" He stared at the manuscript. And within those precious few moments before allowing the space for a response, he abruptly shut it down when he added, "... never mind."

From the corner of my eye, I watched him continue working on coming to terms about who his daughter was. I whipped up a couple of eggs and poured the frothy mixture in the skillet over the vegetables. He watched as I turned the omelet onto a plate, then grated a few slices of parmesan on top, set the plate on the counter, and then pushed it towards him.

"Where's the bacon?" he asked, checking the oven where I usually placed food to keep warm.

"We're out," I replied, relieved to return to our normal everyday banter.

"Any toast?" he asked, taking a seat on the barstool.

"You're in luck. I snagged a few packets of yeast in the grocery store the other day so I was able to bake a couple loaves of bread. Toast should be ready in a minute," I responded, checking the toaster oven.

"Mmm, I prefer your homemade bread anyway. It tastes much better than store-bought."

"I'm happy to hear that because finding a loaf of bread has gotten rough these days."

He dug into his breakfast with gusto. "You're not eating?"

"Not anymore. I lost my appetite. Too much on my mind."

"I understand, but you still need to eat," he said between bites, watching me closely, noticing a change in my attitude. "What's up, Zumi?"

I sighed before speaking, "I think you might be right. Maybe I should wait before rushing into this. After all, it's been years since Kenya disappeared. What harm is it for me to wait a bit longer to make sure what I'm doing is the right thing?"

"Good to hear you're thinking about the consequences beforehand."

"I guess I'd better. No telling what kind of trouble I can get us into if I don't." I leaned forward on the counter as a question formed in my thoughts. "Honey, can I ask you something?"

"Sure..."

At that very moment, a sound, like a strong gust of wind came from the living room.

"What was that?" I asked.

"I don't know," Gerald replied, jumping up from the counter. He rushed towards the living room. I followed closely behind.

We watched in bewilderment as the Holy Bible that Gerald had placed on the coffee table earlier, now laid open. The pages mysteriously turned as if powered by unseen wind. We waited for the fragile pages to become still before making a move. I approached the coffee table, turning to and fro trying to determine from where the breeze had come. The ceiling fan was off. All the windows were closed. The A/C hadn't yet kicked on. There was nothing that could have opened the book. No way those pages should have turned on their own.

"W-w-what just happened?" Gerald asked.

"Kenya?" I asked into the air. "Is that you?" Inasmuch as I knew there was no one physically in the room with us, something or *someone* supernatural was. Considering the past day's events, it would not surprise me if Kenya suddenly materialized.

"What are you doing?" he asked, staring at me as if I had lost my mind. So in order to preserve his, he picked up the Bible. "That's strange. I never earmark the pages. I always use a bookmark, but this page is folded as if it's directing me to a particular passage."

"Which one?" I asked, leaning forward for a closer look.

"Luke 8:16". He began to read the text, " *'No one lights a lamp and hides it in a clay jar or puts it under a bed. Instead, they put it on a stand, so that those who come in can see the light...'* "

I gasped in amazement. I felt faint. Before the fringes of my vision grew dark, I lowered myself to the couch before my knees gave out. Tears trickled down my face as I listened to my husband read aloud. I whispered, "Is that *'The Parable of the Sower?'*"

"No, the one after it. *'The Parable of the Lamp',*" he replied.

"Hmmm," I replied. "What does the rest of it say?"

Gerald continued to read, *"...For there is nothing hidden that will not be disclosed, and nothing concealed that will not be known or brought out into the open...'* "

"You know what this means?" I whispered, as he read through verse 18.

"I'm still not sure, but it looks like we'll be publishing *Out of Nigiro,*" he replied in awe, taking a seat beside me. "Now what was it you wanted to ask me earlier?"

I opened and closed my mouth several times trying to recall what seemed so important just a few moments before. "Never mind. I've forgotten what I wanted to ask."

"Well, it if was important, it will come back later," he said, returning the Bible to its rightful place on the coffee table.

Chapter Three

Later that Sunday... Malcolm, his wife Drena and our granddaughter, Mali Zambia, named in honor of her Aunt Kenya, stopped by the house for our weekly Sunday dinner. Sunday dinners were a tradition instituted by my Nana to keep up with the St. Louis family. It was an occasion when the aunts, uncles, nieces, nephews, cousins, and a few good friends—whoever happened to be around—met over at my grandparent's house to partake in a delicious downhome cooked meal with all the fixings. Once Nana transitioned, GrandPapa went shortly thereafter. A few years ago after both my mom and dad retired, they wanted to remain in Missouri so they relocated to a small mostly black town on the outskirts of Cape Girardeau where several family members had previously moved. My mother is now happily volunteering in a homeless shelter, spreading joy to whomever is within reach. My daddy finally got the chance to paint that 'masterpiece' he always spoke of. Despite the ongoing various global pandemics, we visit with them as often as we can just to see their smiling faces and for me to get one of my father's awesome bear hugs.

My youngest son, Stokely, elected to remain in St. Louis to attend college. He and Kenya were really close, thus her disappearance left a huge hole in his young life. Although we all had gone on with our lives, none of us gave up hope for her safe return. In our minds, against all rhyme or reason, we knew she was not forever lost.

From the kitchen, I heard my son before I saw him. He'd let himself in with the key we provided in case of emergencies; despite us never having an emergency, to both his father's and my amusement.

"Hi Mom," Malcolm said, leaning over to plant a kiss on my cheek.

Shoulder length dreadlocks that smelled of fresh coconut and spicy aftershave tickled my face. "Hey son.

Hi Drena," I said from the kitchen table now used as an extension of my office. The draft of the book was splayed out in two stacks. One consisted of pages I had already typed, and another for those yet to be transcribed. I was only on page seven of two hundred and eighteen.

"Where's Dad?" he asked, peering into the empty oven.

"He's either in the garage or the living room," I replied, continuing to peck each word into the laptop, periodically hitting 'save' during my progression.

"What are you doing?" he asked, sniffing the air searching for signs of dinner being prepared.

"I'm transcribing Kenya's book." I carefully typed each word exactly as it was written.

"You're writing a book about Kenya?" he asked, picking up one of the pages.

"No. I am *transcribing* her book," I explained, motioning for him to return the page to the table.

"Really?" Malcolm asked, studying the text typed in an unfamiliar font. "I didn't know she had written a book."

"You didn't tell me your sister wrote a book," Drena addressed Malcolm. "I think that's awesome! I've always wanted to write a book but never seem to have the time."

I smiled lovingly at my daughter-in-law. Drena had proven herself to be a God-send in a short period of time. She and Malcolm were married after a brief courtship. Drena's parents were Oklahoman Native American— Creek Indian to be specific—and of Croatian heritage on her paternal side. She was strikingly beautiful with emerald green eyes, thick curly black hair that seemed to have a mind of its own, and naturally tanned skin the color of milk caramel. In my eyes and in my heart, neither her color, race, nor ethnicity mattered because she loved my son with a passion. When Malcolm told me Drena was pregnant, my son getting married was the furthest thing from my mind. Initially, I was hesitant to give my blessing to a relationship that had yet to be tested through an entire season, but Malcolm seemed so sure she was the right one. Gerald thought he was filling a void left by Kenya's disappearance and gave the marriage a year tops. But I knew true love when I saw it. Those two were destined to be together. And as a bonus, I was gifted with a wonderful granddaughter. Mali is a beautiful blend of both parents in appearance and temperament.

"Mom, did this sudden urge to become an author have anything to do with yesterday?" Malcolm glanced over at Drena.

"Son, weren't you listening?" I said, trying to not become exasperated. "I didn't write the book. I am *transcribing* it."

"What are you saying?" he asked.

I briefly hesitated before continuing, unsure how to break the news of his sister's return. So, I decided just telling the truth was best. Let the chips fall where they may, as they say.

"This is your sister's testimonial. Each and every word of every sentence is attributed to Kenya."

"Where did you get this?" he asked, looking perplexed while reading a random passage.

"It's a long story," I replied.

He glanced first at me, then Drena before shrugging. He finally said, "Looks interesting. But it doesn't sound like Kenya to me."

"Trust me. This came from her. I tried to change a word with one that I thought worked better, but would you believe this laptop does something weird so I can't change anything."

"Can I see it?" Drena asked, reaching towards Malcolm.

"Don't worry, you'll both get a chance to read it. When I am finished," I said, gently removing the page from his hand.

Malcolm pulled up a chair across from me. His interest, no longer focused on the status of dinner, became set upon those printed pages. "Mom, what is going on?"

"This may sound a little strange."

"Mom, I'm your son. I'm used to strange," he teased. "Go on."

I took a deep breath to calm myself before continuing. I said, "Remember this past Thursday night when I was in the backyard getting ready to watch the meteor storm..."

He nodded.

"I told you I saw a really bright light in the yard..."

"Yeah, you saw a light. Same as me. We agreed that it came from a helicopter."

I shook my head. "It wasn't a helicopter. It was Kenya coming to see me."

Malcolm leaned back in his chair with disbelief written all over his face. Same as his father did initially, proving the apple does not fall far from the tree.

"Now I know how this sounds, but just listen to me."

Drena put the baby down in her carrier and joined us at the table. I marveled at how quickly her pregnancy weight had come off her now slender frame. She attributed breastfeeding to dropping those extra forty pounds while also clearing up her complexion. She told me the bouts of acne that scarred her face had all but disappeared once the baby was born.

"Go ahead, Mama Zumira," Drena said in a soothing voice. She placed her hand atop Malcolm's arm. "No judgement. We're listening."

"That night I heard a very loud noise. It was weird because there was nothing that it could have come from. The sky was clear. But it sounded loud, like a freight train rumbling down the tracks. Then this bright light appeared in the backyard. Like it dropped from the sky right in front of my eyes! When I reached out to touch it, I felt Kenya."

"What do you mean, you *felt* her?" Drena asked.

"Not physically. I sensed her presence. It's a connection a mother has to her child."

"Like how I know when Mali's upset? Like that?" Drena interrupted.

"Something like that. But I not only sensed *her* presence, but also the presence of the ancestors. It was as if they were all joined together as One. Shining through eternity in a brilliant light..."

"Mama Zumira, since I became a mommy, I know that a mother's intuition is real. Maybe that's what you experienced."

"Could be a mother's intuition was part of it, but what I experienced was so much more..." I tried to explain the inexplicable.

"Mom, you don't sound like yourself. I'm going to get Dad."

Drena gingerly tugged Malcolm's arm to encourage him to remain sitting. To just listen.

I addressed my son, "Look, I know how irrational this all sounds because it feels crazy coming out of my mouth. Funny thing was, I wasn't scared when it happened. I felt only pure love permeating from that light."

"W-w-what happened next?" Drena asked.

"Kenya pulled me inside that light with her. It was the most amazing sensation! Then we kinda floated up into this thing that must've been a space ship."

Malcolm was still not convinced. As a matter of fact, he appeared to be even more skeptical.

Drena shot off one question after another. "Is Kenya all right? Did she tell you what happened? Where is she now?!"

To avoid faltering in my determination to tell them what had really happened, my eyes went from Drena, back to Malcolm, and finally resettled upon my daughter-in-law who gratefully didn't look at me as if I had lost what was left of my natural mind. On the contrary, she was very supportive.

"Mom, what's really going on?" Malcolm became frightened by the thought of his very practical mother losing her grip on reality. "Are you all right?"

Intentionally ignoring their questions, I continued on as if I were reliving the moment, "She was only on the ground for a few minutes before we ascended up through the clouds into that UFO. She wanted to see you, Malcolm, so we headed over to your apartment." Thankfully, Drena was hanging onto my every word which gave me courage to continue. I turned to my son and said, "We saw you on the rooftop setting up your telescope, but we had to quickly leave. There was also a helicopter out there that night, so chances are that was the light you saw."

He snickered when he said, "I think I'd be able to tell the differences between a helicopter and a flying saucer."

"Kenya told me that Man's cutting-edge technology is nowhere near the Nigiro's. But that's not why we left," I tried to explain.

"C'mon, Mom... Really? You actually want me to believe that my little sister returned to visit you in a UFO?" Malcolm guffawed, just like his daddy.

I shot him a look that reminded him I was still his mother.

"I'm sorry" he apologized with a profound humility. "Please, go on..."

"She gave me this..." I handed the small metallic object thing to him. "...and asked me to share her story with as many people as possible. It provides an account of what happened from the day she was abducted. It also contains a warning about what is going to happen to us."

Drena, taking note of my last comment, sat back in her chair, vacillating between being excited or scared out of her wits.

Malcolm turned the gadget over in his hands trying to figure it out. "What is this thing?"

"I think it's some kind of hard drive or storage device. Last night when I figured out how to turn it on, it projected the pages onto the wall and then automatically connected with the printer to print that stack of pages you see here. But I can't get it to work again."

"Did you tell Dad all this?" he asked incredulously. He was even more of a pragmatist than his father.

"Of course, I did." I frowned at his persistent cynicism. "I told your daddy everything I just told you. He was there and watched as this text was transmitted to the printer."

"What did he have to say?" Malcolm asked suspiciously. His scientific background resulted in him focusing only on what could be proven. In his mind, nothing about this story had anything to do with facts.

"Hi Malcolm. Drena..." Gerald said, casually entering the kitchen.

"Hey Dad! Hi Poppa!" they replied in unison.

Peering into the refrigerator, Gerald added, "I overheard part of your conversation. And believe me son, when your mom woke me up in the middle of the night and told me what she remembered, I was even more skeptical than you are now. In fact, I'm still trying to process it."

Malcolm remained silent, not wanting to challenge his father in front of his wife. Or mother.

After retrieving a beer from the fridge, he said, "Once your mother showed me what came from that thing. Well, I must admit, I'm still not 100% sure what this all means."

Malcolm chuckled uncomfortably. "Well, we already had this conversation about me and mom missing a day." He tapped the object against the table while searching for a seam to pry it open. "It's just that I didn't expect we'd still be talking about it this morning. I thought it was settled."

"Same here, son. But after we got that visit from the NSA after you left last night..."

Drena perked up right away. "Wait a minute! Did you say the NSA came here?! To this house?"

Gerald rummaged through the utensil drawer for a bottle opener, found it, and then popped the lid off the bottle before taking a swig.

"What did they want?" Malcolm asked.

Gerald calmly explained, "Last night around seven, two men..."

"*White* men," I added.

"Like I was saying, two white men came to the door while your mother and I were having dinner. They said they were polling the neighborhood to see if anyone had seen or heard anything suspicious."

"Anything suspicious like what?" asked Malcolm. "What were they looking for?"

"Did you ask for identification?" Drena added. "Maybe they were trying to scam you."

"We checked their ID's," I explained. "They seemed legit."

Malcolm then said, "Why are you two acting so weird? You're acting like its normal for the government to send agents to your home."

I shrugged before explaining, "At first, I thought the neighbor across the street had something to do with them coming here. Now, I'm not so sure."

Gerald added, "I've also been thinking about why those two *X-Files* wanna-be's showed up when they did. The only sensible explanation is, the government must have been tracking that UFO your mother said she saw out back."

I added, "You might be on to something, love. But they're not going to get any info from me."

"Oh my goodness! That is amazing!" Drena remarked, excitedly.

Malcolm stared first at me, then at his father, and finally shot his wife a disapproving look. Clearly, he wasn't happy that her reactions only seemed to encourage us on.

I sat back in my seat, crossing my arms over my chest. "If you don't believe that something was in the backyard, go see for yourself."

"I'll go look," Drena said, rising from the table.

"There is a patch of green grass that wasn't there the day before," I offered.

"Be right back," she told Malcolm.

In the backyard, Drena came across a fairly large area of newly sprouted grass. She knelt down and pressed her hand into the six-inch growth of tender blades. After determining there was nothing odd about the grass other than it should still be dormant, she then surveyed the entire backyard area. Nothing else appeared out of the ordinary. The small garden was a hodgepodge tangle of dead vegetation. *Look at this mess! I was supposed to help Mama Zumira clean this out and prepare it for planting after the last spring frost. I'd better add this on my list of things to do right now.* She promptly returned to the house through the kitchen door.

"Well?" I asked. My lips pressed tightly together. If there was one thing that annoyed me more than anything else, it was having my integrity questioned.

"It's true. The grass is green in that one spot—in a large circular pattern, but the rest of the yard is still brown," Drena said.

Malcolm shook his head trying to wedge loose a credible argument. He stood up and began to pace the floor before taking a look in the ashtray. He picked up a half-smoked blunt and held it up accusingly.

"That's not it, son. I wasn't smoking that night and besides, weed doesn't give you hallucinations." I shuffled the pages together.

"I don't know, Mom... The new strains they're developing with higher amounts of THC has sent some people to the hospital," he retorted. "You don't know what you're smoking anymore. Some of those dispensaries are selling GMO weed because it gets people higher."

Gerald came to my defense when he said, "Oklahoma is one of the states with legalized medical marijuana so using it is not against the law. And even I know that the most important aspect of cannabis is its medicinal value. When it is used correctly."

I added, "I trust the owners of the dispensary. The sisters are very knowledgeable about the benefits of marijuana. Besides, I mostly use it to ease the pain of my arthritis," I replied. "Lately, I've been having flareups in my hands."

Malcolm explained, "For the record, I'm all for legalization *and* decriminalization of cannabis. After all, it is just a plant. I'm just saying that you need to be careful."

I smiled lovingly at my oldest child and replied, "You don't have to worry about me. I am not going to get hooked on drugs."

"We appreciate your concern, son, but cannabis had nothing to do with a visit from the NSA," Gerald addressed Malcolm.

"And it for sure didn't cause me to hallucinate my child's return."

"Honey," Drena said to Malcolm gently. "Why don't you read it before you jump to any more conclusions?"

"That's what I would advise," Gerald added, taking another sip of beer. "See if the story resonates. If it does, then we can have another conversation."

Malcolm picked up the draft. "Might as well read since there's no food cooked."

I laughed. "Don't worry. I'm going to make dinner. I was just waiting for your daddy to let me know when the coals are ready. We're having barbeque."

"Yummy!" Drena rubbed her hands together in anticipation.

Gerald peeked out the backdoor and reported, "Coals are ready now. Let's get the food on the grill before it goes out because that's the last of the charcoal."

"Mama Zumira, we rarely eat real meat except when we're here," Drena confessed watching her husband head off to the living room.

"Is that right?" I asked, surprised at her admission.

She nodded and explained, "Actually, if it weren't for my employee discount, I'd probably never buy meat because it's gotten so expensive."

"Well, we had to get rid of those pork ribs we had in the freezer. Might as well cook 'em now," I explained to Drena before removing the marinated meat from the fridge. "But be warned, after you read Kenya's story, you'll probably never want to eat pork again. Or any other animal product, for that matter."

"Give up meat entirely?! Is it really that serious?" she asked.

I nodded. "Yes. Fortunately for us, it *is* that serious."

~ ~ ~

It was nightfall before Malcolm put down the last page. Drena and Mali had fallen asleep on the couch watching a movie with myself and Gerald to pass the time. Every now and then, I went to check on Malcolm who had taken up a quiet spot in my office to read. He'd be sitting there staring off into space, totally immersed in the imaginative words from his sister, describing another reality he thought impossible. Although he had to fight back his urges to totally dismiss what he was reading as foolishness and dribble, he knew these were Kenya's thoughts and dreams. There were too many details of her life in the words for the story to have come from anywhere else. At one point, I watched him weep. And being a mother witnessing her child suffer, I went to him, but he waved me off. He had to power through the story on his own to allow his misconceptions, prejudices, and the wall of the only reality he had known all his life to come tumbling down.

When he finally joined us in the family room, he plopped down on the couch next to his sleeping wife and child. Gerald paused the movie because hearing Malcolm's thoughts were much more important than watching Kevin Hart's latest caper.

"Well?" I asked my oldest, noticing the vacant look in his eyes. I recognized it as the same as my own from hours before. "What do you think?"

He dropped his head and gazed lovingly at his sleeping baby, wondering what kind of future was in store for his little girl. He remembered the first time Drena told him she was expecting. Despite their precautions taken to avoid becoming pregnant, and their misgivings about bringing a child into a pandemic filled world teetering at the precipice of WWIII, his daughter, Mali Zambia was determined to be born. And now that she was here, Malcolm vowed to do everything within his power to protect her.

Drena woke up to find her husband looking forlorn. "Sweetheart?" she said, searching his eyes. The dazed expression he wore was not someone who had seen a ghost; it was of one who had discovered the truth. "Are you all right?"

He nodded, but remained quiet as he gathered his thoughts.

"Malcolm!" called out his father. "Say something, son. What do you think after reading your sister's story?"

He picked Mali up out of her carrier seat and gently kissed her on the forehead. "Mom. Dad. I have a confession." He looked at Drena. She nodded her support.

"What is it?" Gerald asked.

"Tell us, son," I added.

"I had a really weird dream last night."

My eyes went to Malcolm, then to Gerald, briefly rested on Drena and then returned to my oldest child. "What are you saying?"

"I'm not convinced of anything yet, but..." Malcolm admitted, "... after reading this, I think it may have been Kenya trying to contact me. To tell me what happened to her. But, I pushed her away."

Drena silently encouraged him to keep going.

"I dreamt of Kenya last night. It was so real. Like she was trying to tell me something. I told Drena about my dream when I woke up. Now that I've read this... I really don't know what to believe."

Words escaped me. Our entire conversation had taken on a surreal quality touching on ancient forbidden topics. Religion, spirituality, and somewhere in the middle—in a place where the truth of those two philosophies collide. *A space that only exists within the offbeat of life...* It was the kind of conversation that Gerald and I called 'high talk', experienced when one was extremely high. But that was not the situation here. We were all sober.

"Mom, I want to believe you. And as crazy as it all sounds, I know you believe that Kenya is still out there..."

As I listened to my oldest son speak, I did not realize I had been holding my breath until I heard an audible sigh escape through my lips.

He looked at me with the eyes of a child, seeing the real world for the first time. "I'm not entirely sold on how you acquired this story, but if you intend to move forward with it, you have to know that publishing this book is going to change our lives. And in the short term, probably not for the better."

"How do you mean?" Gerald asked.

"Her story is a lot to take in," he explained. "What she covered in those pages goes against what we've been taught all our lives."

Drena rubbed the sleepiness from her eyes. She sat up and listened to her husband speak.

"Mom, technically speaking, Kenya is still a missing person. You're going to have to publish it under *your* name. As if you were writing it from Kenya's viewpoint.

And you cannot classify it as non-fiction because among many other reasons, you're not citing documented historical information."

"What do you suggest, son?" Gerald asked, leaning forward.

"Dad, I think Mom should publish it as fiction. A fantasy novel. Or maybe under science-fiction with an emphasis on the supernatural and spiritual elements."

"Malcolm, I understand what you're saying. But this isn't some fantasy. Neither is it science-fiction. This is a true story! A spiritually inspired story!" I spoke stronger than I intended, but this was my conviction.

"Mom, I understand you believe Kenya's story is the truth, but no one else will believe you if it's written as such," he explained.

I sat back deflated. He was right. Even I thought those people who claimed to have been abducted in the middle of the night by little green men were not playing with a full deck. "You're right. As much as I don't want to, her story has to technically be classified as 'fiction'."

"I haven't read the book yet, but I think Malcolm is right," Drena added. "You don't have to limit it to only one genre. It can be published under several. Spiritual, science-fiction, metaphysical, fantasy, mystery, paranormal or any combination thereof. Those who have discernment will see right through to find the true meaning of what her story is trying to convey. How it's promoted to the people is all in the marketing. I can help with that."

"Look, Mom, I know you and Dad don't intend to exploit Kenya's abduction just for the sake of selling books."

Gerald interrupted, "You got that right, son. This isn't about selling books."

Malcolm exhaled long and deep before saying, "And despite the anxiety I have about getting involved, you can count on me. I'm in."

"Me too!" Drena added, excitedly. "What do we do next?"

The relief I felt that my family was behind me one hundred percent was overshadowed only by the tremendous assignment at hand. Time was not on my side. Kenya did not say when the rescue would happen, only that it was imperative that I get the word out. Our world was coming undone one day at a time. The last thing I wanted was for the Nigiro to suddenly appear in the sky above when this book could have warned everyone before it happened.

Chapter Four (Sistah Kenya Returns)

Greetings Sistahs and Brothahs!

During my brief existence on planet Earth, I was more commonly known as Kenya Mali Zambia Williams. I am now recognized by a high vibrational frequency of Love. For those of you with questions after reading about my spiritual journey in the book titled, OUT OF NIGIRO, I confess the story that I shared with my mother is true. The book was *intended* to cross several genres to cause the reader to ponder whether they were reading fact or fiction. What I can tell you is, an important message from The Teacher was woven into the storyline of Out of Nigiro. Those with discernment will recognize the prophecy behind the words; whereas others may never quite understand. Ultimately, I hope that the truth behind the words makes its way through the reader's eye, so that it may be processed with a sound mind, and settle down deep in the heart where it takes root in Love.

~ ~ ~

Many have been called to help awaken God's children. I am one of the Chosen—a spiritual conduit of The Most High God; The Creator; The Almighty; The One. She sends me to places— physically and spiritually—to help others progress along their journey to find the Way. I go where I am told to go. I say what I am instructed to say. I do what I am told to do. Thitherto, I am prepared to spread The Creator's message as instructed, without question.

My tribe is comprised of Artists. I live with an awesome group of Elders which include actors, musicians, painters, poets, and of course, writers. I transcribe stories obtained from the ether to open the inner eye (third eye) of the spiritually 'closed' off brothahs and sistahs. I use my gift of writing to help spread the word about the return of the Nigiro.

There are many ways to reach the children, including using the fine art of music—a popular method to bring peace, harmony and love into the world. Music is a spiritual gateway into the subconscious mind. Therefore, listen to old school artists such as; Earth, Wind & Fire, Marvin Gaye, Mandrill, Cymande, Maze featuring Frankie Beverly, David Sanborn, Teena Marie, WAR, Nina Simone, Stevie Wonder, Hall & Oates, Donald Byrd, Lionel Richie, Prince, George Benson, Sting, The Commodores, Kool and The Gang, Roberta Flack, Count Basie and the list goes on and on. What I have learned is, only a true musician can weave both uplifting and inspirational messages within the notes of their song.

The Elders are always busily creating wonderful artistic masterpieces to be put out into the world to help spread the word of the Nigiro. As for me, they are pleased that I also appreciate many of their other interests like gardening, cooking, reading, and birdwatching.

Speaking of the Elders, let me tell you about one who resides in our village. I met a beautiful Nigiro woman who was so ancient, so spiritual, and so powerful, that she had no need to speak. Her vibration literally translates as, *Seshat*, whom researchers of ancient Egyptians have titled 'the goddess of writing'. However, if any woman was entitled to be called 'Queen' or 'Her Highness', Seshat would be it. Because in every sense of the word, that is what she is. Regal, elegant, beautifully made inside and out, and filled with the vibration of Love. She communicates to me through ultra-high frequency vibrational energy. Seshat has taught me so much about life in a very short time. I'm always curious and asking questions about what I don't understand. She tells me there are great things in store for me. I only have to remain obedient. She revealed that I am her favorite because I do what I am told; when I am told to do it. I am reminded to never question the guidance I receive from the Teacher. And to maintain my faith in The Creator because The Creator is Who we all serve.

Unbeknownst to anyone, I have been in constant spiritual contact with my mother ever since I gifted her with the story about the Nigiro. As a matter of fact, I often slip into the realm of another dimension where I see her balancing a demanding job, family responsibilities, and carving out the necessary time to get my book out in good enough shape to publish.

The Teacher knows the importance of the task given to my parents. Thus, he provides them with supernatural wonders, but never more than they can handle. Natural occurrences such as thousands of white turtledoves gathered together in a cluster of highway-side trees; heavy snowstorms that 'magically' appear on special occasions; a brilliant rainbow that tinges the sky yellow after a strong thunderstorm rumbles by. One time my parents were outside catching some rays when a curious out-of-season honeybee playfully buzzed my father's face as he read aloud a bible passage from the book of Kings. The Teacher was delighted that he uncharacteristically brushed it away instead of stomping on it.

With The Teacher's recommendation, I steered them to purchase two beautiful Ankh rings as reminders of The Creator's eternal Love. The rings include a stylized heart shape representing 'Sankofa', the concept of *'it is not wrong to go back to that for which you have forgotten'.* (My mother thinks the heart-shaped symbol resembles a mighty Queen more so than a backwards facing bird carrying an egg in its beak.) She calls the symbol the 'Queen of Hearts', which amuses the Teacher. My mother and father are both doing wonderfully, but I see the toll all this has taken on them. When weariness sets in, it is important for my parents to keep the faith that my story will reach its intended audience.

After I presented the metallic object containing the account of my journey to mother, I returned to Nigiro filled with a newfound peace. By providing an early warning to the brothahs and sistahs about the impending Nigiro rescue mission, I hoped many would take the amazing story to heart. Although I realized I had placed a tremendous burden on my mother, I have every confidence she would be successful in spreading the word about Nigiro to as many of God's children as she possibly can. Sadly, with no knowledge about the existence of other worlds, they believe that the world they live in is all there is.

The existence of planet Nigiro is known worldwide by scientists and researchers alike—although they have intentionally kept this knowledge hidden from the general public. Earthlings have been trying to communicate with Nigiro, but have been unsuccessful because they are using infantile technology. They might as well be children trying to make a phone call using two tin cans strung together by a string; it would achieve the same result.

I first discovered highly melanated people lived on other planets purely by accident. While in flight training, I was trying out the orb's navigational system because I heard it could zoom all the way down to ground level view. I wanted to see how it worked, so I picked a random planet with an atmosphere that was similar to earth's. I remember how excited I was hoping to see a real alien lifeform! Imagine my delightful surprise when I saw the 'alien lifeforms' resembled distant family members. I later discovered the aliens were actually Nigiro!

Now, when I tell you our planet is paradise, I only speak the truth. Forget the pictures of paradise you've seen in magazines. Those images do no justice to help describe our beautiful planet. The temperature is always comfortable. I can go outside without freezing or becoming overheated. The air is so clean it smells sweet. Like a marketplace filled with freshly cut flowers. You can drink water straight from a stream. And the sky! Oh my goodness! If you think you've seen wondrous colors when you've vacationed in the Islands...! Your eyes will never want to close when they gaze upon this magnificent world. I love the colors turquoise, mango, and sea-foam green! The colors orange, cherry red, deep blue, and fuchsia are naturally found everywhere! However, purple is now my most favorite color. Velvety purple flowers abound here in so many beautiful vibrant shades, it makes my eyes tear with joy just thinking about them.

To compare Nigiro to a tropical island left untouched by colonizers is the closest description I can get to being accurate. When I inhale the fragrance of the land, it reminds me of how dirt on Earth used to smell, before my father and every other family in the neighborhood started using chemical-based fertilizer treatments to help keep the weeds in their yards at bay. But the best part is, everything I plant grows! The vegetation receives an extra dose of chlorophyll courtesy of the immense amount of sunshine.

My familial seaside compound is comprised of numerous stately homes dotted throughout the luscious landscape of rolling hills blanketed by blue-green grass and colorful wildflowers. Ancient cypress oak-looking trees draped with sheets of hanging moss grace the inlands, while tall palm trees of every variety grow wild and free along the coastlines. Everything on Nigiro is beautiful! I feel like I am living in a resort villa in the Dominican Republic, similar to the one where my family vacationed, but so much better!

Our two-story mansion was built so long ago, the elders don't even remember when it was constructed, nor why it was located on the top of a hill facing the sea. I am thankful though, because I absolutely love the unobstructed view of the turquoise water from the balcony! Sometimes I fall asleep listening to the waves come ashore. But as nice as it is, I rarely spend time in my suite, unless I am sleeping, which I rarely do now. I discovered that I don't need as much rest because there are no stressors here for my body to recover from!

The décor of the home reminds me of old photographs showing how African royalty lived during a time when they ruled their own countries. Before the colonizers arrived on the continent and set up shop. Although the mansion is truly magnificent, a spacious courtyard located right off the kitchen is one of my favorite places to hang out. An humongous tree that looks as old as the mansion itself, grows in the center of the courtyard in dirt hardened by centuries of use. The tree is so tall that I cannot see the top, and its above ground roots have grown so high that I can easily walk underneath—the much taller Nigiro sistahs, not so much.

Pretty plants and colorful flowers sprouting from decorative terracotta pots fill the sunny space of the courtyard. Butterflies in all different sizes, shapes and colors love to flutter over the fragrant flowers while they curiously watch me. And on those rare moments, when I want a quiet place to read or just think, I grab a healthy snack and then plop down on one of the surprisingly comfortable wooden benches in the shade of the ancient tree. The relaxing sounds of brightly colored birds singing songs of love, makes the area that much more pleasant.

The Nigiro are a loving and peaceful people, so I am safe here. The villages I have visited are all marvelous in their own unique way. I live in a beautiful house, in a beautiful village, on a beautiful land. Everyone is family, thus the word 'stranger' is not in the lexicon. Love abounds in all we do. There are no rich; nor are there poor. There are no guns, murderous rampages, or wars imposed on innocent people. Crime does not exist. We all have exactly what we need to enjoy a prosperous bountiful life. To tell you this, you would not believe me unless you see it for yourself. One day, I hope that you will!

There are many men who graciously tend to landscaping the compound grounds, so I don't have to be concerned with doing those chores. For real though, it doesn't take much to make the grounds of what amounts to paradise any more beautiful than how it naturally grows. Just a bit of pulling a few weeds here and there and the rest takes care of itself.

The main garden is tended to by everyone who lives in the house so all will know how to grow food. The elders have shown me how to help plants become bountiful. Yes, there are many insects and some are poisonous, but when left alone none seem to bother us. My family—I say family because we are all related in some form or fashion—often walk barefoot through the thick grass with not a care in the world of injuring themselves.

As we live near the sea, I am blessed to be able to walk to the coast—day or night—and dip my toes into the cool water. As the sun settles in the eastern part of the sky, when the first of two full moon rises, one shortly before the other, I listen to the gentle waves lapping against the shore, being lulled asleep by the soothing rhythmic sounds courtesy of the lunar nature cycle.

On those rare days when I am feeling a bit blue—from missing my earthbound family and friends—I wander just a short walk from the compound to my very favorite spot at the seawall to watch the sunset. The winding gravel road takes me along a path of breezy shade trees that opens up to the beach. Mangrove-type trees, some with branches drooped to eye-level heavy with oddly-shaped fruit that sometimes prick my skin as I make my way to the water. It's worth it though, because it leads to a very peaceful setting where I can watch the sun set. I love how the wind uses the waning sunlight to paint the wispy high clouds differing shades of pastel colors, just because it is delightful to see.

There is ample time to relax, and although my days are loosely structured, I make good use of my time while I am here. For example, in addition to my daily lessons, I am studying seven spiritual aspects: Truth, Holiness, Faith, Wisdom, Power, Grace, and Glory. What I continue to discover is, there is so much more to learn!

I am also learning how to use my mind to move small objects. When I am stronger, I will have the ability to move larger, heavier objects with only a thought. I once believed telekinesis was the coolest lesson until I discovered levitation by accident! Learning how to teach this heavy body to fly is much more difficult than I ever imagined, but I vow to continue learning until I grasp that as well. I have discovered that I do well at practically everything I put my mind to.

Since I no longer physically reside on earth, my body has become hypersensitive to stressors in the earth's atmosphere. I discovered that constant exposure to a toxic environment rampant with ultra-low frequencies had a negative impact on my body. Therefore, I am learning how to raise my vibrational frequency. In time, I will have the ability to master every cell of my body to resist all harmful viruses, bacteria, illnesses, diseases, ailments, maladies, afflictions, and cancers.

~ ~ ~

Brothahs and Sistahs, I have shared much more than I intended, but I want you to know there is so much more to life than any human eye can see. Look inside yourself! There you will find the most beautiful spirit waiting to be discovered. I could be here all day telling you about my wonderful life on Nigiro, but as great-Nana reminded me in the astral plane, *'Times a wastin'!'*

The Teacher often stops by to check on me because my journey is not yet complete. He said that when I first became his pupil, I was only using about 15% of my brain's power. Now, I'm using closer to 48%, and increasing by the day.

One beautiful sunny day, I was out planting seeds in the garden for next season's crop when I felt a powerful presence. I stopped what I was doing, stood up, and then shaded my eyes as I looked towards the entrance of the compound's graveled path. I was filled with delight when I spotted the emerald green sparkly exoskeleton spacesuit. It was The Teacher! He stood near the gatepost, patiently waiting for the right moment to catch my attention. My heart leapt inside my chest when I realized he had returned! I rested the tiny vegetable seeds on a leaf I found on the ground, and then placed a small white stone on top so I wouldn't lose track of them.

Before I realized it, in my excitement, I was levitating again! With nothing more than the powerful thought of seeing the Teacher, I flew-floated at least three feet off the ground towards him with my arms outstretched. I dropped down at his feet and relayed, *"Teacher! Teacher! What a nice surprise!"*

"Braveheart, it is so good to see you again. I see you've done well with your flight instruction," The Teacher relayed in return.

"Thank you so much for stopping by!" I said, catching my breath. "Flying is so much easier when I simply 'let go' and stop thinking about what my body is doing."

He spoke aloud, "Where the mind goes, the body follows." Tiny crinkles appeared around his eyes as he released the most beautiful smile that lit up his already sun-kissed face. He was just as delighted to see me as I was to see him.

"Teacher, you did not tell me that Nigiro is a real-life paradise! It is more than beautiful here!" I gushed, unabashedly. "And I have learned so many interesting things about myself. And the Elders... Oh my goodness! They are positively amazing!"

"Indeed," he replied, amused. Then, he said in a voice barely above a whisper, "It is time."

As I knew this day would ultimately arrive, I relayed, *"I think I know why you have returned."*

"Tell me," He commanded, telepathically.

I did as requested, relaying, "I presented ourstory of the Nigiro to reach The Creator's children. A precious few comprehended the story as intended. Others, unable to discern the message behind the words, dismissed it entirely. What saddens me most is way too many never got around to reading the book at all."

The Teacher did not speak, listening to what he already knew was true.

"Because I now know who I am, I must return to help awaken more of The Creator's children; not only in my family, but to those scattered throughout the world. The children are in deep trouble. Evil is running amok amongst them and most don't even realize what is happening. I must also remind them to be mindful when using man's technology; for the ruler of the kingdom of the air is now at work."

The Teacher relayed back, *"You are correct, Braveheart. Living in this world has resulted in mass confusion within the minds of the children."*

"What more must I tell them?"

"Remind them to pray. Morning, noon, and night. Tell them to remain steadfast and vigilant. To persevere. To honor The Greatest Commandment cited in Matthew 22:37-40."

"Thank you, Teacher." I said, as a flash-back of vacation bible school surfaced from my memory. Although we had stopped attending church, my daddy wanted us to at least know how to read the bible, "Is there any particular passage they should focus on?"

"Reciting The Lord's Prayer aloud provides comfort," The Teacher explained.

"I remember The Lord's Prayer. I was taught to recite it from the King James Version like this..." I bowed my head and prayed, **"Our Father, who art in Heaven, Hallowed be thy name; Thy Kingdom come. Thy Will be done on Earth, as it is in Heaven. Give us this day our daily bread. And forgive us our trespasses, As we forgive those who trespass against us. And lead us not into temptation, But deliver us from evil. For thine is the kingdom, The power, and the glory. Forever. Amen."**

"Perfect!" He relayed. *"You did very well."*

"Thank you. My parents always said I was a good student." I smiled just thinking about them. We walked towards the house; stopping near the vegetable garden.

"Braveheart, you are a quick study. I know you will do as instructed."

I nodded, graciously accepting his approval.

"I see you've been busy." He replied, while surveying the garden plot.

"Yes, Teacher I have been very busy with my lessons, but also with this. I've discovered it doesn't take much effort to grow plants here. Doesn't matter what seed I place in the ground—fruit, vegetables, flowers—everything grows as if I've doused it with Miracle Gro, the stuff my mother once used."

The Teacher turned to focus on the compost bin I started in a section of the garden. Upon the recommendation of an Elder well versed in horticulture, he recommended the food scraps be located away from the main house to avoid drawing insects. Upon discovering compost, I learned the best fertilizer comes from nature.

He relayed, *"There is no need to improve upon what The Creator has perfected, for the soil is extremely fertile on Nigiro. Adding chemicals would only serve to compromise the integrity of the plants."*

"Sunshine, water, and natural fertilizer is all that's needed." I agreed, plucking an aggressively growing weed from between two rare tomato plants. I tossed it right in the garbage container before it had a chance to root and take over.

The Teacher stood to his full height, towering over me. In a gesture that only he could pull off, he gracefully crossed those long arms behind his back, resulting in him appearing even more dignified than before. He relayed, *"Braveheart, I want you to put aside your gardening for a moment and focus. Why have I come for you now?"*

I surprised even myself when I shouted out, "It is time to return to save the Brothahs and Sistahs from generations of bondage! To help free the minds of the Nigiro! They must know the truth about who they are. Through the delicate weaving of words I presented to my mother, many will be able to follow me on my journey to reach the truth. The MA 'at. The Almighty One. The Way. All hands on deck!!!"

"Very good, Braveheart. You understand perfectly."

"Teacher, I need a few more days to make sure I have everything to complete my assignment. I want to make sure I get everything done correctly,"

"Absolute perfection is not attainable by humans." The Teacher relayed his response, *"Evil is knocking on the spiritual doors of The Creator's children searching for ways to get inside. What the children do not know is, once they invite evil in, whether intentionally or not, it takes effort to get rid of it. With diligence and prayer, removing unclean spirits from one's space is possible. That said, I understand."*

"Thank you," I replied. Though he had acquiesced to my request for more time, I instinctively knew we didn't have time to waste.

"Go on..." He encouraged me. "What else?"

I spoke aloud the thoughts transmitted into my mind by the Teacher. "I must tell the brothahs and sistahs to be very careful about who and what they allow into their homes. Many fast-talking people will try to entice them with empty promises and extravagant gifts. They must use discernment. If someone's spirit doesn't resonate highly with theirs, do not engage any further. Nor should they feel obligated to accept invitations. This advice is given freely to the children for those rare moments when they are feeling overwhelmed by negative vibes; call on The Creator for backup. Because we are never alone in this fight against evil forces."

"Well done, Braveheart. I shall return in three days."

"Thank you, again," I sighed with relief.

The Teacher raised the teleportation-object to chest height, stepped forward, and instantly dematerialized into the tropical air. A momentary vibration outlining his body fizzled away until nothing remained. Several waves of intense ultra-high frequency vibrational energy moved through me, as if I had wandered in the midst of an electrical field. Then the energy was gone. I stood alone, momentarily pondering my next move.

As I prepared myself, physically and spiritually, to return to the earth, I figured that temporarily wading in the low vibrational field was worth it if I can at least wake up others spiritually. Truthfully, I do not wish to remain down there any longer than is necessary. My plan is to get in and get out unscathed. When it is time for my return to Nigiro, I pray that renewing my mind won't take as long as it did the first time. The 'real' world may sully my spirit temporarily, but I am positive I will find my way home again.

I am appreciative that the Teacher has a good sense of humor. He occasionally likes to surprise me with something totally unexpected that puts a smile of delight in my spirit. Instead of providing a complete solution to my problem or question, he often gives me clues or riddles to solve. I never know what he's going to tell me, show me, or give me. But I know he already knows I need a little more time. He knows everything.

A gust of warm air came out of nowhere to gently ruffle the scarf I wore to protect my hair when I gardened. Yes, even on Nigiro, I still had to consider my haircare routine. As I gripped my scarf to prevent it from flying away, I knew the breeze came from the Teacher. Thus, a big smile covered my face when I realized that because I followed his instructions carefully, I had pleased him.

Sistahs and Brothahs, I want you to know, that the very moment The Creator declares 'Now!', we will arrive in less time than it takes to blink an eye. Swooping down like powerful birds on a mighty wind to clear away the filth and corruption of a chaotic world in order to prevent its total collapse. Believe me, no one will see us coming.

Chapter Five

Traffic on I-35 headed to downtown Oklahoma City was a total mess on Monday morning because of light rain. I passed by at least four accidents on my way to work. While listening to the DJ banter of the local morning talk radio show, I glanced at the name tag attached to my old battered *St. Louis Cardinals* lanyard hanging from the rearview mirror. 'Carmen *'Zumira'* Williams', it read. The funny thing is, I no longer recognized who that name represented. My entire attitude had shifted in the span of a weekend with the discovery of my child's well-being. Learning that our ancestors came from a mighty ancient civilization that originated from a different world, had awakened me to see life differently. Just the thought of spending eight hours at the job and an hour traveling to and from the office, felt like a huge waste of my precious time. What seemed so important when I left work on Thursday, no longer mattered today.

I finally made it to the office, after checking in with the guard assigned to screen all employee and visitor temperatures upon entering the building. Thankfully, today, mine was normal.

As I settled in my cubicle, listening to my coworkers piss and moan about the lack of live sports and their disappointment that another sports season had been cancelled due to the ongoing global pandemics, I wanted to scream at them all to 'Wake the fuck up!'. Whether we knew it or not, we were all living in a great big lie.

Doing my best to take my mind off how to publish my daughter's book, I focused on the hundreds of unread emails that had flooded into my inbox from last week. Just as I was about to respond to one marked 'urgent', I was surprised when Meredith, my supervisor, sent me an instant message requesting my immediate presence in her office. "Really?! It is too early for this shit," I uttered under my breath. Because I had missed work on Friday without calling in, I had a nagging suspicion this was what the unscheduled meeting was about. I was not about to let my guard down. I gathered my wits about me, scooped up the laptop, and headed to the woman's workspace. I knocked briefly on the open door.

"Carmen, come on in," Meredith said, glancing up from whatever she was working on. "Have a seat."

Only at work was I addressed by my given name; I preferred it that way. I did as requested, my eyes scanning over dozens of pictures of dogs and horses that graced the walls of her office.

"How are you?" she asked, looking for a longer response than I was prepared to give.

"I'm fine, Meredith," I replied, hesitantly. "How are you?"

"You know... Taking life one day at a time."

"I hear ya." I looked at Meredith closely. Something was different about her today. It wasn't her weight. Aha! She had a new hairstyle! And it was dyed platinum-blonde! I sat amazed watching each strand move in succession with the others whenever she made a sudden movement of her head. The pageboy cut was intended to accentuate one's jawline, but hers was not well defined. The style was not flattering on her. I searched dull expressionless eyes that occasionally changed color like a mood ring from back in the day. Today, they were grey. Which put me on notice that nothing good would come of this meeting.

"I see you got a new haircut," I said, flatly. Although I had picked up on her melancholy mood, she remained clueless as to mine.

She suddenly giggled like a teenaged girl instead of a thirty-six year-old woman. "Yeah, I had it styled over the weekend. I wasn't sure about the cut though..." She replied, fishing for a compliment.

"It's a great hairstyle..." I replied honestly, but I didn't finish with the most critical part of the sentence, '...it just *doesn't look good on you. And that color?! Girl, what were you thinking?!'*

"Thanks. I was hoping the look wasn't too... extreme," she stated, self-consciously touching her hair.

No longer interested in discussing her choice of hairstyles, I asked, "So, what can I do for you?"

Meredith squirmed uncomfortably in her chair before blurting out, "Carmen, is there something I should know?"

"What do you mean?" I asked, noting her discomfort. I fought back the innate urge that overtakes many older black women—the urge to make others feel comfortable, especially white people.

"Anything I should know about... outside of work?"

I shook my head. "Nope. All is well."

She continued to flounder her words, "Great. Nice. Yeah...Um, that is awesome to know. Things are going well..."

I nodded, hoping she would get to the point. I had work to do.

Meredith twiddled a pencil between her fingers. Struggling to find the right words, she muttered, "Well... Uhm.. Look... the reason I asked you to my office is, I need to know why you didn't come to work on Friday. You didn't even bother calling. What's going on?"

I sat back in the chair, allowing my thoughts to gather before I spoke. I was not about to say something I would regret later. The memory of my child's strange return and the magnificent story she presented were too fresh on my mind.

Meredith placed her crossed arms on the desk. She leaned forward taking an authoritative posture, because that is what she was taught to take when having difficult conversations with employees.

"It's personal," I replied, defensively. "But I promise next time I need to take the day off, I'll make sure I call in first."

"That's fine. Just don't let it happen again."

Meredith obviously missed me rolling my eyes and twisting my mouth sideways at her. Or she choose to ignore it.

"Carmen, remind me again. How long have you been with us?" she asked, glancing at her computer screen.

"Two and a half years," I replied. "Same as you. We attended the orientation together. Remember?"

"Oh yeah, that's right," she chuckled softly. "I forgot."

I held back mixed emotions when the truth behind Kenya's words threatened to send me flying across that desk. Reading about the Nigiro opened my eyes to the possibility that an entirely different world exists. If that was true, I had nothing to lose. I boldly said, "Meredith, when we first met, you told me that until you got this job, you had never held a regular job in your life. I never thought about it until now. How did you reach your thirties and never have a job?"

She responded honestly, "My family is in the casino business."

"I thought you had to be Native American to operate a casino..." I interrupted, staring at the one of the 'whitest' women I have ever seen.

"My family's names are on the Dawes Roles," she explained with a wink.

"Oh..." was the only response I could muster. My husband often spoke with disdain about the so-called 'five-dollar Indians' whose ancestors paid money to have their family names added to the *Dawes Rolls*.

"So anyway, up until this job, I never had the need to work for a living. But when we had to shut down the family business because too many of the workers were getting sick from the virus, I had to get a job. So, as a favor to my daddy, my uncle hired me to learn the ropes of his company. Now look at me! The head of my own department! My family took bets that I wouldn't last six months."

"Well, you sure proved them wrong," I responded, amazed by her continued lack of self-awareness that the only reason she'd gotten the job and a promotion was due to nepotism.

"Yes, I did. But that's enough about me," she quickly shifted her demeanor. "Now, back to you. Let's see here..."

"What's the problem? I already told you that it won't happen again." I was this close to telling her what she could do with that job.

She snickered while she continued to peruse the screen.

"What are you doing?" I asked, trying to maintain my composure.

"Just reviewing your HR file." She made several more keystrokes before hitting the print function. She spun around in the chair to retrieve the form from the desktop printer. The obedient haircut followed a millisecond later. "I need you to sign this form, please."

"What is this?" I asked, carefully reading the paper.

"I've put you in for a raise and a bonus. I just need you to sign your acknowledgement. It'll show up in your next pay check."

"What?" I asked, perplexed. "What did you say?"

She smiled as she explained, "You have been such a huge help to me these past couple of years. I couldn't have advanced this far had it not been for your support."

"Wow, Meredith. This is unexpected. I had no idea. Thank you." I scribbled my name at the bottom of the form and handed it back to her, still feeling a bit unsure about what had just transpired.

"Perfect!" she exclaimed, cheerfully. "Give me one minute and I'll make a copy, then you can be on your way."

I was shocked that she had taken the time to acknowledge my hard work. This was so unlike her. So I waited patiently while she huffed and puffed her way around the copier. When she glanced my way, without her uttering a single word, I understood she was waiting for me to offer assistance. Because that's what I always did. When she couldn't figure something out, whether it be how to use a spreadsheet, setup a multiple person conference call, pull up a file from a secure website, or how to use the printer, she called for me.

"Um..." she grinned, embarrassment coloring her cheeks a brighter shade of crimson. "Can you please help me with this thing?"

"Sure," I replied, going around the desk to push the necessary buttons. In a matter of moments, the printer kicked on. I retrieved the form and handed it to her.

She initialed the copy and then returned the paper to me.

"Thanks," I uttered,. "I really didn't expect..."

Meredith's office phone rang interrupting our meeting, rescuing me from embarrassing myself any further. She accepted the call and characteristically waved me off.

I returned to my cubicle. I stared at the letter feeling some kind of way. *What just happened? I expected a reprimand, but instead get a raise and a bonus?!* My hands suddenly began to tremble from an influx of adrenaline rushing in. My heart raced. I tried to catch my breath by gently pressing my hand over my chest. An overwhelming feeling of déjà vu overtook me as I sat in my chair. But something was off. Meredith was rarely kind to me.

Holding on to a decent paying job, particularly in a field that was becoming dependent on artificial intelligence for mundane functions, was becoming more of a challenge each day. With the direction technology was going, there was no telling how long my services would be needed. Whereas Meredith's position was firmly secured in their family business, mine stood precariously in the balance.

Reading Kenya's summary of the state of the United States of America had opened my eyes. I recognized we were all living an illusion. The threadbare quilt of the

American landscape was slowly unraveling, being tugged apart one piece at a time.

~ ~ ~

Later that evening when I made it home from work, I was exhausted—mentally and physically. I went straight to the bathroom, emptied an entire bag of scented salt into the tub, put on some mellow inspirational jazz, and then sank into the hot water. Gradually the stresses of the day melted away and subsequently snaked down the drain when I pulled the plug. Toweling off in the mirror, I took a good long look at my face, wondering who the woman staring back truly was. My daughter had learned the truth of her greatness when she was only sixteen. Here I was, a middle-aged black woman living a middle-class existence in America. Up until a few days ago, I thought I knew who I was. I believed Gerald and I had 'made it'. We were living our best lives. But now, I began to question if my entire life had been built upon an ugly lie.

It was well past seven before I made my way to the kitchen to peruse the contents of the refrigerator. Gerald would be home at any moment. We still had plenty of leftover baby back ribs in the deep freezer, although now the thought of eating pork no longer seemed appetizing. However, we couldn't afford to waste food, especially meat, which was becoming more and more scarce. So I popped half a rack in the oven, tossed in a couple of new potatoes and made a salad. Then I sat down at the kitchen table and began to transcribe where I left off yesterday.

Gerald walked in fifteen minutes after I'd only gotten through about half a page.

"Hello love," he said, leaning over to plant a kiss on my cheek. "How was your day?"

"I had a very interesting conversation with Meredith."

"Really. What is little 'Miss White Privilege' up to now?"

"You won't believe this, but I am getting a raise *and* a bonus for all the hard work I've done for the company."

"What?"

"Yeah, she called me in her office and gave me this," I handed the copy of the letter to him.

"For real!" he smiled, reading the letter. "That's great news!"

"It is..." I twisted my mouth sideways. "But it isn't. Not really."

"What do you mean?"

"Don't get me wrong. I mean... I am thankful that my hard work was recognized and rewarded. But..."

"But what?"

"Just the fact of that woman having the authority to make decisions about my life leaves a bad taste in my mouth. If she can put me in for a raise means she can do almost anything. We started working for that company on the same day. I do all my work, plus most of hers. But since she is the owner's niece, she gets the promotion to be my boss. It ain't right!"

"Which part, Zumira? The nepotism? The white privilege? How about an entire capitalistic system that was setup to specifically be against black and brown people?" Gerald sat down to untie his shoes. He slipped them to the floor with a sigh of relief. "Well, at least you're getting paid well. We can do a lot of good with your bonus."

"You're right," I released a weary sigh. "It's just that ever since reading Kenya's story, nothing feels the same anymore. It's like once my eyes were opened, I cannot close them to any injustice. For real, I'm not sure how much longer I can work at that company."

"I understand." He nodded with empathy. "My day wasn't any easier to get through."

I replied, "Meredith seemed different today."

"How?"

"She was acting weird. Something about her behavior that was 'off'. Plus, she came to work with that crazy hairstyle," I said.

"Whatever it was, I'm happy you benefited from it," Gerald replied. "We can use that money to fix a few things around the house."

"Yeah, I guess," I sighed, realizing I was putting way too much energy into thinking about my supervisor. "Even though the company finally recognized my hard work, it bothers me that someone like her—with no education or experience—can basically walk in off the street and get that far ahead of me. I can run circles around her with what I know."

"Baby, all you have to do is say the word. I make more than enough to take care of us, if we cut a few luxuries. Unfortunately, Stokely's tuition payment for the next semester is coming due. So is his rent to your brother, Ricky." He shuffled through the stack of mail in his hands. "Not to mention the first and second mortgages, utilities, car payments, and insurance due at the end of the month. Shall I go on?" he said with a smile.

"Don't worry. I'm not going to quit. Not yet, anyway..." I glanced at my husband imagining the full weight of our financial burden resting squarely on his shoulders. We could make it on his pay, but just barely. If we cut lots of corners, got rid of my car, and told Stokely he'd have to find a better paying part-time job to help pay for school. But neither one of us wanted to go down that road. We'd figure a way to make it all work. Just as we always had.

"I'm not worried," he said with a grin. Changing the subject, he proclaimed, "I was thinking about the book earlier today. What if it takes off and becomes a best seller? Then you won't have to work."

"That's a wonderful thought, but I believe the book becoming a bestseller is not the point."

He shrugged. "I was just thinking. If the book takes off, you can quit your job."

"No telling how well it's going to be received, so that is not an option at this point." I sighed.

"Can you take some time off work to finish?" he asked, inhaling the fragrant scent of the ribs warming in the oven.

"Not really. My workload has gotten to the point I can't even take an entire day off. And now that I'm getting a raise, I'll be expected to work even harder." I picked up another page to continue the transcription. "But I'll tell you what... I am going to get this book finished if I have to get up early every morning and stay up late every night. Even if I have to quit that job, my baby girl's story is gonna get told."

"I hear you," he replied. "So on that note, I'll let you get back to it."

"In case you're looking for dinner, we're having leftovers. You can serve yourself whenever you're ready to eat. The food is warming in the oven. Salad is on the counter."

"That sounds great." He dropped the mail—mostly advertisement flyers—in the waste basket for shredding. "Be right back. Got to take a quick shower."

"Hold on!" I quickly realized my oversight. "I almost forgot to tell you what else happened."

"Why aren't I surprised?" he grinned. "There's always more."

I laughed because he was right. I became very serious when I uttered, "I had the strangest feeling this morning after talking to Meredith. After I returned to my cubicle, I got the feeling that we'd had that conversation before."

Gerald remained quiet, listening.

"I must have been daydreaming. Or perhaps it was wishful thinking. Because in my mind, our roles were reversed. I was a different version of myself. So was she. I was in charge and Meredith was the employee."

"Now that's an interesting twist."

"Tell me about it... *I* owned the business," I responded with a smirk.

"With all that experience you have, your being the owner of your own company doesn't surprise me one bit!" he replied, kissing my cheek again. "I'll be back in a few minutes after I change."

I got back to it, slumped over my laptop, carefully typing each word as it was written. As I read each page aloud, I was once again captivated by the imaginative stories, proudly noting that Kenya's writing skills had dramatically improved from the B level work handed in during the previous semester of her Honors English Composition class.

Gerald returned to the kitchen wearing sweat pants and his favorite t-shirt sporting a faded picture of *Parliament* across the front. Every time I tried to toss the tattered t-shirt in the trash, he reminded me this was the same shirt he had purchased on our first date. At this point, the shirt was more nostalgia than clothing.

He fixed two plates and handed me mine, taking his dinner to the living room to not disturb my concentration. Between bites of salad, my fingers flew across the keyboard, stopping occasionally to make sure I didn't lose my place. The challenge I quickly discovered in transcribing was to not get caught up in reading what was akin to my daughter's journal. As a mother, it was my duty to protect my child and her private thoughts from potential ridicule from critics or even well-meaning individuals. The more I thought about it, the more I was convinced the decision to publish her story as fiction was the best way to ensure her name wouldn't be dragged through the mud. Especially since technically her legal status remained as 'missing'.

The alarm on my cell phone chimed as a signal it was time to quit. Before I realized it, hours had passed.

"Zumira!" Gerald called out from the living room.

"Uhm huh," I replied trying to find a place to stop.

"Sweetheart, it's after ten o'clock. Are you coming to bed?"

I glanced at the digital clock on the laptop before closing it. "I suppose this is as good a time as any to stop. I am exhausted."

"How far did you get?"

"Not very far at all. At this pace—a couple hours in the morning and a few hours after work—it's going to take a month to retype the complete manuscript."

"Anything I can do to help?"

"Just keep me supplied with your infinite kisses. And occasionally making dinner will help out tremendously."

"I can do all that," he smiled, joining me at the table. "Have you thought about which publisher you want to use?"

"Not really. Drena said she would do the marketing so maybe she has some inside information on getting it published," I replied, releasing a loud yawn.

He reached for my hand and with a sweet whisper said, "C'mon dear writer. Time for you to get some rest."

"I know," I replied, wearily. "Tomorrow morning will come around soon enough and we'll have to do it all over again."

"You said a mouth full, my love. But for now, let's go to bed."

Chapter Six

Shortly after moving to Oklahoma City, I became aware that on Saturdays at noon, a siren blasted out over the entire metropolitan region. No matter where I happened to be in the city—at home or out shopping, I heard it. At first, I had no idea what the loud high-pitched sound was, other than it was annoying. What I eventually learned was the siren was a test of the early warning system for tornadoes. When those sirens blared any day or time other than high noon Saturday, Okies knew to take shelter because more than likely, a twister was coming their way. The only exception to the weekly test was if there was already an active storm in session. City officials understood that testing the system while storms were in the vicinity could possibly send the metro into a frenzy.

The early mail notification we received from the post office indicated a letter postmarked with a return address from a prominent New York publisher would be delivered today. As I stood in my doorway waiting patiently for the mail carrier, I glanced at the decorative clock sitting on the foyer table, noticing the time was 1:11 pm. I realized the warning sirens had not sounded. A flash of lightning momentarily drew my attention towards the sky.

I spotted the familiar mail carrier van just two houses down. That's also when I saw the source of the lightning. A line of thunderstorms had formed not too far off in the distance. Waves of rumbling thunder preceded the storms arrival. Its ceiling was so low that you could actually watch the dark tumultuous fast-moving clouds heading our way.

"Honey?! Can you please get the mail before the rain starts?" I shouted to Gerald who was somewhere back in the house. "The mailman is almost here!"

"Be right there!"

"Hurry! It's about to start raining!" I shouted.

Gerald rushed past me just as the van pulled away. He called out, "I'll be right back!"

I could barely contain my excitement about the content of the letter. Of all the publishers I submitted the book's excerpt to, I was sure this one would be good news. I hoped this agency would be as enthusiastic about publishing Kenya's story as I was getting it published. After all, the publishing company was owned by a black woman.

"Got it!" Gerald shouted as he ducked back into the house barely missing the first heavy drops of rain. He dropped the mail on the narrow table alongside a small container where we kept the car keys.

I leafed through the stack of mail looking for the letter. At that point, our phones began to simultaneously sound off. I put the mail down. The letter could wait. According to the weather alerts, a strong cold front had developed in the southwest bringing with it the potential for high winds and very strong storms. Bolts of lightning lit up the western portion of the sky indicating the storm was nearby. Five seconds later, a round of thunderous booms shook the whole house. Everyone was normally on edge this time of year because it was tornado season.

"It's coming down pretty good out there!" he remarked, wiping the rain from his face.

I sniffed the air. "Do you smell that?" I asked, monitoring the approaching storm from the safety of the doorway. The unique fragrance of electricity charged the air as negative ions coming down through the clouds connected with positive ions emanating up from the ground. I was surprised to learn that when it comes to 'ions', increasing the negative ions in one's environment is much better than increasing the positive.

"Yeah, I do," Gerald replied, changing the television to the local news. "Let's see what's going on out there."

I watched in fascination as the darkest clouds I'd ever seen slowly begin to rotate. Entranced by the natural phenomena fueled by the power of the wind, I whispered, "It's beautiful in an awe-inspiring sort of way."

"Well, let's hope beautiful doesn't turn ugly," he muttered to himself, focusing his attention on the weather report.

A low-hanging wall cloud, dark grey with an ominous greenish tint—the strongest storm that I'd seen in a while, threatened to drop and further rotate. The howling wind was fierce, soon showering down quarter sized hail in such large quantities that the street appeared to be covered with snow. As I listened to the high-pitched, adrenaline-tinged voice of the weather man shouting to the tornado chasers on the ground—becoming more excited than he probably should have—I spotted something very strange embedded within the approaching storm clouds. Whatever it was, it was massive! Then I became aware that I was about to experience something magnificent.

"What in the world...?" I whispered, poking my head out the front door. Sheets of rain were coming down sideways preventing me from going out any further. I closed the door and ran through the house to the kitchen hoping to get a better look from the back door.

"Where are you going?!" Gerald called out excitedly, his eyes glued to the television.

My husband was normally a very calm man and rarely allowed any situation to get to him. Since he had grown up in a little town outside of Tulsa, he recognized the warning signs associated with tornadic activity. So when he began to get nervous, I clearly understood we might be in danger. Nevertheless, ignoring my husband's rising concern, I cautiously opened the backdoor to watch the storm develop. A succession of lightning flashes lit up something within the clouds. I stood as still as possible to avoid losing sight of whatever that thing was. I watched in fascination as the rain rapidly dispersed around the object like beads of water falling from a freshly waxed vehicle.

"Honey! Come out here! Something's in the storm!" I called over my shoulder. "Hurry!"

"Zumira, get away from the door!" Gerald yelled, running towards me. "A tornado was spotted just a few miles away! It's headed in our direction!"

Listening to the weatherman practically screaming for everyone to take shelter had almost put me on edge too. Most Okies learned from childhood that the safest place to survive a tornado was underground. When we found a house built with the next best thing—a reinforced walk-in closet that also doubled as a safe room and shelter—we were sold.

A thunderous bolt of lightning must have connected with something on the ground nearby because an indescribably loud noise that sounded like the sky itself was ripping apart, came from above the house. Suddenly, the electricity went out, leaving us in a darkness more akin to nighttime than the middle of the afternoon.

"Hold on!" I shouted, stepping outside. "I want to get a closer look!"

"What are you doing?!" Gerald shouted. He tugged at my arm, his voice raised by adrenaline. "We have to get inside!"

"Wait a minute," I said, almost too calmly. Kenya's words came to mind. *'The Nigiro can disguise the arrival of their spaceships within the midst of powerful storms.'* I don't think this is a tornado."

"Zumira! This is not the time to argue! We have to take shelter! Now!"

"Gerald! Listen to me! This ain't no tornado!"

"What are you talking about?! One was spotted just a few streets over!"

"Look! There's something in the clouds!" I quickly motioned for him to join me under the overhang of the patio. I wasn't afraid. That fact alone should have frightened me. But I felt no fear. None at all. And it was an exquisite feeling.

"Woman, get your butt inside this house!"

"Wait a minute!" I shouted, pointing to the sky. "Look!"

"What's so important that you're trying to get us killed?!" Gerald yelled, reluctantly stepping outside to the patio.

And all at once—just like the snapping of fingers—the wind stopped howling. The rain ceased to fall. The powerful sounds of thunder grew silent and the bolts of lightning flashed no more. The sun now shone brightly in the partly cloudy sky. With the exception of the calming sounds of nature, it was quiet. Too quiet.

Gerald turned to me and whispered, "Zumira... What the hell is going on?"

"I don't know," I replied, resting my hand on his for reassurance. The rapid pace of his heartbeat was in total synch to mine.

He looked to the sky and said, "What happened to the storm?"

As we were both trying to figure out what was going on, our attention was drawn overhead. What I had first spotted cloaked within the storm was now fully visible in the sky. Now I probably should have been terrified, but I wasn't. On the contrary, I was astonished to see a real live unidentified flying object!

The UFO was so huge, it probably covered the entire neighborhood! It hovered above the ground about the same altitude as an airplane does when it's coming in for a landing. It looked nothing like any of those flying saucers so many have claimed to have seen. It was not round, oblong, or cigar-shaped. It didn't look like the Star Trek Enterprise or any other manmade Hollywood space ship. This thing was otherworldly! It appeared to be 'built' of some kind of 'fluidy' iridescent metal—like metallic paint that changes color dependent upon how the light hits it. In spite of its immensity, the only noise it emitted was a high-pitched whine, similar to tinnitus, what my doctor had diagnosed me with years earlier.

A small pod underneath the spaceship emitted several bursts of pulsating bluish lights. I watched in fascination as the entire surface of the UFO shifted to mimic the blue sky—fluffy white clouds and all! Then just as quickly as it became invisible, it momentarily reappeared in its original metallic form before shifting back to become invisible. After several iterations of shifting color schemes, I figured that whatever was inside that vessel was reaching out to me. Witnessing the magnificent spectacle unfold before my very eyes, I was absolutely mesmerized! In my humble opinion, only an advanced alien 'race' could have created such an amazing feat of technology.

"Zumira!" Gerald shouted, "Snap out of it!"

I turned to face my husband, not sure what had come over me. I tried to get my thoughts back to where they should be. In the present moment. But I couldn't help staring up at that magnificent spaceship, wondering if there were Nigiro inside. I was enthralled, but I also wondered why my husband wasn't. I needed to know that I was not hallucinating. I asked him, "Don't you see that?!"

"Yeah, I see something," he replied, looking up guardedly. "That's why I'm trying to get us inside!"

I felt Gerald tugging me back towards the safety of the house. And I would have complied, had it been possible. But I couldn't move. My feet were glued to the spot. Then the ground shook.

Gerald relaxed his grip, before uttering, "What the hell was that?!"

In the blink-of-an-eye, the entire neighborhood disappeared. There were no houses, no cars, no animals. And no people. We found ourselves in the middle of a wildly grown meadow bordered by tall majestic trees. Nothing was the same. I touched my husband's arm just to make sure I wasn't dreaming.

"W-w-where are we? W-w-what happened to the h-h-house?!" I stuttered, trying to maintain my faltering grip on reality.

"I don't know," he whispered.

We looked up simultaneously. The UFO was still there.

Totally unaffected by this shift in our reality, two brightly colored Cardinals swooped underneath the spaceship, fluttering about the exterior, almost as if searching for a way inside.

My attention was drawn away from the birds to witness an even stranger phenomena taking place. As my husband and I watched dumbfounded, less than twenty feet away from us, fragments of misty light were gathering together to form the outline of a body. Once the fragments solidified, a young black woman wearing a glittery gold jumpsuit and enveloped in an aura of glowing golden light appeared.

"Kenya?" I asked, unsure what I was looking at. I reached out my sweaty hand to grip Gerald's for support. "Is that you, baby?"

The figure turned to face us and spoke in a voice as clear as my own. "Greetings Mother! Greetings Father! It's so nice to finally see you both again!"

"Is this... Is *that* what you saw that night?" Gerald whispered, from the side of his mouth.

I shook my head, trying to not draw any attention to myself. I whispered back, "Last time she came in an orb of light. I physically laid my hands on her."

Gerald continued to listen, staring at what he thought looked like more of an apparition than their child.

"Plus, the spaceship she took me up in was much, much smaller than this," I continued, whispering in hushed tones.

"Mother, you're wondering why I look and sound differently. It is because you're looking at my hologram. It is a projection. I am actually in the mothership above," Kenya's voice explained.

All of a sudden, everything seemed very surreal. Like I was fighting my way through a thick blanket of heavy air that divided two worlds. My vision became blurred. I felt woozy. Sick to my stomach. Unable to breath. I clutched onto Gerald in case I fainted.

"I know this is a lot for you to process, but there is no need to be afraid. The Nigiro mean you no harm," Kenya's image shimmered as it spoke. "The space vessel you see is real. We have journeyed many earth years to return to you."

The breath I had subconsciously held in was released with a long sigh of relief. This specter standing before me wasn't my flesh and blood daughter; it was scattered pixels of light, like images from a movie projector. But much more advanced. I glanced up at the spacecraft wondering, *Can she really see me? Are the others also watching?* For a moment, I expected I might see the tall black alien again. He had disregarded me the first time. But that was before I read Kenya's account of the Nigiro.

"Kenya?" Gerald asked, hesitantly. "Are you really up there?"

"Hi Daddy. Yes, I am," her hologram replied, sounding like her old self again. "I just want you to know that I love you very much! I don't blame you for anything. This was my destiny."

"I read your story," he replied, wiping a tear from his eye. "I thought it was really good."

"Thanks Daddy. That means a lot."

"Baby, are you okay?" he asked, gently.

"I have never been better. I know who I am. I discovered the true purpose for my life," said Kenya's image as it began to fizzle out. "I have returned to help you and others discover the same."

In that moment, Gerald inwardly released every pent-up emotion he didn't realize he'd held inside since his child first disappeared. Grateful for this moment, he breathed a deep sigh of relief, comforted in the knowledge that his little girl was alive and well.

"Kenya," I interrupted, gently. "I finished transcribing your story. Your brother's wife, Drena, is going to help us get it published."

My child's holograph-imaged facial features scrunched into what I would describe as being perplexed.

I was more than happy to guide this surreal conversation into more familiar territory. "That's right! You don't know about Drena! She and Malcolm were married a couple years ago. He has a baby girl. He named her Mali Zambia after you!" I gushed, looking at the image of my futuristic daughter who hadn't aged a bit, but had matured beyond belief. It took me aback. There was no other sensible explanation. She had to be who she said she was.

"I already know about Malcolm, Drena, and the baby. And I am happy they named my niece after me, but that's not what concerns me."

"What is it, then, sweetie?" I asked, feeling my mother-child connection begin to reconnect.

"Malcolm is having a difficult time accepting my story. You must help him to understand. My testimony describing my rescue by the Nigiro is more than a tale of fiction."

"I'll do my best," I said, looking towards Gerald. "We both will."

"I know you will," she responded, beginning to pixilate. "I've come to speak with you about the troubles you're having finding a publisher."

"Wait a minute! I just had that exact thought," I said to myself. "How did you do that?"

Kenya telepathically relayed, "As I explained in my story, Nigiro communicate telepathically. I know your thoughts when you do. Since you're my mother, our connection is very powerful. Besides, I check in on you often ..."

I stared up at the pulsating blue light, wondering what other extraordinary abilities my daughter possessed. I asked tentatively, "Kenya, did you... Did you just communicate with me telepathically?"

Kenya's image nodded. "*Yes, Mother. I did that so you can know that I have the means to communicate with you directly through your thoughts.*"

Gerald appeared even more confused than I was because he had not received Kenya's telepathic transmission. So he asked, "You can get inside her head? Just like that?"

"*Not always. But I don't have enough time right now to explain. I just wanted to drop in to see you both. And to offer mom encouragement to stay the course. If the big publishing companies will not publish the book, you will have to publish it on your own.*"

"Do it myself?" I asked, pondering what was more than a notion. I didn't have a clue how to go about publishing anything.

"*You'll figure it out.*" Kenya's now familiar holograph smiled. "*We've been told 'his' story for much too long. It is now time for "ourstory" of the Nigiro to be known.*"

"Ourstory?" I uttered, trying the word out loud for the first time. "I think I really like that. *Ourstory* as opposed to *history*. It sounds so much better."

"*I think so too. Before I go, I want to show you something I think is significant. Please open your minds and locate the love inside.*" Kenya motioned towards the far side of the meadow. "*Ready?*"

We both nodded.

In the blink of an eye, Gerald and I were transported to a summit's crest which provided a panoramic view of a beautiful countryside. I did not know if that UFO was still overhead or not, but the sky had changed to the shade of indigo with pastel pink and orange clouds lazily passing overhead. An oversized yellowish-orange sun, the likes of which I had never seen, blazed down through an atmosphere free of pollution. The warmth of the sun was intense, as if it were late summer or early autumn. A light breeze coming from the southwest filtered through tall shade trees which offered some relief from the heat.

"W-w-where are we now?" I asked Kenya's hologram.

"Is this some kind of an illusion?" Gerald added, gawking at the incredible sights taking place right before his eyes.

"Wow! This is amazing!" I uttered, looking about in every direction, feeling a sense of wonderment.

"The Teacher has transported you and Daddy here..."

"The Teacher? Is he up there with you?" I asked, looking upwards, hoping I'd get the chance to see him again. Gerald too.

"Yes, he is here with me." She nodded and explained, "The Teacher also has the ability to manipulate spatial-time at will. You were brought to this particular place in time because you must know that the very land your home was built-upon once belonged to our ancestors countless generations prior. They were children of the Nigiro. The images you see before you represents our family. This country—this hallowed ground you stand upon—once did, and will soon again, belong to us."

The ancestral village was populated by hundreds of melanated people from the same family. *These homes sheltered people who resembled my relatives.* They lived in adobe-style type houses topped by thatched roofs that were constructed of dried prairie grass and red clay.

On the outskirts of the village was a large community garden where all kinds of fruit-bearing trees and colorful vegetables sprouted abundantly from the rich soil. The garden was being tended by dozens of young women and children. I noted their smooth dark skin resembled the color of the ground on which they toiled under the hot sun. Most of the older woman wore their thick hair plaited into two ropelike braids, while the younger girls' hair was braided in a manner similar to the rows of corn in the field. Stooping down to pick their selection directly from the garden, I ascertained they were busily filling their baskets with bounty in preparation for the upcoming meal.

A small group of men—a few old, but mostly younger—rode into the village on horseback. They didn't look like Indians portrayed in the olden days or even the

Native Americans we see today. To me, surprisingly they just looked like 'black' men dressed in a fashion similar to what is shown in the historical pictures of the modern-day Native American Indians. The bandanas tied at their necks were used to protect their mouths and noses from dust flying about as they rode their horses through the countryside. Any part of their faces left uncovered was turned ashy from the dirt being kicked up.

The men dismounted from their horses near a fence constructed of aged tree branches tied together with sturdy vines. After thanking the horses individually for a good journey, they loosely tied the reins to a post which allowed the beasts to dip their nose into the water bin for a refreshing drink. Not too far from the stables, a small building that might have been used as an outhouse, was covered in the vines of aromatic plants.

I turned to look in the direction where I thought our house previously stood. I was surprised to see a large thatched-roof, open-air structure sitting in its place. Two young men sat cross-legged on carpets of grass, beating their drums in mesmerizing rhythmic ceremonial songs as the crowd continued to gather. As I watched in awe, a sacred coming-of-age ceremony for children who'd recently entered puberty was about to take place. The dozen or so boys and girls all proudly wearing the color Indigo were quietly making their way to the stage. They walked like royalty. How I knew all of this, I do not know.

Kenya explained, "The reality you previously knew no longer exists. When the storm passes, you and daddy will move through another dimension. If you continue on this journey, from this moment forward, you will question the physical world you left behind. The people who thought they knew you well, will wonder if you are the same person. You may sometimes begin to doubt even yourself."

"What do you mean by 'another dimension'?" I asked, looking to Gerald for confirmation that he too was experiencing the same concerns. The confused expression on his face caught me off guard.

Kenya spoke reassuringly, "Do not be concerned. Your physical life shall remain as it is. The dimension you have entered is a spiritual one. This concept is indistinguishable to the average human's 'ways of knowing'. But those with discernment will understand."

I stared at my daughter's hologram, only now truly comprehending the power of the Nigiro. This was not the same teenage girl I last said good-bye to on the morning of her sixteenth birthday. For a split second, I became saddened by the knowledge that I never fully understood Kenya as a child. But in the very next moment, my heart swelled with love for the young woman she had grown into.

Gerald remained quiet, taking it all in. Dozens of thoughts swirled inside his mind.

"Poignant questions may cause you to seek spiritual guidance from others. I caution you to not be moved by false teachings from those who say they have the answers but who know not what they teach. Seek guidance from The Creator. For She is the only one who can provide what you need to move forward."

"What are you saying?" I asked her image.

"Please. Continue to watch. And listen," Kenya advised.

While we spoke, a beautiful woman dressed in an ankle-length turquoise dress with gold accents, and wearing a matching ceremonial head covering, took center stage of the wooden structure that resembled a large pergola. Dozens of gold and turquoise bracelets graced her bronzed arms, brilliantly flashing speckles of light over the gathered audience as the sunlight bounced off the precious metal and stones. The woman spoke passionately to the children who now sat at her bare feet, in a language I did not know. A man with dark glistening skin, equally elegant in appearance and stature, stood in the background watching the woman speak. The sparkle in his eyes led me to believe he might be her husband.

"Wow! She's telling the children a powerful story about their ancestors! The Nigiro!" I uttered. "But wait a minute... how is it possible I can understand what they're saying?!"

Kenya's hologram simply smiled.

"Is this for real?" Gerald asked, astonished by what he was witnessing. His family always said they had 'Indian' blood in them from ancestors way back when. Now he realized they were doing more than trying to be someone they're not.

"This vision is courtesy of the Elders."

Kenya made a quick wavey motion with her hand. With that small movement, Gerald and I were placed from the outskirts to standing within the crowd. We were close enough to hear the children's excited chatter. As if we were actually there with them in real time.

"You are not here physically. The children can neither see nor hear you. This vision provides a glimpse of who we were before you became who you are now. This is what once existed before history became ourstory."

Upon a closer inspection, I noticed the regal woman bore a very strong resemblance to my deceased paternal grandmother, Kenya's great-grandmother.

"Mother, this is a vision of our ancestors from numerous generations past. The matriarch you see was a proud woman who dedicated her life to ensuring her people practiced the culture and traditions of our people. Her husband served alongside as village Chief. They established a safe community on this very land for their family—an indigenous tribe of Nigiro."

"This is incredible!" I gasped aloud.

"For many centuries, long before some of our ancestors were stolen from Africa and then enslaved in the Americas, various indigenous tribes lived harmoniously in their respective villages with nature and each other. This includes the land now called 'Oklahoma', *home of the copper-colored man*."

"Why don't I know any of this?" I posed a very difficult question to my child. "How did we lose the true narrative about our past?"

"According to their history, in the late 1800's, thousands of greedy colonizers, historically romanticized as 'Boomer

Sooners', set their sights westward, including the land called Oklahoma. For our people, it was the beginning of the end. From the moment the early gentrifiers arrived to the so-called 'unassigned lands' of the designated Indian Territory, they made it their business to terrorize, maim and murder our ancestors, just to steal their land. After laying claim to the stolen land by squatting, the government ultimately awarded those murderous thieves millions of acres for nothing other than a proclamation of "squatter's rights."

Gerald chimed in, "I know this story. I've heard a similar one from my relatives up there in Tulsa. They stole the land right from under their feet."

"That's right, Daddy," Kenya replied. "After our ancestors were displaced, they traveled far and wide searching for other safe spaces in which to build their communities. Consequently, as soon as they rebuilt, those towns too were destroyed. Thus, our culture was all but forgotten."

"Is *this* the land of our ancestors?" I asked, observing the ceremony taking place under the thatched-roof structure. Everyone's faces looked so familiar, I felt as if we were standing in the middle of a family reunion that had taken place long before this country began. This vision was so realistic, we could have been on a movie set filming an indigenous scene starring black people.

With a swipe of Kenya's fingers, the indigenous ancestral village disappeared, only to be replaced by a vision of an all-black community from the 1950's. Gerald and I found ourselves standing in the middle of a newly paved street staring at two small tidy homes fenced-in together on a large family plot of land. Both houses had covered front porches. My focus was on the house on the left, the one with the two uneven concrete steps leading up a porch covered by a green awning. The one requiring a skeleton key to unlock the front door. There was someone special living inside that home, but I had no idea who. Or how I knew.

It was the beginning of a hot summer day, probably a Sunday. The morning sun had just started to settle high in the sky. The fragrant scents of bacon and country ham frying in a cast-iron skillet wafted in the air. A rooster from the chicken coop situated in the backyard of the house to the right crowed, 'cock-a-doodle-doo!'. A young woman with a scarf tied about her head shooed the rooster away while she tossed kernels of dried corn to the clucking birds. Between the two houses, in a small strip of grassy yard, a mature weeping willow tree that provided shade in the summer *and* green whipping switches in the spring, danced gracefully in the warm breeze.

As breakfast was being prepared by the women inside, an elderly man with skin the color of earthen clay sat in a rickety rocking chair outside the kitchen door. Several young children sat mesmerized on the hardened dirt at his feet. The children's father stood nearby happily listening, chuckling here and there. He'd heard these same stories when he was a child. The older man, the children's great-grandfather, was busily spinning his favorite tale from his youth. He used expressive hand gestures and voice characterizations to make his characters come alive. When he finally told the punch line, all the children burst into happy laughter. All except one little girl who was about four or five. She became afraid and started to cry. I looked on in fascination as the father of the little girl knelt down, hugged, and then lovingly told his daughter, *'Don't mind papa. He's just tellin' tall tales again.'*

"Zumira! Zumira!" Gerald shouted, returning them both back to the present moment.

"Huh?" I said, feeling light-headed.

"So let me get this straight," Gerald said, finding it difficult to comprehend the incomprehensible. "You're telling me that this house we bought in Oklahoma City of all places; a city where neither I nor your mother had ever considered living until you disappeared, was built on the land where Zumira's ancestors in the Americas originated?"

"Yes."

"But how is that even possible?" I asked, feeling more like myself.

"Your moving to Oklahoma was not by chance. Nor was it a coincidence. The Elders made it possible for you and daddy to be here because they foresaw what was happening in the world. The path opened for you to get jobs, and this house was made to be available when you were ready to move. It was all part of The Creator's plan."

I think I understand," I responded, considering the ease it took to locate the house. Everyone—from the realtor, to the broker's agent, to the bank officer who assisted with the loan—bent over backwards to ensure the process went as smoothly as possible. Now I understand I had nothing to do with it.

"The Almighty God has a plan for my life. For your life. For all our lives. A purpose. A clear destiny. If you pay attention to the signs and use discernment, you will know The Universe is always communicating."

Gerald remained quiet and simply listened. He no longer recognized his child, nor the serious words she spoke.

"Mother, I am going to ask you a question and I want you to be totally honest with your response."

"Okay," I said to her image, warily. "Go ahead. Ask."

"Forgive me in advance, but do you imbibe in cannabis?"

I blushed at the question posed by my child. "Yes, but I have a medical condition," I answered, defensively. *I furrowed my brow thinking, the last thing I want to do is discuss the use of cannabis with my daughter, especially so soon after having a similar one with Malcolm.*

Kenya's image replied, "Do not think I am judging you. Only The Creator has the ability to do that."

Then I remembered she could read my thoughts anyway so I answered, "I use cannabis to reduce the pain of my arthritis. Plus, it helps calm the anxiety caused by living in this crazy mixed-up racist society."

"The herb causes various reactions in those who imbibe. It can put one in touch with one's spiritual side and may even help to open their internal vision—what some refer to as the 'third eye'—to visualize the true reality of who they are. It can temporarily push back the curtain to show you the world as it really is. An illusion."

"Why do you ask?"

"Understand that cannabis is akin to taking a boat across a mighty river. Once you have crossed the river, the boat is no longer necessary. It then remains docked at the shore until you need it to cross the river again. Many only need to use cannabis occasionally; others may need it more frequently. Some don't need it at all."

Gerald and I both relished the wisdom spilling forth from our child.

"There is no shame in using what God has provided." Her projection pixelated again before reemerging. "But be very careful of what you consume. Certain strains of cannabis—those that are genetically altered or tampered with to produce higher levels of THC—can produce unintended side effects. Whereas one's intent may be to raise their level of consciousness, if there is a propensity to do evil, or harbor unclean thoughts, those are the spirits that individual will attract. It really depends on how spiritually enlightened the person was before they began using."

"That's good information to have, sweetie. Thank you," I replied.

"Mother, I have another question, if you don't mind," Kenya said.

"Go on..." I said.

"Have you noticed any strange occurrences around the house lately?"

"Like what?" Gerald asked.

"Anything that seems unusual or out of the ordinary."

"Over the past few years, ever since moving to this house, every now and then I see flashes of light from the corner of my eyes when I enter a particular room."

"Anything else?"

"*Tell* her, my love," my husband prodded me, hoping to solve the mysteries of what actually happened that night.

I sighed, then averted my eyes before admitting, "Well... Sometimes I feel a rush of adrenaline that originates deep within my core and then spreads outwards like tiny ripples in a pond. Like a wave of energy—or a great 'presence' has overtaken my body. I'm left with a feeling of anticipation that something great is heading my way," I replied, watching the look of surprise register on Gerald's face at my admission.

"Do you remember the first time you felt the presence?" Kenya asked.

"Yeah, I do," I said recalling it for the first time. "It was a day that I'll never forget. It was a few months after we moved to Oklahoma. I was in pretty bad shape. I couldn't eat. Couldn't sleep. I was literally sleep-walking through my life. But something happened that woke me up."

"What are you talking about?" Gerald turned to face me.

"Late one Friday evening, you were working late. I had settled down to watch TV. I stumbled across an old B&W video with footage of an elderly black man who believed *Elohim* had charged him with telling others his truth."

"Go on," she encouraged me.

"As I listened to that old man speak, something fascinating happened to me. All of a sudden I felt a strong presence in the room. It overtook me. As if a wave of energy passed right through me. I immediately dropped to my knees with a profound knowledge that the Almighty God was speaking to me through that man's voice. I don't know how I knew, I just did. When I got up from the floor, I thought I had hallucinated the entire episode. Or that I was super high. But the downloads kept coming throughout the evening reminding me that God is always with me. He never left me. After that moment, I knew something wonderful was going to happen."

"You never told me that," Gerald added, looking perplexed.

"Until now, I had forgotten all about it," I explained, innocently.

Kenya's image tilted her head as if she were listening to someone unseen. She then explained, "The Teacher tells me the presence you felt was a powerful spiritual force. Your senses have been heightened to receive it."

"Cool!" was the only appropriate word I could find.

"What about the flashing lights? Anything significant about that?"

"Daddy, those flashes represent light energy. Opening the spiritual eye allows one to see what was previously unseen. Those 'lights' are the ancestors reminding you they are with you. You may think of them as your guardian angels."

"That's awesome!" I gasped my astonishment. "I don't know what to say."

"Where you stand now, this is the land of the ancestors. Our land. Your land. Familial land. They wish to welcome you home."

"Kenya, you're telling me our ancestors drew me to this house?"

"That is correct."

"Why?"

"I did not want to be the bearer of troublesome news, but the land under your home is consecrated."

"What do you mean by that?" I asked.

"This land is sacred because it was used as an ancestral burial ground."

"For real?!"I asked.

"Many of the ancestors died while trying to reach this land. Those who did make it had to fight off men who believed they did not belong here. Many family members died while protecting this land under this subdivision. They are buried here. In an unmarked mass grave."

Gerald's eyes grew wide in astonishment.

"Just as this government intentionally flooded dozens of all-black towns throughout this country in the 1900's, and then made them into lakes located in national and state parks, developers intentionally plow over graveyards in the name of progress. Parking lots, shopping malls, housing developments, prisons, schools... Dig deep enough anywhere in this country and you'll find the remains of the ancestors."

"I had no idea," he replied.

"This entire country was built on bloodshed."

I was stunned by this revelation. "Are our ancestors' spirits with us now?"

Kenya's hologram smiled. "Yes, in spirit, they are always with you. Me as well."

"Like how you described when you were in the spiritual realm with your great-Nana?" I asked.

"Something like that. Even though Nana watches over me in the spiritual realm, in time, you will see it is The Most High God connecting with you spiritually through the powerful vibration of Love."

I placed my hand against my forehead. This was too much information coming in at once.

"But that is not the only reason why I have come. There are many entities who wish to prevent you from accomplishing this important assignment. Just know that you, and all those in this family, are protected. Not only physically, but most importantly, spiritually."

"Wait a minute. My parents—your grandparents— were from around Tulsa," Gerald blurted out. "I wonder if something similar happened to my side of the family?"

"Yes, Daddy." Her image wavered, like a glitch in the reception. "Many of our ancestors built the all-black towns throughout Oklahoma."

"I have a question, baby," he asked, hopefully. "Will I also receive the insight that your mother is receiving? That telepathy ability?"

"Daddy, you must be open and receptive. Then if you follow all you are instructed to do, you too will receive the insight."

Gerald straightened his back just a little more. He possessed the knowledge that his ancestors, who also suffered under a cruel system of white oppression, had not only survived, but thrived in spite of it.

"You and Mom are both in the process of re-awakening, but your timelines and the messages you each receive may not be the same. You both have been given a spiritual gift. However, until all is revealed, The Teacher has placed you here to assist mother with the monumental task I have presented to her. Unseen evil forces will provide distractions and temptations to try to prevent Mom from doing what she was instructed to do. You must resist!"

He nodded, accepting his very important role.

"Mother, the ancestors brought you to Oklahoma to this house for a specific purpose."

"What purpose is that?" I blurted out, unexpectedly.

"Please forgive me, but that is not for me to disclose," she whispered.

"When will I know what it is? How will I find out what I'm supposed to be doing?"

"Pay close attention to your dreams. Either myself or great-Nana will contact you in the spiritual realm with more information. The Teacher will begin working through others to give you further instructions, so don't be distracted from whom the message originates. Also look for the signs. These small crumbs are scattered everywhere—on street signs, t-shirt slogans, bumper stickers, license plates, billboards—seemingly random words that will provide information to help guide you along the Way. After your daily Bible readings, remember to pray often throughout the day."

Gerald went to the hologram for a closer look. He was no longer frightened. Just curious. He reached out to touch his daughter's face, but his hand passed right through.

"I must leave soon. The storm is beginning to dissipate." Kenya's mostly transparent form motioned where the spaceship, no longer visible, now blended in with the clouds.

"Can I ask a few more questions before you go?" I shouted, as I joined Gerald in the field where he stood next to her image.

Her image fizzled out completely, before returning to its full-strength projection. She nodded.

"When will I see you again?" I asked, hoping the spaceship would drop its stealth mode so I could get a better look. *I also hoped I'd catch a glimpse of the Teacher, too. Not only for my sake, but for my husband's.*

"I do not know when I will see you again."

Although disappointed by her response, I had to ask. "Soooo, about getting the book published... How much time do I have?"

"Mother, when you work diligently, the time it takes you to complete the book is all the time you'll need. But your progress must be intentional." She cocked her head to the side as if she were receiving an incoming message from someone unseen.

Gerald asked, "I think what your mother wants to know is, is there a timeframe it must be finished?"

"Daddy, if you are asking me will you have adequate time to publish the book... What I have learned from my lessons on time is fairly simple. The time it takes to accomplish the task will be sufficient."

"I think I understand," he replied. "If it takes thirty days to complete the transcription, publish and then distribute the book, then that means a month's time is enough. But if it takes longer, time will tell us how much more of it we need."

"Exactly." She smiled that old familiar smile exposing the dimples her great-Nana proclaimed was the spot where she had been kissed by an angel.

Though Gerald was satisfied, I still did not understand what her theory on time had to do with me getting the book published. I suppose my confused expression led to her further explanation.

"Time is constant, but the rate of how time passes is relative. It is measured in seconds, minutes, days, weeks, months, and years. But not everyone measures it the same."

"Really?" I stated.

"What is not commonly known is there are several calendars in use throughout the world today. The west uses the Gregorian calendar; a 12-month, 365-day with one leap year day every four years. On the other hand, the Ethiopian calendar, though consistent in the number of days as the Gregorian, uses a 13-month year. The 13th month has only 5 or 6 days, dependent upon a leap year, and was once referred to as Pagume or the 'forgotten days'. Furthermore, those two calendars differ by eight years. My point is, the date you have been led to believe to be true, is arbitrary at best."

My mind momentarily drifted away remembering where I was and what I was doing on that New Year's Eve of 2013 when the world was supposed to end. Although I was not surprised when the world didn't end, it was the first time I'd ever heard that there was another type of calendar in existence. I remember diving into the internet to find out if there were any more out there.

"Many prophesized the modern world would end in the year 2012; ushering in a new world. However, that date was incorrectly attributed to the ancient Mayan civilization who, by-the-way, were also the ancestors of Nigiro. As you know, the world did not end on December 31, 2012, as was predicted."

"Since the world didn't end in 2012, will the world end soon?" I asked, nervously.

"Only The Creator knows the answer to that question."

"Well, can you at least tell us the date this *new world* you mentioned will come into existence?" Gerald said.

"Man in his arrogance tampered with the original calendar to prevent the general population from ever knowing that others exist. So what is today's actual date? So who knows the exact date of when the new world that was prophesized about long ago will come into existence? It all depends on whose calendar you're using. But the Mayans were believed to have based their calendar on the 'one that has yet to be named'."

"Kenya, my love. While I appreciate the lesson on 'time', there are so many other questions I have, like... Like..." Gerald struggled with choosing the right words to express himself. "Disregard. My mind just drew a blank."

"Just know that we are always close by. And if you are ever in the midst of severe weather that pops up out of nowhere, chances are the weather disturbance is being caused by Nigiro spacecraft, picking up or dropping someone off."

I nodded, although I didn't really understand how picking up or dropping off Nigiro affected the weather. I wondered *if any of the extraterrestrials were our neighbors or 'friends', put in place to provide assistance when the UFOs begin to arrive. One thing was for certain, I'd have to start paying better attention to the people whose circles I moved within.*

"By now, you are also probably wondering when the rescue will happen."

Although I was still slightly uncomfortable with my child's newfound ability to monitor my thoughts at will, I appreciated her straight forward way of asking with no double-speak.

"I can only tell you that the Nigiro will deploy upon instructions received from The Creator."

I didn't know what else to say, so I did not say anything.

"Take care of yourself, angel," Gerald added. "I'm so very proud of you!"

"Thank you, Daddy." Her hologram began to blur at the edges. "Mother, by the way, the Teacher's inattention during your first encounter with him was not intended as rudeness. It's just that he places his attention on those who have the desire to know the truth. Until now, he did not see a yearning for the truth within you. But now that your heart has lightened, do not be surprised or alarmed when The Teacher reaches out to you directly."

'I keep forgetting she can read my mind!' I crossed my arms protectively across my chest, trying my best to hide my embarrassment.

"I want to give you one more tidbit of information that may help with the timeline for the completion of your task."

"We're listening," I said, after confirmation from Gerald.

Though Kenya's image was now almost transparent, her projected voice was clear. She said aloud to us both, "The moment I presented the book to you was the moment you began your spiritual journey to rediscovering yourself and reconnecting with The Creator. The gifting of ourstory was not a mistake."

"What's going to happen to our family?" I asked, reaching for my husband's hand.

"Be not fearful of what will come. Continue to pray. Watch for the signs, especially the wonders found in nature."

"I'm not sure what to look for, but I'll keep my eyes and ears open," I replied.

"I will do the same," Gerald added.

"There are infinite ways The Creator sends the message of Love. In time, you will learn discernment. In the meantime to help you remain focused, The Teacher has given me this message for you, 'There will come a day when you are outside reading a passage from your Bible. A beautiful hummingbird will suddenly appear as if it just stopped by to say 'Greetings!'. And just as quickly as it came, it will quickly flutter away. This will happen three times'."

"I can't remember the last time I've seen a real live hummingbird. So when it happens, I will definitely remember that you told me first." I replied. I allowed the lovely images to take hold of my heart, having faith it would happen. When? I did not know, but I vowed to remember the joy I felt when she described what was yet to come.

"Mother, one last thing before I go," Kenya relayed.

I heard a barely audible voice inside my mind as she relayed, "The cough was not just a cough. You may notice a small blemish within the space between your shoulder blades. Tiny clusters of cancerous cells had grown on your lung and eventually appeared as an irregularly-shaped mole on your back. Unbeknownst to you, The Teacher removed the malignant growth and all remaining cancerous cells from your body. I just want you to know that you are forever cancer free."

Gerald's facial expression registered as astonishment. He turned towards me for he too had heard the utterings of that quiet voice's very fortunate news.

"I love you, Daddy. I love you, Mommy," she relayed, her hologram now barely visible.

"We love you too, Kenya!" Gerald and I shouted simultaneously.

As for me, I thought the dry cough I had experienced for almost a month was the leftover remnants from a bad cold virus, not cancer. With this realization, I didn't say another word. Just took in several deep breaths of the freshly rain-washed Oklahoma air, grateful to be able to do so.

I relayed to the Teacher who remained shrouded within the spacecraft above, a heartfelt, *"Thank you."*

Chapter Seven

The trance was broken. Gerald and I once again found ourselves standing within the confines of our backyard, in the waning storm, with gentle warm raindrops falling on our upturned faces. We shielded our eyes, capturing another glimpse of the spaceship—or UFO as most people would have called it—watching it vanish completely within the thunderstorm. White-hot bolts of lightning lit up the darkened afternoon, yet only an indecipherable ripple in the air remained where the humongous vessel once was. The tornado sirens once again sounded in the distance. Although we no longer felt the need to take shelter, we did want to get out of the rain.

I did not want this special moment to end, but I begrudgingly followed my husband inside the house. We remained silent for many minutes before speaking. He was, as was I, lost in quiet contemplation about what we'd just experienced.

"Zumira, what just happened?" he asked, stepping out of soaking wet shoes, propping them up near the door to dry. "I felt like I was in a different world."

"Yeah, that was something else..." I agreed, pulling off my wet clothes at the patio door, watching him do the same. Dressed only in my undergarments, I padded to the linen closet and pulled out a towel for Gerald and a bathrobe for myself. I returned to the hallway where he stood dripping wet. I tossed him the towel, then said "Can you...?"

"Shhhhh," he abruptly said, maintaining the presence of mind to remember that we lived in a constant state of being monitored. "Where are the cellphones?"

Picking up on his thoughts, I replied, "On the kitchen counter."

He made a 'shooshing' sound holding his finger over his mouth.

I watched as my husband placed both phones into the lead-lined box we kept on the kitchen counter. We actually owned two safe-communication boxes. The other one was in the bedroom. Anytime we wanted to have a 'private conversation' we stored away the phones to prevent the potential of eavesdropping.

Only when the phones were safely put away did he lose his restraint. He shouted, "Zumira! That was amazing! Not only did we see a real live UFO, but we spoke to Kenya's hologram transmitted down from it!"

"I know, right?!" I absent-mindedly scratched an itch on my head. I struggled to find the right words to describe how I felt, but they remained out of my grasp. "Ya know... I thought I had seen it all that night when Kenya showed up in a ball of light. But what happened today... this was *way* different than last time."

"I still don't believe my eyes! That spaceship was so big it's impossible that no one else saw it!" Gerald shouted, rushing to the living room window, expecting to see the neighbors gathered outside going nuts. "And getting transported to your ancestors' indigenous family village?! That was incredible!"

"I'm glad we experienced it together." I looked at my husband with fresh eyes, forever bonded by our shared experience. I told him, "You don't have to worry whether anyone else saw what we did. According to Kenya's story, the Nigiro are pretty good at being elusive. They are only seen when they want to be seen."

"Wow! Our baby girl... She is part of something so much bigger than what we could have ever imagined," he remarked. "I am so proud of her."

Nostalgia replaced trepidation as I stared at the pile of loose papers stacked on the table with the story of a child I never really knew. Kenya always seemed to be on a different vibe than the rest of us. I guess it took her getting abducted—I mean rescued—for us to realize how truly special she was. And *is.*

"If the Nigiro are the original humans, *this* changes everything," Gerald said with a grin, casually resting his hand on top of the draft copy.

I added, still shaken from our encounter, "Kenya *is* truly gifted *and* blessed. We just have to catch up to believe what she says is true." A feeling of calm overtook me as a memory formed in my mind. One that always seemed to pop up when I thought lovingly of my child. "She always had her nose stuck in some book reading about who knows what."

Gerald's gaze rested on the backyard, staring at the spot where the echo of the vision continued to resonate. "Strange how life works out," he uttered. "What are the chances that we'd end up living on the same land that originally belonged to your ancestors long before this was even a country?"

"Or that we'd end up living on an unknown unmarked burial sites..."

"Good thing we never considered putting in a swimming pool. No telling what they may have uncovered." He laughed before thoughtfully adding, "But then again, maybe we should research what used to be here before they built these houses."

"You know what, even though the thought of living on top of a sacred burial ground bothers me, I'm more concerned about what happens next."

Toweling his bald head dry, he said, "Still, I wish I could have seen Kenya in person. Held her once to know that she really is truly happy."

"I'm sorry you didn't get that chance, but she seems like she's doing better than fine. She's doing what she was meant to do."

"You're right. It's just that I miss her so much," Gerald said, finally accepting the inevitable. "Hey, I have a question for you. Kenya referred to God as 'She'. What do you think that was about?"

"I don't think she was referring to God as either 'male' or 'female'. I think that since English is the only language we understand, the pronouns we use are limited to one gender or the other. Man or woman. He or she. In reality, The Almighty has no gender."

Gerald stared at me as if I had grown a third eye in the middle of my forehead. He'd never heard me speak so freely about God.

"What?" I shrugged. "I'm trying to get in better touch with my spiritual side. With all that's happening, I think I'm finally beginning to comprehend that God *is* real!"

"I am happy you feel that way, but to consider The Almighty as *"She"*... That's quite a stretch," Gerald said, falling back on his old religious background where patriarchy was the rule rather than the exception.

I replied gently, "Changing people's minds to refer to God as *"She"* would take an entirely different way of thinking in terms of religion. I don't know if the people are ready for that." I added, "But what I do know is, aliens are real!"

"Zumira, do you think aliens... I mean, Nigiro, are living amongst us?"

"Yes, I do. And so would you, if you believe what Kenya said is true."

"Yeah, she was pretty convincing." Gerald nodded in agreement before whispering, "She said they only come down when they're dropping off or picking up someone. What did she mean by that?"

"According to her story, the Nigiro are all around us. Hiding in plain sight. Gathering up information and using it to plan their rescue." To bring back a semblance of normalcy, I wrapped myself in a towel and went to the foyer to retrieve the mail. The storm had weakened considerably as it moved out of the area.

The electricity kicked on with the loud popping sound of a generator coming back online. The television once again blared out reports about the weather. By now, the weatherman had removed his jacket, loosened his tie, and rolled up his sleeves in preparation for a long afternoon of updates. The thrill of finally having actual weather to report had increased the man's adrenaline level to the point that his voice was now two octaves higher than normal. Storm chasers livestreamed videos of wall clouds lowering and then beginning to rotate. When a tornado equivalent to an EF2 on the Enhanced Fujita scale did materialize, they provided concise locations, down to neighborhoods and street level. *We were no longer concerned about tornado warnings. Whereas, the threat for those in its path were real, to us it had all been a ruse the Nigiro used to mask their arrival.*

"Maybe I should read this again," Gerald said in reference to the book. "In my excitement to get to the end of the story, I might have missed a lot of details during the first read."

"Yeah, maybe we should both re-read it," I agreed.

As I tidied the kitchen table, a light blue envelope amongst the stack of mail caught my attention. The envelope with a major New York publishing company's logo in place of the return address, was addressed to me. I promptly ripped it open.

"Well, what does it say?"

"Honey, listen to this," I said, tossing my hands up in disappointment.

"Another rejection letter?" he asked, using the remote to turn off the television. Giving me his full attention.

"Yes, but it's not as bad as the others. I actually think this one may have considered publishing our book. I read the letter aloud, *"We find the concept of your novel very intriguing. Unfortunately, the subject matter is not appropriate for our core audience. However, we have referred your manuscript to another group that specializes in this type of story. We wish you the best in all your future writing endeavors'..."* I placed the letter on the table, sighing. "I'll give you a dollar if you can guess who their 'core audience' is."

"Well, it looks like they are interested, but no telling how long it'll take for their other group to get back to us.

So since time is of the essence, I guess we'd better find out how to do this ourselves." Gerald pulled on a sweatshirt and shorts, from a basket of clothes waiting to be folded, and then plopped down on the sofa.

"Yep, I suppose so," I sighed again, wearily. I had placed way too much confidence in hoping that a major publisher would understand the importance of the story. Those agencies were all about the bottom line. Since I had received the latest response to my inquiry, the task at hand once again felt momentous.

"At least they didn't outright turn you down," Gerald tried to console me.

"You're right," I replied. "I had no idea Kenya's visit would zap so much of my energy. I'm going to take a bath to recharge."

Once in the bathroom, after pouring in an entire bag of scented sea salts, I drew my bath. As I waited for the water to fill the free-standing clawfoot bathtub, Kenya's declaration came to mind. I picked up a hand mirror and maneuvered my body to get a better look at my back. The reflection of me in the bathroom mirror took my breath away. I spotted a healed sore between my shoulder blades.

"Gerald!" I shouted. "Come here!"

"Just when I was getting comfortable," he huffed, pushing himself from the comfort of the sofa.

"Honey, come to the bathroom!" I called out again.

"I'll be right there!"

"Hurry!" I called out impatiently.

"What's wrong?!" he shouted coming through the door. "What is it?"

"Look at my back!"

"Woman, I thought something was wrong with you," he replied, exasperated.

I turned my back towards the light so he could get a better view.

"What am I looking for?"

"Look between my shoulder blades. See that little spot where my skin is healed-over?"

"Yeah, I see it," he said, running his hand over the scar. "How did you do this?"

"Before Kenya left, she told me that her teacher had removed cancer from my lungs. Now why would I have cancerous cells growing in my lungs? I don't smoke…"

"When did she say that?" he asked, slightly confused.

"Right after her hologram returned to the UFO."

"What exactly did she say?"

"She communicated with me telepathically. She told me the teacher healed me of a cancer I didn't even know I had. I can see the evidence on my back of something, but the thought of having cancer never crossed my mind." I whispered, mentally reviewing the past several years of my medical history, "Nobody in my family has ever had any form of cancer that I'm aware of."

Gerald took a deep breath before speaking. He blurted out, "Baby, I think we both received the same telepathic transmission. Out of nowhere I heard this tiny voice, explaining that you are cancer free!"

"You heard it too?! For real?!" I looked at him grinning at yet another supernaturally shared moment. "This is sooo crazy!"

Gerald proclaimed, "What I must say about what we just heard is, don't question why the cancer was removed, just say, 'Thank You'."

"You do have a point," I said, turning the water off. "I am very grateful."

"Enjoy your bath. I'll be out here reading."

With a newfound sense of gratitude, I stepped into the tub and sank down into the fragrant warm water. "This is really funny…" I whispered, more to myself than to my husband.

"What is?" he asked before he could close the door.

"Everything! Today we both witnessed an actual spaceship! We watched while a hologram of our missing child made our entire neighborhood vanish right before our eyes. Our child can use telepathy to communicate with us. The teacher can heal a disease I didn't even know I had. We went either backwards or forwards in time...to the point I don't know where we are now!"

"Well, when you take all that into consideration, we did have a mind-blowing afternoon," he remarked, closing the door. "Enjoy your bath. See you in a few."

I was in a reflective mood listening to music softly play in the background while I gently splashed the warm water over my face. I replayed the fantastic events of the day over in my mind. Inhaling the tropical coconut scented fragrance triggered a pleasant memory of our family vacation in the Dominican Republic. That was such a wonderful trip! An entire week of sunshine, sand, and fun spent in a beautiful villa with my husband and our children had brought us all closer. I recalled an episode with Kenya that at the time left me puzzled, but now I clearly understood what was happening with her. My baby is a gifted spiritual conduit. She was blessed to communicate with highly evolved heavenly spirits who no longer have the ability to do so in the natural realm.

With this epiphany, I regretted the many times I told her to be quiet when she asked difficult questions about subjects I had no knowledge of, because I was too ashamed to admit I had no response. How I wished I could hold her one more time and lovingly express how proud I am of her. She brought a ray of sunshine to a world fueled by darkness.

Chapter Eight

The house phone in the hallway rang several times before Gerald picked it up. As soon as I heard my husband's hearty laughter, I knew that our youngest son, Stokely, was on the other end. Other than political robocalls and telemarketers, he was the only one we knew who used that number. The reason we had a landline in the first place was because it was already installed when we bought the house and I came to find out that landlines were crucial to have during power outages. Or when the cell phone towers went down due to strong winds—which was a high probability in Oklahoma. Nevertheless, Stokely only used the house phone when he wanted to discuss something personal or sensitive, thus I knew whatever it was, it had to be important.

I quickly got dressed and joined my husband in the hallway. He motioned for me to get the other phone, so I hurried to the kitchen and picked up the extension.

"Stokely!" I said, happy to hear his voice again. "I was wondering what you've been up to. It's been over a month since we've last spoke."

"Hi Mom! I'm hangin' in," he replied in a deep voice, sounding more like his older brother each day. "I was just tellin' Dad that it's been too long since I've seen you guys. I wanna come home this weekend, if that's alright."

"You know you don't need an invitation to come see us. Of course! I'll even ask Malcolm and Drena to be here when we get home."

"That sounds great, Mom," he said, but without the usual cheerfulness coloring his voice.

I immediately picked up that something was off. Stokely was my youngest child, the one who never let anything get to him. He was supersensitive, yet took everything in stride. When Gerald and I told him about the move to Oklahoma City and that we were selling our house, I was surprised when he told us that he wanted to remain in St. Louis. We expected he would have wanted to get away from the constant reminders of his missing sister. But when all was said and done, he did not want to leave his hometown or his extended family.

Since he was technically an adult, he made the decision not to move with us. Although I wasn't happy about his living so far away, I had to give him the space to fully experience his life. His grades were excellent enough to warrant a scholarship to the university. He had a part-time job to help pay his living expenses. Thus, we agreed he could stay *if* he lived with my brother and his wife while he attended the university. Stokely was on the accelerated track to get his undergraduate degree and was making plans for graduation in two more years. He made me proud.

Gerald was as perceptive as I was when it came to our children. And before I could say anything, he uttered, "What is it, Stokely? What's going on up there?"

He hesitated momentarily before speaking. "I didn't wanna say anything..."

"Do you need for us to come get you?" I jumped in.

"Actually, I do," he replied. "My driver's license expired. I don't wanna chance getting stopped on the drive down. Things are getting bad up here. Those cops are lookin' for any little reason to lock us up."

"Wouldn't it be easier if you just renewed your license?" I asked.

"Yeah, you would think so. But because of this virus, the state of Missouri wants proof of vaccination before anyone eighteen and older can renew their driver's license. Same applies to gettin' passports. My shots ain't up to date."

"Why don't you just get the vaccine?" I asked.

"Mom, I already took three shots because the school mandated it to return to class," Stokely replied, "...but don't nobody wanna get vaccinated every six months, especially the people who got sick from takin' their first round of shots. I told the people at the Motor Vehicles that I'll get another booster shot as soon as 'they' figure out what the long-term effects of takin' all these different vaccines are. Til' then, I guess I'm stuck without a license."

I sighed wearily, listening to my son's dilemma.

"This is getting out of hand," Gerald added. "Next thing you know, we're going to have to show our shot card just to travel to another state."

"Some of my friends took a road trip a few weeks ago. They said the Missouri state patrol is settin' up road blocks at the borders. They're randomly pullin' cars over. Checkin' travelers' temperatures and askin' about where they're goin'."

"What?!" I shouted. "They can't do that!"

"Yes, they can, sweetheart," said Gerald. "I've heard the same thing is happening in several states."

"That ain't all," he lowered his voice. "Uncle Ricky was arrested last week. He was charged with disturbin' the peace, just 'cause he invited me and my friends over to the house. We weren't doing nuthin' 'cept hangin' out in the backyard."

"What?! Is he all right?!" I shouted.

"Yeah, he was released the next day, but he don't seem the same, Mom. I think they did somethin' to Unc while he was in jail. He keeps sayin' they put a 'chip' in him."

I placed the phone to my chest and exhaled. Now was not the time for anger. I had to think about my son.

"What happened?" asked Gerald.

"Uncle Ricky an' Auntie Sharleen thought it would be cool for me to invite a few friends over to the house to blow off some steam after studyin' for finals. We was just hangin' in the backyard listenin' to music, playin' cards, and talkin' smack. About an hour after everyone showed up, Auntie started servin' the food. She got a phone call and seemed kinda worried. She said somethin' to Unc because he took off into the house. When he came back outside, they started talkin' real loud. I asked them what was goin' on. Even before Auntie or Unc could explain, the po-po rammed the gate open! About a dozen cops dressed like a swat team rushed into the backyard with their weapons raised and yellin' at us to put our hands up. They acted like they was breakin' up some terrorist group!"

"Are you okay?! Was anyone hurt?!" Gerald asked.

"We was all scared, but we stayed cool. What got me Dad was it was a brotha leading the team. That head-nigga-in-charge walked through the gate like he owned the place. He had this look on his face I've seen before... Excuse my language Mom, but he looked at us like we wasn't shit when he asked whose house it was. Uncle Ricky was real cool when he told him, 'He was the owner'. Unc didn't lose his temper or nuthin'. He just asked him what was goin' on."

I felt my temperature begin to rise. My brother was well-versed in dealing with the police because he had lived in St. Louis all his life. Unfortunately, frequent encounters with the police was a way of life for black and brown men, then and now. The uncharacteristically angry manner in which Stokely spoke indicated he'd had several encounters with the police since moving in with my brother.

"That nigga had a smirk on his face when he said they got a complaint of loud music."

"That's no reason for them to bust into their yard!" I screamed, fighting to quell the rising tide of anger within.

"While the HNIC was talkin' ta Unc, one of the white cops asked all us for some identification. We didn't want no trouble so all we gave them our school ID's. When he found out we was college students, he told the HNIC. I guess that pissed that nigga off. He acted like he didn't like the fact that we went to school. He snatched my ID from that white cop and laughed. He had the nerve to ask me if I thought I was *Stokely Carmichael*."

"So, what now?! You're telling me that educated young adults can't get together on a Saturday afternoon?" I said through clenched teeth.

Stokely momentarily choked up when he explained, "I tried to talk to the HNIC because I thought that since he was a brother, he'd be a little bit more understanding. But that nigga told me to 'Shut the fuck up!'. That really pissed off Unc so he called him a 'damn sellout'."

"Oh no...." I whispered. "I can only guess where this is going..."

"He told Uncle Ricky he was under arrest. Auntie kept explain' that they hadn't done nuthin' wrong. Told them fools that we was just havin' a friendly get-together to blow off steam, because it was finals week. But they wouldn't listen to her, me, or any of my friends. We watched them shove Unc against the fence an' put handcuffs on him."

"Son, I can only imagine how it must have felt watching them do that to Ricky."

"Dad, it took every ounce of control for me to stand there and do nuthin' while those cops put Uncle Ricky into the back of that squad car. What really pissed me off was the neighbors who came outside to watch. All those white faces starin' at us like *we* didn't belong there. Their kids didn't even try to whisper the stupid stuff that they were sayin' out loud about Unc. They were too busy laughin' and takin' videos with their damn phones to really see what was happenin'."

"I am so sorry you had to experience that, Stokely," I said, feeling my son's despair seeping through the phone.

He continued, "I looked up and down the street at them big expensive houses with their nicely manicured lawns. At least one luxury car was parked in each driveway. Seein' the scared expression on Auntie Sharleen's face, and knowin' there was nuthin' I could do to help... That is when I knew we had been lulled to sleep."

While listening to my child describe an all-too-common occurrence, I had an epiphany! *Stokely just made a reference to being asleep. When Kenya was just a child, she often spoke about being awakened. I never knew what she meant until I read her book. Now I wonder if he is going through a similar experience.*

"They've been livin' in that house for over twenty years and not one of his lame-ass neighbors stood up for him?" I asked, naively.

Gerald declared, "Just because those people were Ricky's neighbors, they were never part of *his* community. I told them they shouldn't have moved into that neighborhood."

"Honey, you're not helping," I said.

"All those so-called progressive liberal white folks don't want to live near blacks even if they are professionals," Gerald scoffed. "Can't say it's much different here," he added under his breath.

"Mom. Dad. I'm ready to get out of this damn city!" he said. "I can't even go for a bike ride without being stopped. No matter where I go, or what I'm doin' there is usually some white person tryin' to question me to see if I belong. For real though, I'm scared I might get myself locked up if I don't get outta here."

I'd heard enough. No longer able to contain my emotions, I said, "I swear to goodness, I am so tired of having to hear about this incessant talk about 'white supremacy'! Those people aren't any better than anyone else. It is time they finally realized it!"

"The system won't change until people's attitudes change," Gerald said. "All that talk about defunding the police a few years ago actually did the reverse. Now they're better equipped than ever."

"I'm starting to believe racism will never end. As a people, we've been fighting for the right just to be human for as long as this country has been in existence," I said.

"I feel ya, Mom." Stokely was thrilled we had become more woke, but he still hadn't gotten quite used to what he called our 'light-weight radicalism'.

"Back in 2012, *we* thought our lives would improve with the re-election of President Barak Hussein Obama. Don't get me wrong, while I still love and support our brotha, looking at the big picture, after his serving eight years in the highest office in the land, he really didn't do much to improve the lives of black people." Gerald spoke about a time when, collectively, we hoped had ushered in the change we so desperately needed. A time before we realized we'd all been duped. "So the question I asked then, and I continue to ask now is, When will we learn that electing a president—Democrat, Republican, Independent or whatever—does nothing to make our lives better?! Only *we* can make this world a better place!"

"That's right, my love. We always get the same old bullshit!"

"Language, Mom," Stokely teased, breaking the tension.

"I'm sorry. You know what happens when we start talking politics," Gerald laughed heartily.

"So what's goin' on with y'all?" Stokely asked.

I used every bit of restraint within me to bite my tongue and not say anything about the events from earlier in the day. Thankfully, before I could utter a word, Gerald answered for us both.

"Same ol', same ol'," Gerald replied. "We're just trying to live our best lives, son."

I covered the receiver with my hand, grateful that Gerald and I were on the same page. Whereas Stokely did need to know about Kenya, this wasn't the right time to break the news of her reappearance. Not over the phone. He already had a lot on his mind and burdening our son with an unfathomable story would only add to his current woes. A discussion about the return of his supernatural extraterrestrial sister was better suited for an in-person conversation. So, for that reason alone, I was thrilled he wanted to come for a visit despite the awful circumstances surrounding his decision.

"So what's a good day to come get you?" I interrupted.

"I got finals all this week so probably the following week would be better. I already told Auntie an' Unc that I'm gonna move back with y'all. Auntie doesn't want me to go, 'specially with how Unc's been actin' lately."

"What's wrong with Ricky?" I asked Stokely.

"I'm not sure. Only that ever since he came home from jail, he's been actin' different and sayin' weird random stuff."

Gerald cut in, "Hey Zumira, Ricky's been buggin' me for the longest time to come down to check out his new outdoor kitchen. This'll give us the perfect opportunity to check on them."

"Sounds good to me. How about we overnight on Saturday then get on the road first thing the following Sunday morning."

"If it's good with Stokely, its fine with me," Gerald said.

"Sounds good. That'll give me enough time for me to get my things packed," he said.

"Great! We'll see you the following weekend," Gerald said. "Until then, try to lay low and keep your head down."

"I promise I'll be safe. Love you, Mom. Love you, Dad."

"We love you more," we replied in unison.

"And tell your Aunt Sharleen I'll be giving her a call sometime this week," I added.

After we said our good-byes, Gerald joined me in the kitchen. The storm was gone. The afternoon sun appeared just in time to raise the humidity to an uncomfortable mugginess for the remaining hours of the day. Unfortunately, the storm in our home was just beginning to brew.

"What in the world is going on?" I plopped down in a chair, feeling as if the air had been punched from my lungs.

"I wish I knew," he replied.

"If the visit from a hologram of Kenya courtesy of a UFO wasn't strange enough, now we have to worry Ricky getting arrested and Stokely being harassed by the police." I rested my head in both hands, feeling the beginnings of a headache creep into my temples.

"Zumira, they'll both be fine," Gerald declared, confidently. "Stokely has a good head on his shoulders and two parents who love and support him. With that, he's already ahead of most young black men his age."

"Yeah, you're right." I stood up, taking several deep breaths to help calm my nerves. "It's just that our son is a young black man living in a city run by criminals slowly trying to turn it into a police state. I am afraid for him. For his future and the futures of all those like him. And now I have to worry about the safety of my brother..."

Considering where they lived, Ricky's nocuous situation could just as easily have been his. With this realization, he sank down into the kitchen chair and said, "Stokely mentioned something about Ricky believing he was chipped..."

"You know my brother. He's always going on about government conspiracies. Microchipping the entire population to keep track of us without our knowledge or consent is one of them."

"Zumira, I know all about Ricky and his conspiracy theories," Gerald smiled. "We talk frequently, remember."

I laughed because my brother could sometimes be difficult to 'take'.

"Well, now I know why I wasn't able to get ahold of him last week." Gerald sighed. "But anyway, a couple weeks ago, he told me that the military is secretly testing out new nano-technology. Some kind of biological warfare for population mind control administered through vaccines," he explained.

"Dang..." I uttered. "Is he for real?"

"I'm only telling you what he told me. He said the government is using the ruse of mandatory vaccinations to insert nanochips into 'certain groups' within the population."

"I'll bet I can guess which part of the population they want to control," I said, trying not to shudder at the prospect of a living in a country where white people proudly proclaimed they wanted to return to the good ol' days. My question has always been, *whose good ol' days are they talking about?* Certainly not my ancestors.

"Ricky thinks 'they' can bounce signals off of all these new cell phone towers they're putting up every few miles. He believes once activated those implanted nanochips can alter one's behavior. He even mentioned that young brotha who shot up the Navy base a few years ago. It's rumored that he was under the influence of mind control. He told investigators that he heard voices in his head that made him do it."

I replied, remaining unconvinced, "See, that's the problem with conspiracy theories. Most are like fairy tales that no matter how ridiculous they sound, become more plausible with each passing generation. And those true theories, the ones that are based on facts, get lumped in with all the others."

"Ya know what, Zumira... There was a time I wouldn't have considered any of Ricky's conspiracies, but today... After what we just went through. And after reading this..." he said, referring to Kenya's book. "Well,... it's not hard for me to believe that those cops did something to him."

I interrupted, "But inserting a nanochip through a vaccine?!"

"It does sound farfetched," he snickered, with an unexpected twinkle appearing in his eyes. "But remember what the green-eyed woman told Kenya about the pharmaceutical industry. After that story, I now believe anything is possible."

"Yeah, I remember. And I do agree that the pharmaceutical industry does some foul stuff for money. But I don't believe they're putting tracking nanochips in vaccines," I retorted. "Speaking for us, I, for one, am glad we got our shots. I don't believe The Almighty God created the coronavirus, but I know He provided us with the means to keep safe from it."

"How so?" Gerald asked.

"Have you ever heard the story about *'The Drowning Man'*?"

He shook his head, "No, I don't think so."

"I believe it's a parable about faith. A man learns that God continuously provides us with help even when *we* don't know He's doing it. In the parable, there was a man stranded atop a roof during a flood. Praying in faith, the man asks God to save him. All the while he was stuck on that rooftop, three different men arrive—one in a rowboat, another in a motorboat, and the last in a helicopter—with offers of rescue, but the man waves them all off telling them he was praying for God to save him. Well, eventually the floodwaters overtake the house and the man drowns. He finds himself in Heaven talking with God. The man asks God why did He let him drown? God explained that He had sent a rowboat, a motorboat, and a helicopter to rescue the man. What more did he expect Him to do?"

"I get it," he chuckled, "but what does that parable have to do with Ricky getting a vaccine?"

"My love," I exhaled. "This is so much bigger than Ricky. One day it just occurred to me; that story is a correlation to the coronavirus and the vaccine. Who knows for sure whether or not that virus was created in a laboratory, but what we do know for certain is, it is in the world killing our people. My point is, God gave man the knowledge to develop an effective vaccine to keep us from becoming sick. And "Christian" brothahs and sistahs professing that God will protect them against the coronavirus are not looking at the complete picture. Like the man in the parable praying to God to save him, these vaccines were developed to save *you*. So, if anyone is still waiting for God to save them and choose *not to* get vaccinated, they are passing up an incredible opportunity to receive His Grace."

"Where did all that come from?" Gerald eyed me suspiciously.

"I don't know," I felt my head begin to swoon. "It just came to mind and I felt I had to say it."

"Interesting..." he murmured. "You just might be on to something profound."

"Woosah. Woosah. Woosah..." I uttered several times, calming my elevated heartbeat.

"Woosah is right!" Gerald exclaimed, picking up the draft. "Take the rest of the day off and chill while I read this again."

"Thank you," I mouthed, gratefully. Feeling better and much more relaxed, I went to the cupboard, retrieved Gerald's pint of Hennessy and two shot glasses. I placed the glasses on the table, filled both almost to the rim, and then handed one to my husband. From this moment on, everything we once knew was no longer. But perhaps that wasn't such a bad thing. The world as we know it could use a little shaking up.

"What's with the Hennessy?" he asked.

"I know it's not traditional and we normally don't drink when saying a prayer... But with everything that's happened today, we should consider this a very special day. So let's begin with a toast and end with a prayer."

"Sweetheart, forget about tradition! Let's start doing things our way. Besides, I could use a drink about now."

I boldly declared, "Here's to a new beginning. We will do our part to help make this world a better place, not only for our children, but for *all* God's children." Though I was no longer stressed, words from Kenya's testimony quietly entered my thoughts, '*You are protected. Your family is protected. Physically, yet most importantly, spiritually. As was each previous generation, and those yet to come.*'

We clinked our glasses in a toast.

Gerald bowed his head and recited a simple prayer, "May the Grace of The Almighty Lord be upon us as we travel along this wondrous journey."

In perfect unison, we prayed, "Amen."

Chapter Nine

Malcolm held the paperback novel in his hand, staring at the abstract painting depicting an unknown universe on the front cover. Gerald and I had decided to order two copies of the final version for the quality check before ordering more. The first drafts were delivered today, which worked out perfectly because we were heading up to St. Louis early the following morning to pick up Stokely. I could barely contain my enthusiasm when the mailman rang the doorbell after placing the small box on the door step.

"What do you think?" I asked Malcolm, removing the second book from the package. "How does it look?"

He merely shrugged his response. As far as he was concerned, although the artists' rendering was very impressive, the cover was the least important aspect of a book. What truly mattered was what was inside. That old adage of not judging a book by its cover was one he strictly adhered to. He had seen way too many books with dazzling covers that included what amounted to a load of crap inside.

Drena went to the bedroom and returned with Mali who had just awoken from her nap. I didn't babysit my granddaughter often, but whenever I did, it was a day filled with pure joy. Besides, taking the week off work to help finish the book and prepare the house for Stokely's return was a mini vacation I hadn't realized I needed. My supervisor wasn't pleased about the short notice—especially considering the recent bonus, but in my mind I said, '*whatever*'. I had much more important familial situations to focus on.

"I can't believe you and Drena were able to format the book, design the cover, and get this published. All within the span of a week!" Malcolm marveled. "I thought publishing a book took years."

"Had I pursued the traditional route of trying to find an agent to represent me with one of the big-time publishers, it probably wouldn't have happened at all. Those agents I did query always responded with 'thanks, but no thanks' if they provided a response at all. Without having connections in the industry, it's extremely difficult for unknown authors to break through."

"Mom, you actually published this yourself?" Malcolm asked, looking impressed.

"Apparently self-publishing a book isn't as complicated as I thought. Unfortunately, there is a stigma attached to being a self-published author. The problem is, *because* it is so easy to do, poorly written books have flooded the market," I explained, after learning this information from my research.

"No problem, Mama Zumira!" Drena gushed excitedly. "You're going to shatter that 'stigma' to pieces. We'll be marketing to as many sites as possible. I designed and ordered marketing swag—t-shirts, pencils, and author cards to hand out during events. Those should get here next week. We can even do a marketing blitz by setting up a booth in front of stores... I can call my friend over at the supermarket. Maybe we can do it there."

"Wait a minute, Drena! Don't get ahead of yourself," I chuckled, examining the cover of the second draft, checking for grammatical errors or misspellings on the cover. I planned to read it cover-to-cover during the trip tomorrow. "Let's make sure the book is good before we push forward. I want this to be as close to perfect as possible."

"You're right," Drena said. "I'm just super excited about the book and I want to be the first one to buy an autographed copy when it's done."

"Autographed?" I asked.

"Yes," she replied. "You are the author. Who else is going to sign it?"

"But I didn't write *Out of Nigiro*," I said, feeling for the first time like a plagiarizer. "How can I claim right and take credit for something I didn't do? This is Kenya's story."

"You certainly can't say that Kenya Mali Zambia Williams is the author," Malcolm added, candidly. He opened the pages and casually flipped through the book. "After all, technically, she is still missing."

"I didn't think about that..." I replied, taking a seat. My enthusiasm was replaced with trepidation about how to move forward.

"Maybe you should think about it. Because once that magnificent story is released into the universe, people are going to want to know how you came up with it," Drena added.

Malcolm laughed out loud. "I don't think she'll have that problem. After all, no one is going to believe this actually happened."

"Why not?' I asked.

"Mom, really?" he scoffed. "I know that something mysterious happened to you and dad last week during that tornado, but that doesn't mean others will be as quick to accept what's between the covers of this book as factual."

"Mama Zumira, don't listen to Malcolm. The people who need to receive the message will. No matter how they get it. Like Pops loves to say, *'Let those who have eyes see, and those who have ears, hear.'*"

"Stop encouraging her," he said to Drena. "They're the ones, especially Mom, who is going to have to come up with a cover story."

"I thought you were on board with us on this," I said, with no attempt to hide my displeasure with his change of heart. "When you left last Sunday, you were all gung ho. What happened?"

"Nothing happened. It's just the more I thought about this, the more I'm starting to wonder if publishing this book is a good idea."

"I don't know what you mean, Malcolm," I said.

"All this talk about spirituality. Supernatural beings. Extraterrestrials. Unidentified Flying Objects. Conspiracy theories. And not to mention the blatant reverse racism that is written all over this book. What do you think is going to happen to your jobs when it gets out how *you* feel about white people? Or the Tricksters, who we know are *Jewish*." He tossed the book on the table. "In today's cancel culture, people are being ostracized for saying anything negative about *those* people..."

"Son, I don't have any feelings one way or the other about Jew-*ish* people. If they believe they are living righteously, who am I to question them? I'm just delivering the message. You know what they say about not shooting the messenger..."

"We live in a different world than the one you and dad grew up in. I have a daughter to think about."

I stared at my son with fresh eyes. And for the first time since my initial contact with Kenya, I had to take into account how her reappearance had affected the entire family. Just as her disappearance and the resultant trauma had threatened to tear us apart. This was not his battle. I had no right to pull him into a promise made between me and his sister.

"You're right. I don't want to do anything to threaten yours or anyone else's life."

The relief on Malcolm's face was palpable. He gently took Mali from Drena's arm and held her close, placing a fatherly kiss on her forehead. He was his child's protector and if antagonizing his parents was what he had to do to keep his baby safe, then so be it. If there was one thing that resonated from his sister's story, it was the importance of remaining in Mali's life to raise her to the highest form of herself.

I thought about his brother Stokely and the precarious position he'd been placed in just a few days ago with that encounter with the police. I wasn't aware if Malcolm knew about that incident or not. I hadn't asked. With the simple act of a phone call about a group of black students gathered to enjoy a Saturday afternoon, he could have been tossed into jail. Or worse. Instead of progressing in our attitudes to embrace one another's differences, society has double-downed on white supremacy and blatant racism.

"I'll publish the book as fiction and I won't place it in any one category. I'll provide a foreword that explains the story was inspired by my missing daughter. And if it blows up in popularity, who knows. Maybe by then, the conversation will be much different and you won't have anything to worry about."

"That's right, Mama Zumira. If anybody gets upset about what's inside those pages, just tell them it's fiction. And if they really start to make noise, remind them that only the dog who yelps is the one who gets hit when the rock is thrown. That should shut them up."

"That's not quite the analogy I'd use, but I get the picture," I chuckled. "Drena, since you haven't read *Out of Nigiro*, take this copy. Gerald already read it twice. But you need to know what you're getting yourself into, as well."

"I'll start reading it as soon as I get home," she responded enthusiastically, settling down to breastfeed the baby.

Malcolm began gathering up any remaining baby supplies scattered around the adjoining family room.

"Thanks for having my back and all your hard work, Drena. But I totally understand Malcolm's position. No one ever said that doing the right thing would be easy. And I guess I'm about to find that out first hand. After we return from St. Louis with Stokely, I should be able to make revisions during the drive up and back, and then finalize the novel for release by next week."

"I sure hope you guys know what you're doing, Mom," he stated, uneasily.

"Son, I know you're having a difficult time coming to terms with all this. I have to admit it's been hard for me and your daddy too, but I made your sister a promise. I trust that she knows what she asked of me because she is working for a higher power. The Highest Power. So if I have to experience some discomfort, then that's what's going to happen." I stacked the book atop my laptop. Then added a pad and pencil for notetaking to the pile, since I was old school.

"Not to change the subject, but why is Stokely coming for a visit now? Shouldn't he be studying for finals?" Malcolm asked.

I 'tsked-tsked' when I responded, "It's obvious you two haven't spoken lately. Otherwise you'd know why he's coming down,"

"Sorry. I've been meaning to call to check on him," he replied sheepishly. "I've just been so busy with work..."

"There's no need to now because he'll be here on Sunday. We're leaving first thing in the morning, and then plan to spend the night with Ricky and Sharleen. Knowing your daddy, we'll be back on the road at first light so we should be home by two o'clock. I'll expect you both to come over for dinner."

"You're planning on cooking after that long drive?" Drena asked.

"It's no big deal. I already made a lasagna earlier this morning. All I have to do when we get home is throw it in the oven and make a quick salad. But... since you're concerned about me cooking, you can bring the garlic bread and dessert."

"I know what would be good for dessert, Mom. Can you pick up a Gooey Butter Cake while you're up there?"

"If we have time, I'll stop by the store," I replied, surprised that my son managed to keep his weight down despite his sweet tooth.

Drena chimed in, "I hope you do bring one back because Malcolm has talked that cake up so much, I have to try a piece for myself to see what the big deal is all about."

"It's a St. Louis thing," he explained.

"I admit, that cake is delicious," I conceded. "But it's made with everything that's bad for you. White sugar, butter, cream cheese, bleached flour... With all the decadent desserts, fried ravioli, white castle burgers, and MSG laced Chinese food... I'm surprised more of us aren't on kidney dialysis."

"It's really not that serious, Mom. It's just cake. It's not like I'm totally changing my diet overnight."

I laughed because what he said was true.

"Besides, I'll run a few extra kilometers next week to make up for it," he said, patting his six-pack stomach. "Just remember you have to go to the bakery on the southside to get a good one. Not from the grocery store. Those are gross."

"Don't worry, I know where to buy your cake." I went to the refrigerator to retrieve the extra breast milk Drena had pumped and stored frozen in single-serving BPA free bags. Mali wasn't a fussy baby, but she definitely preferred the breast over the bottle.

"What time does Dad get home?" Malcolm asked while glancing at the clock on the wall that perpetually seemed to lose time.

"He should be home any minute," I answered. "He probably stopped to gas up so we don't have to in the morning. You know how your daddy likes to get an early start."

"I'd like to stay until he comes home, but we'd better get going. It's my turn to cook dinner and if I don't get started soon, we won't be eating until ten o'clock tonight." He laughed.

Drena joined in. "He is not exaggerating. One night the food wasn't ready until eleven so we skipped dinner that night and had it the next day. And it was delicious."

~ ~ ~

The next morning, Gerald and I got into his SUV and headed east on I-44 towards Missouri. Watching the beginnings of the sun peak above the horizon, I was grateful the weather had cooperated and the forecasted storms hadn't gathered. Long distance traveling was bad enough, but there was nothing worse than driving on the highway in the middle of a downpour. I had planned on reading the book first thing, but since it was not yet dawn, we listened to soft music as a backdrop to our conversation.

"Did you talk to Sharleen?" he asked.

"I did. And she's a mess. She says Ricky is convinced he was drugged while at that police station. He actually believes they inserted a microchip in him."

"Why in the world would the police be interested in your brother? He's a mailman who delivers letters and packages for a living."

"I don't know, but apparently he believes they are trying to shut him up. For whatever reason."

"Zumira, what do you think is really going on?"

"I wish I knew, my love," I replied, slightly troubled.

Gerald and I were quiet for a few minutes as the strains of an old school song by Maze played on in the background. As we listened to the lyrics of 'Happy Feelings', it was nice to not have to think about the troubles of the world, if only for a brief moment.

"Zumira, I'm thinking about looking for another job," Gerald blurted out, unexpectedly.

"What? Why?" I sat up in my seat and turned down the radio. "Did something happen?"

"Nothing happened. Not yet, anyway. But these white boys are up to something."

"Something like what?"

"Not sure. But the white people I used to think were cool, well, most of their conversations are now focused on buying guns, ammunition, going to target practice. I can feel it in my bones that they're up to no good. Hell, they even take their families to the gun range on the weekend and call it a family outing."

I frowned, listening to my husband speak about strange matters. He tended to not let 'worldly' matters bother him. So when this topic did, I listened.

"I'm not just talking about wives and girlfriends. They take their kids too. I'm telling you, Zumira. These yahoos are preparing for something big."

"That's weird," I frowned. "Why would anybody, especially a woman with children, want to spend their family time at a gun range?"

He shook his head.

"What are they so afraid of now, Gerald? The government has had *us* living under martial law for years. The police are killing black people like it's open season. Hunting us down like we're animals... or dogs in the streets."

"Yeah, I agree with you with one exception. They consider us to be lower than dogs because if you shoot a dog in the street, your black ass will immediately be put in jail. White man intentionally shoots a black man and chances are they'll walk free. Or maybe get a slap on the wrist."

I stared out the window as we zoomed down the highway maintaining the posted speed limit. We didn't want to do anything to draw a state trooper's attention. The serenity of the countryside belied the simmering cauldron of racism overtaking the nation. We heard too many stories of black people being stopped and harassed by small town cops for no other reason than the amount of melanin in their skin. Thus, many of us opted to trade in our expensive luxury cars for something less flashy to decrease chances of being pulled over. Overt racism against black people exploded with the election of 45; causing the collective to wonder if we were indeed reliving the 1960's. It didn't seem possible that half a century later we would still be fighting the same war for fair treatment and equal rights. Yet, here we are again.

Our ancestors struggled to move us forward with each successive generation. That progression was thwarted in 1968 with the assassination of Martin Luther King Jr.. The 'Baby Boomers'—a term developed to categorize those born between 1946 and 1964, is the generation thought to have dropped the ball when they allowed themselves to get caught up in a capitalistic system that celebrated individualism. Far too many others were lured away from their communities by opportunities in the military or high-paying government jobs that came with benefits. They had indulged themselves in all the trappings that came with living a 'white' middle-class lifestyle. I reflected upon our lives. For all intent and purposes, we were worse than the 'Boomers' for we too had fallen for the okie-doke. Hook, line, and sinker. Comfortably living in the suburbs away from our people and the struggle, we inadvertently had become part of the problem by forgetting who we were.

As I listened to my husband hum along softly to the music—singing along without saying a word—his vocal chord vibrating in tune with the melody, I now understood the possibility of communication through vibrations.

I recalled an interview I'd heard the other day on my way home from work between an urban talk radio host and a semi-famous musician. At the time his theory on the evolution of music seemed ridiculous to me, now I wasn't so sure. '*When the ancestors were enslaved, they discovered they could communicate through songs. Music is the universal language and that's why we are so drawn to it. Record companies discovered music was an effective way to market to black people, so they dangled unimaginable sums of money in those artists faces and required they sign ironclad multi-million contracts. Artists who used to sing songs of empowerment and enlightenment resorted to recording songs about the 'gangsta life'. This new style of destructive music glamourized drugs and gangs, and only pushed us even further away from knowing the truth of ourselves.*'

"You're pretty quiet. You okay?" Gerald asked.

I snapped out of my daydream, noticing the sky had brightened significantly. We were driving east, heading directly towards the sun. I spotted a sign notifying us we were approaching the Missouri state line. But first, we had to get through the final Oklahoma tollbooth. Gerald scanned his credit card over the meter reader, I looked up and saw a line of red taillights ahead.

"What's going on up there?" I shouted to the tollbooth operator.

Her tone indicated I was not the first traveler to ask that question. She replied in a monotone voice, "Troopers been routinely setting up roadblocks for temperature checks and testing for the virus. That one up ahead should be the last checkpoint before you can leave the state. But I heard they're doing the same thing once you cross the border inside of Joplin."

When the machine didn't automatically print out the receipt, Gerald requested one. Most people would have disregarded requesting the receipt and driven on. But one thing we had learned over the past few years of living in a police state was to always carry receipts, even if it was just for a candy bar.

"Here you go," the tollbooth operator replied, handing him the printed credit card receipt. "You folks have a good day. And I hope neither one of you has a fever. Because if you do, that can definitely ruin your day."

"Thanks," Gerald said, taking the receipt. As the two lines of cars slowly crept forward on the highway, I leaned my head out the window, trying to get a better look.

"Can you see what's going on up there from your side?" he asked me.

"Yeah. Four state trooper vehicles with their lights flashing. And they're stopping cars. Maybe a dozen or so people wearing yellow hazmat suits walking around. Looks like they have dogs with them," I replied, in disbelief. "Dang, this is worse than I thought it was out here!"

"Zumira... Look at what those assholes are doing!" He motioned to the activity on the shoulder ahead.

"Wow!" I exclaimed, watching three more cars being pulled over. All the people who exited out were black. The trooper signaled a fourth vehicle to stop. When that driver stepped out of his car and joined the others on the side of the highway, I noted he was a young Hispanic man. From my vantage point, it appeared 'minority' drivers were being singled out, while vehicles driven by whites were waived straight through. I pushed down the anger threatening to erupt from the pit of my stomach. "This is some bullshit!"

"Calm down, love. We don't want any trouble. Let's just do what they say so we can get out of here."

When it was our turn to move forward, I made out a young white woman's face behind the clear plastic face shield of a hazmat suit. She motioned for us to pull over. Gerald complied. Then she instructed us to lower both the driver and passenger windows. With my eyes focused on the woman, and before I realized what was happening, a Missouri state trooper, a middle-aged white man sporting dark sunglasses, approached Gerald's side of the car. The more I stared at the scene unfolding on the side of the highway, the more I thought the state troopers' uniforms resembled those of German soldiers—before East and West Germany became two separate countries.

"Where are you going today?" the state trooper asked, in a pleasant enough manner while studying Gerald's recently issued universal driver's license.

"We're heading to St. Louis," he replied.

"For how long?" he asked,

"We're going to pick up our son for the weekend. He's in college." Gerald added, "We'll probably return sometime later tomorrow."

He looked in my direction, probably determined in a split second that I was not a threat, and offered me a quick perfunctory smile before glancing in the backseat for any other passengers.

"Here you go, Mr. Williams. You folks can go on thru," he uttered in a way that seemed to surprise him as much as it did us. He returned the driver's license to my husband and rejoined the trio of officers he'd just left.

"That was *different*," Gerald said, as he pulled away from the shoulder being careful to not make any sudden moves.

"Yeah, it sure was," I agreed.

"What makes us the lucky ones who didn't get pulled over?" he said, in reference to the brothers and sisters, young and old, standing on the shoulder getting their temperatures checked.

"I don't think we are lucky at all," I stated, watching them pull over the car behind us, which included a black couple who appeared to be about our age. "I'm starting to think we may have a higher power working on our side."

"I think you're right," he said, glancing in the rearview mirror for signs that the troopers had realized their 'mistake' and would be coming after them at any moment. He accelerated until they were cruising slightly above the speed limit.

I peeked at the speedometer when I heard it begin to beep. We were over the posted speed limit by 10 MPH. The automatic indicator that automobile makers were recently mandated to install in all the newer models, was our reminder to slow down. I cleared my throat and remarked, "While it might be true that we have a higher power watching over us, there is no need to speed."

"You're right," he said, decelerating. "No use tempting fate."

Chapter Ten

It was shortly after two o'clock in the afternoon when we pulled into the driveway of my brother's home. An inground sprinkler sprouted up from the next-door neighbor's yard, watering Ricky's walkway more so than the wilted chrysanthemums and geraniums dying in their own flower bed. We had to walk through the grass to avoid being sprayed.

Ricky and Sharleen lived in an older section of St. Louis; a neighborhood that included several historical estates once occupied by wealthy black families from the early 1800's and up through the mid 1900's. Ricky had learned the house was being put up for sale from someone on his mail route. Apparently, the retired African-American couple whose family had owned the house for several generations had decided to sell it to fund their retirement home in Florida. It was an architecturally sound house, beautifully designed and constructed with the finest of materials, unlike the cheaply built homes of today. When none of their family members could afford to buy the house, the previous owners were hesitant about selling it to a Caucasian family because most houses within the subdivision had already been snapped up by 'gentrifiers'. He and Sharleen met with the owners. They offered the previous owners a fair price and subsequently bought the house at a huge discount.

When my brother and his wife first moved into their home, the neighborhood was still predominantly black. Sadly, as the elderly homeowners began to pass on, they often willed their properties to family members who had no connection to them or the city. More often than not though, the elderly who lived primarily on fixed incomes and social security fell behind in paying property taxes. This often resulted in the city placing tax liens, which accumulated interest, against the property. And when they passed, whomever the house was left to would either have to pay the accumulated taxes with interest, or sell. Sadly, how the story too often played out was the heirs didn't have money to pay the subsequent tax liens and were forced to sell those magnificent homes at a fraction of their value.

Hungry real estate investors with an eye for opportunities to make quick money would swoop in and easily pay the tax liens, buying up properties from the city usually for pennies on the dollar. After a few cosmetic renovations, they'd quickly flip the houses and then sell at a price triple what they paid; usually to white homeowners looking to relocate back to the 'urban core'. Unfortunately, the heirs typically had no idea of the true value of the property or if they did know, did not have the financial means to pay the tax lien. What those investors understood is, money comes and goes, but the land remains forever. Unfortunately, as more familial homes exchanged hands into those of gentrifying whites, the composition of the neighborhood had gradually shifted the entire makeup of the once thriving black community. Since my brother and his wife were now only one of a handful of black residents who remained, their presence was no longer desired. And thus, now barely tolerated.

I rang the doorbell. From the depths of the hallway, I heard the musical chimes ringing out the first few bars of an old familiar song.

Ricky answered. "Sis! Gerald! So good to see you both. We were just about to have lunch," he said, unlocking the storm door. "C'mon in and join us."

"Hey big brother," I said, allowing him to envelop me in a bear hug. "Stokely's up in his room packing."

"Whassup man!" Ricky said, greeting Gerald with a brotherly hug. "How you doing?"

"I'm good, brother. Just trying to stay alive to see another day."

"I hear ya," he said. "C'mon back. Sharleen's in the kitchen putting lunch together."

We followed Ricky through the foyer. I had always loved this house from the first moment I stepped inside. Even though they had renovated the kitchen with stainless steel appliances and modern fixtures, most of the historical details were incorporated in the overall design. Unlike the cookie-cutter style houses springing up in new developments, their home had character.

Sharleen and I greeted one another with a love shared by biological sisters, rather than one of in-laws. "It is so good to see you again!"

"You too!"

"Zumira, I can't tell you how much I miss driving over to your house on a Saturday morning, picking you up, and us girls spending the entire day shopping. You, me, Kenya and Jewel..."

"Yeah, those were the good ol' days," I said. "Although Kenya was not a fan of shopping, she sure did like hanging out with her cousin."

"I'm so sorry," Sharleen apologized for her faux pas, "I didn't mean to bring up Kenya."

"Don't worry about it," I said for the first time realizing the pain of my child's disappearance no longer weighed heavily in my heart. "Speaking of Jewel, how is she?"

"She's in her second year at Howard and is doing wonderfully. She is so happy she decided to attend an HBCU instead of attending in-state. According to her, the teachers are fantastic, especially her African-American studies professor. She says that man has expanded her young mind to incredible heights.

"Good for her!" I responded.

She dried her hands on a threadbare dishtowel after peeking into the oven. "Chicken's on the grill. The baked beans should be ready in another twenty minutes."

Ricky pulled a bowl of potato salad from the refrigerator and set it on the table. Despite the warnings about leaving potato salad sitting out too long, he believed it always tasted better at room temperature. A dish covered by foil rested on the counter. "Go on upstairs and show Zumira what we've done to the house. Gerald and I are going to catch up outside over a beer."

"Girl, I forgot how much I love this old house," I said hugging myself. "Feels like home here."

"I know. And that is why we will always keep it in our family. Those nice people we bought the house from... Their ancestors paid for this house with their blood, sweat, and tears. We are not about to sell it to... those people," Sharleen said, glancing out the living room window as we headed towards the stairs.

I joined Sharleen at the window to see what caused her consternation. It was a young blonde woman out walking a large Pyrenees who appeared to be walking her instead of the other way around. In one hand, she held a cellular phone to her ear jabbering away. And in the other hand holding onto the dog's leash, she tightly clutched a small blue bag. The dog stopped walking, circled the grass several times before determining it was safe to shit there, and then hunched over and did its business on the neighbor's lawn. And like a good neighbor, the young woman turned that bag inside out, scooped up the dog's poop, and neatly tied it into a bundle. I watched her continue down the street, holding onto that bag as casually as if she were carrying her lunch.

"Come on upstairs. We totally remodeled the guestroom so you'll be in a different room than usual. Plus, we can catch up," Sharleen said, trying to remain upbeat. Whereas it was great to see the young woman cleaning up after her dog, her presence alone was a sign that gentrification to the neighborhood was in full effect.

I followed her to a guestroom so tastefully decorated, I thought I was in a five-star hotel instead of their home. "Sharleen! Girl, this room is nice!" I said, running my hands over the expensive bedcover. While one wall was designed with terracotta bricks to resemble the historic facet of the house, the remaining walls were finished in some type of wall fabric.

I peeked into the attached bathroom which provided a spa-like quality every bit as luxurious as the bedroom. The granite steam shower was over the top. But the built-in feature of a waterfall gurgling down one wall into a pond below, looked like they must have spent a small fortune.

Sharleen went to the far bedroom wall and pulled back heavy blue velvet curtains to reveal a set of French doors. I opened the doors to a small balcony overlooking the garden below.

"How did you two afford to do all this?" I asked glancing into the garden and taking in all the special touches throughout the room.

"This was my project after we finished the attic for Stokely."

"Thanks again for putting up with my son. I know he can be a handful at times."

"Stokely and Ricky butted heads a few times. He even moved on campus for a few weeks..."

I laughed and replied, "Oh yeah... I remember him calling and begging us to let him move into the dormitory after Ricky got on him about keeping his room clean. But once he got a couple months taste of living dormitory style and sharing his bathroom with twelve other young men, he told me he'd never give you two a hard time again about cleaning up after himself. So, thank you."

Sharleen glanced around the room, still admiring how a few simple details like adding colorful decorative pillows, succulent plants, and scented candles made the small space seem even more inviting. "We don't travel anymore so we're not spending all our money on vacations like we used to. I just wanted a really pretty room within the house. A room that Ricky and I could go into and pretend we're somewhere on vacation instead of being stuck in this city."

"Speaking of Ricky, how's he really doing?"

"You know... We're taking life one-day-at-a time. That incident last weekend... Finding out that one of the neighbors actually called the police on us! Zumira, Ricky and I have held get-togethers in the backyard for as long as we've lived here which is damn near longer than any of them! And now they got the nerve to say we were playing our music too loud! These white people are seriously trying to make us leave our home!" She pulled open the nightstand drawer.

"Why do you say that?" I asked.

"Check out this stack of offers we've received from realtors and investors. I started keeping them when I began to notice we were receiving more than usual. We used to only get these offers to sell our home only now and then. Now they're coming in the mail at least once a day. We even have people knocking on the door offering us twice as much as this house appraises for." Sharleen offered the stack of letters to me.

"Damn, we can't have nothing for ourselves..." I uttered, leafing through envelopes, postcards and flyers with pictures of realtors who'd be more than happy to sell their home.

"Hey Mom!" Stokely chose that moment to happily bound inside the bedroom with outstretched arms. "It's so good to see you!"

"Stokely! Look at my baby!" I hugged him tightly before pulling back for a full view. "Looking like a fully grown man!"

My heart leapt inside my chest upon laying my eyes on my son. He was no longer an awkward teenager, but had morphed into a man's body in the span of a few months. A thick beard now sprang from his chin where a few straggly hairs were the last time I'd seen him. His hair was shaved on both sides, but his locs were pulled atop his head being held together by a hair tie. Last fall before the semester had begun, he was such a skinny little thing, to the point I worried about him playing football because he was so thin. But looking at him now, not only had he grown a couple inches, but had bulked up nicely thanks to Sharleen's healthy meals and regular workouts with his uncle. Taking him in fully, I noticed not only had his outward appearance changed, but his entire demeanor now seemed much more mature than his eighteen years.

"Uncle Ricky sent me up here. He says he's ready to eat."

"Tell him we'll be right there," Sharleen replied, shaking her head, chuckling. "We've been married over twenty years and that man still refuses to begin a meal without me."

"Nothing wrong with that," I chimed in, thinking about how rare it was for Gerald and I to enjoy dinner together. Unless Malcolm stopped by on the weekend, most of our meals were eaten separately or if we did have dinner together, it was usually in front of the television. A sit-down family meal would be nice for a change.

"I'll let him know. Great to see you, Mom," Stokely said before exiting the bedroom.

I stared at Sharleen and asked, "Girl, what have you been feeding my child? He seems so different now."

"*I* haven't been feeding your child anything. Stokely hooked up with some little girl over at his school who introduced him to veganism. She's the one who taught him how to cook healthy meatless dishes. Even convinced him to almost give up meat. Far as I know, he's down to only once a week and that's usually on Sunday when I cook a big dinner."

"Stokely got that big by going vegan?" I asked.

"Um hmm. That and working out in the home gym Ricky built out in the garage."

I was pleased my son had made a decision to become healthy, especially since most those around him hadn't.

"You were about to tell me about Ricky... What happened?"

Sharleen's eyes darted towards the door to ensure their privacy. She leaned in towards me and whispered, "When he was arrested, and after he was processed in the jail, he said before they locked him up, he and a few other men were taken to another location. A clinic or something like that. They told them everybody had to be vaccinated before entering the jail. Said it would limit other inmates' exposure to that new virus that's going around. At first he refused to cooperate because he told them it was against his religious beliefs to be vaccinated..."

"What religious beliefs?" I asked, knowing fully well that Ricky hadn't attended any church in decades. He refused to be led astray by what he referred to as 'pimps in the pulpit'.

"...he only told them that because he didn't want their vaccination. But do you know they tased him and strapped him down! Then they forced him and all those other young black men to take the shot."

"Unbelievable! How can they do that?" I asked, naively.

"Girl, these white folks think they can do anything they want to us, nowadays. We don't have any friends in high offices who are willing to speak up for us. Seems like we are on our own, nowadays."

"I feel you!" I cosigned.

"Mom! Aunt Sharleen!" shouted Stokely from the bottom of the stairs. "We're hungry!"

"Fine! We're on our way!" she called back.

"Stokely says he doesn't want to return to school. Did anything happen that you're aware of?"

She shook her head from side to side and uttered with contempt, "Nothing other than him being harassed on a daily basis every time he steps outside this house by these so-called liberals who have moved in and taken over our neighborhood. The police have pulled him over too many times to count. And now him and his friends can't even get together to decompress after a long week of school."

"What has this world come to?" I asked rhetorically.

"I don't know, sis. Unfortunately, you and I aren't going to solve the world's problems today, so we might as well go downstairs and enjoy a nice meal. No telling when we're going to be able to do this again."

"You are right about that," I said, feeling my stomach begin to rumble as the scent of roasted chicken wafted in the air. "Besides, I haven't eaten at all today so I'm ready for some good food."

I followed her down the stairs and into the dining room. Stokely was helping to set the table by bringing out all the prepared dishes from the kitchen. Gerald and Ricky remained outside finishing up their conversation over a cold beer.

"Hey Mom, look what I made," he said proudly, pulling back the foil to reveal a dish of colorful food.

I went in for a closer look to see what dish my youngest son had created. "That looks delicious. What is it?"

"Garbanzo beans, red quinoa, steamed kale with roasted garlic, roasted red peppers, chopped olives, romaine lettuce, chopped red onions, and organic tomatoes all topped off with a lime vinaigrette dressing."

"You did all this?"

He nodded.

"Sharleen just told me you've stopped eating meat." His confession did not surprise me because he never had been a big meat eater. "When did that happen?"

"My friend first introduced me to healthy eating and veganism about a year ago. I started researchin' the negative impacts to our bodies when we eat the wrong kinds of food." Stokely admitted, "I totally eliminated sugar from my diet when I found out cancer cells thrive on the stuff like it's crack."

"I am so impressed, Stokely." I took out my cellphone and snapped a picture of his dish. "Good for you!"

"Thanks, Mom." He displayed that toothy smile that used to melt my heart. As a matter-of-fact, it still did. "I've been lookin' around at all these people my age getting diabetes and goin' on kidney dialysis and it made me wonder why. Disease in the body is a result of the bad food we've been eatin'. Everybody knows you can mess up a car's engine by using the wrong kind of fuel, so why do it to your own body?"

"I don't see how you got this big by eating just rabbit food," I laughed, gently punching his muscular arm. "Where are you getting your protein?"

"Plants and vegetables are packed with protein. Besides, the largest animals on the planet—elephants and gorillas—are vegetarians. They don't look like they are sufferin' from a protein deficiency."

"Good point, son. I never thought about it that way."

"Listen up, young man! Don't you dare try talking your momma into giving up meat!" Gerald teased good-naturedly, returning from the patio. "I am willing to give up the hog, but don't you dare mess with my yard bird!"

"Hey, I'm only tryin' to help you old folks stay healthy." Stokely laughed.

"Leave the boy alone, Gerald. If only Reggie had eaten better, he'd probably still be here," I stated, forlornly. "I still cannot believe he died from a stroke."

"Rest in peace, bro," Ricky added.

Our older brother, Reggie, had prematurely passed away the year before as a result of a stroke brought on by complications from diabetes. Unmarried with no children, he was only 46 at the time of death, leaving behind hundreds of friends and family. A young man by any standard, he was considered obese and suffered from years of untreated hypertension and undiagnosed diabetes. In our community a lack of healthy living and access to medical care had resulted in heart disease, diabetes, and all forms of cancer and strokes. In addition to practically nonexistent health care, there was also the threat of being killed by another black man which only added more stress to an already stress-filled life. And to top it all off, police were killing black men in record numbers as if it were some kind of warped gang 'initialization'. Considering hundreds of years of living in degradation and experiencing dehumanization, it would be prudent to place black African-American men on the endangered species list. Or at least acknowledge that this country has a race problem. If they can implement protections for a bald eagle, they could at least do it for a human being.

"Food's ready!" shouted Ricky, coming inside with a pan full of barbecued chicken that rivaled any store-bought rotisserie version. "Let's dig in."

"Not so fast! Before we eat, we must first bless the food," Sharleen explained.

Ricky cleared his throat and gave his wife the side-eye. He had given up the concept of praising a white-washed Jesus years earlier and wished his wife would follow his lead. At least the global pandemic had temporarily halted the thrice weekly gatherings down at the church. Although he didn't know the impact of missing all those 'in-person' services had on his wife, their bank account most certainly did.

Sharleen ignored her husband and preceded to give thanks to The Lord God. First for her family and second for the food. We joined hands together in familial solidarity and listened to the glorious blessing.

"... Amen," Sharleen whispered at the completion of giving thanks.

A chorus of 'Amen' rounded the table before plates of food were passed. For the next fifteen minutes or so, the only sounds in the house was the clanking of silverware and the satisfied grunts, moans, and groans from people who were thoroughly enjoying their meal.

Gerald was the first to break the silence when he turned to Ricky and said, "I heard you think those cops did something to you."

Ricky stopped eating. He sat back in the chair, placed his fork on the side of the plate, and wiped his mouth with a cloth napkin Sharleen used only on special occasions. Eyes now on his nephew who busily scarfed down his salad, he asked, "Stokely tell you that?"

"Yeah. What's going on, man?" said Gerald, who also stopped eating to focus on Ricky.

"You don't have to talk about it if you don't want to," Sharleen offered.

"Naw, it's alright. I want them to know what we're dealing with out here. What their son has to deal with from now on if we don't get our act together. As a people," Ricky said, taking a sip of beer.

"Tell them what you told me, Unc," added Stokely.

He pushed back from the table and went to the bar. After pouring a shot glass of Woodford Reserve, he slung the brown liquor back, grimacing as it trickled down his throat.

I watched my brother, knowing full well how he loved to play up a situation. I wondered if this dramatic effect was for our benefit. Growing up, our parents used to tease Ricky that he lost his calling of acting because he not only loved being overly dramatic, but shone brightly in the spotlight of attention.

"After they told me I was under arrest, I was handcuffed and they placed me in the back of that police car," he said, rubbing his scruffy beard. "First time since I was a teenager that I've been arrested."

"We all remember that day, Ricky. Daddy tore your ass up for shoplifting!" I exclaimed.

"I remember it, too. That was the first and last time I ever wanted to get involved in the so-called criminal justice system. And the fact that I hadn't done anything wrong really pissed me off," he replied.

Stokely added, "We weren't doin' nuthin' but getting our eat on and listenin' to music. We made it a point to not be loud."

"It's a real shame how much things have changed in this neighborhood. Loud music coming from the backyard used to be an invitation for neighbors to stop by for a visit. Nowadays, the only thing playing music gets you is a visit from the cops." Sharleen shuddered as she whispered, "It's too damn quiet on this street. Gives me the creeps."

Ricky nodded his agreement with his wife's statement and continued to explain, "Ya know, everything seemed pretty normal during the ride down to the station. I went through the arrest process, they fingerprinted me and took my picture. They took all my personal items. The usual stuff, I guess. But then they told me and three other brothers that because of the pandemic, everyone had to receive vaccines before they could be placed in with the general population."

"Why didn't you tell them no!" I asked. "Don't you have the right to refuse?"

"Sis, you obviously have never been arrested. They don't actually *ask* you anything. They *tell* you what you're going to do."

"Still, it seems that it's your body so you should have some say in what goes in it," I said.

"The guards put the four of us into a van and then drove to the public health clinic. They parked at the back entrance and told us to wait for the health care technician to come out and give us the shot. I told them again that it was against my beliefs to be vaccinated. But those racist cops didn't care about my beliefs because they were following orders of the state. Every single black man who was arrested that day was jailed and received several shots against our will. End of story."

"That's messed up," Gerald said, shaking his head.

"When it was my turn, I told that woman if she put that needle in my arm, I was going to jam it in her fuckin' heart."

"No, you didn't..." I sighed.

"Indeed I did. But as soon as I finished saying what I had to say, one of those rednecks drew his taser and lit me up. I fell to the ground. When I looked up, I saw that asshole laughing like the situation was funny." Ricky exhaled heavily before continuing, "That bitch stuck that needle into my arm so hard, I thought she had broken the tip off. And did you know she had the nerve to be wearing a cross around her neck?!"

Sharleen hugged herself tightly, rocking back and forth in the chair. She whispered, "We gotta pray for our enemies. That's the only way they're gonna stop treating us like this."

"Baby, I know you believe in what you're saying, but I have a difficult time praying for people who say they are Christians, but act more like devils! They better start praying for themselves."

"You're right," Gerald cosigned Ricky.

"So what makes you think you've been microchipped," I asked, feeling less cynical than I would have just a week ago.

"Little things. Nothing I can put my finger on. I just have that feeling like I am being constantly watched," he explained. "This might be totally unrelated, but lately I've been hearing a high-pitched sound in my ears that I never used to have."

"Shoot, that ain't just a feeling. We are all being monitored from the moment we walk out our front doors. In our cars, in the grocery store, at the movies. At work and during school. Or even when we think we're off the grid enjoying nature, we are being monitored." I held up my smart phone. "...Thanks to these convenient little 'government eavesdropping devices' we no longer have any privacy."

"What are you talking about, sis?" he asked.

I looked towards Gerald before proceeding. Once the cat was out of the bag, there was no way to put it back in. He nodded his agreement for me to continue.

"We have something to share with you." I glanced at Stokely. "It's about Kenya."

"Kenya?!" he shouted. "Did they find her?"

"Not exactly..." Gerald replied, eyes now on me with concern about how our son would take the news.

"What about Kenya?" Stokely asked with concern.

"Wait just a minute, son. I brought something that may help explain this better." I left the dining room and went into the foyer. I rifled through my worn tote bag I had left sitting near the door.

"What are you looking for?" asked Sharleen who'd joined me.

I pulled out the draft version of *Out Of Nigiro*. "This," I replied. We returned to the kitchen where the men waited. I paused before uttering another word.

"What's that?" Ricky asked.

"One sec. Do you have anything to block our conversations from being picked up?" I referred to my phone on the table. "Like when you want to have a private conversation."

Ricky nodded and pushed back again from the table. He hesitated momentarily before fully standing, as if he were contemplating something important.

This was all getting to be a bit much for Sharleen so she busied herself with clearing dinner dishes to make room for dessert.

"Can I help?" I asked, noticing her growing unease.

She shooed me away. "You're a guest. Sit down and make yourself comfortable. I got this."

Stokely stared at me and his father. With a frown on his face and lips tightly pressed together, he said, "Tell me what's going on. Did they find Kenya?"

I placed my finger against my lips to discourage his urgent questions. My son was old enough to view the world as it truly was. And because he had lived with his uncle for the past two years, he knew when not to open his mouth.

When Ricky returned to the dining room, all eyes were on him because he now wore a large pendant around his neck. On each wrist, he sported what looked like two oversized watches.

"What in the world are you wearing?" Gerald asked.

"Diodes. Since I don't know what this thing is inside of me, I got me some protection to block ingoing and outgoing transmissions." He repositioned the leatherette chair cushion on the chair before taking his seat. A lead-lined safety box, similar to the one we had at home, was plopped in the middle of the table. He motioned for everyone to toss their phones inside that box. Only then, did we speak.

Sharleen slowly shook her head, rolling her eyes.

"Okay, we can talk freely now," he said, making himself comfortable.

"What's up with the weird hat?" I asked, in reference to what appeared to be a baseball cap dipped in multiple layers of grey paint. The thing was so stiff, it more resembled molded plastic instead of fabric.

"I know my ballcap looks funny. That's because I dipped it in lead paint. It's the only way I can be sure they're not transmitting signals into my brain via satellite or those damn cell phone towers they're erecting every few miles."

Gerald stared at me with a blank expression, although I knew exactly what he was thinking. Ricky had gone off the deep end. At one time, we teasingly called him the 'Conspiracy King' because every single event in American history supposedly had some conspiracy behind it. He believed nothing his government told him. Now, watching him wearing a baseball cap stiffened by lead paint, only confirmed what everyone believed. He was truly off his rocker.

"Before you say anything else, I want to tell Stokely about Kenya." I turned to my son who was still waiting for me speak. I said, "We know where she is, but this is going to sound really strange. I need you to keep an open mind."

"What?! Is she okay?! Is she alive?!" Stokely shouted.

"Yes, to both questions," I answered.

"Where is she? When can I see her?!" he asked, barely able to contain his excitement. "Why didn't you tell me sooner?"

I paused, unsure how to break the news that needed to be broken. All eyes were now on me.

"Zumira?" Sharleen returned from the kitchen with a dish of banana pudding in hand. She placed it on the table, next to the protective box which held our phones. She asked tentatively, "Did you really see Kenya?"

I exhaled long and deeply, dropping my hands in my lap. I glanced around the table at their troubled expressions. This was much more difficult that I had imagined. It was easy telling Gerald and Malcolm because in a way, they had both been involved. But trying to explain the unexplainable to my brother, who appeared to have already lost his mind, and his wife a devout Christian, was nothing compared to how I would break the news to Stokely. He held his big sister in such high esteem, it was scary.

"Mom?" Stokely pressed.

"Well, first let me tell you that Kenya is fine. I saw her last week."

"What?! You saw her last week?!" Stokely pushed back from the table and stood to his feet. His eyes blazed first with anger and then excitement. "Where is she?! Why didn't you guys tell me? Does Malcolm know?!"

"Sit down, son," Gerald gently gripped his wrist. "Let your mother finish."

Stokely did as his father asked, though he dropped his head and tightly closed his eyes.

"Like I was saying, I saw Kenya last Thursday," I exhaled and whispered, "This is going to sound a little crazy. Don't make any judgments until you hear me out."

"Okay," Sharleen said, momentarily forgetting about dessert. "Go on. We're listening..."

"Yeah, go on, sis. Tell us what happened to baby girl..."

I pushed the book towards Stokely. "This is the story that Kenya gave me to give to the world. It's a story about a people called the *Nee-JHEE-row*," I carefully pronounced the name to avoid having them incorrectly read the title.

Stokely slowly opened his eyes and picked up the book. He flipped through the pages, frowned and returned the book to the table. "What are you talking about, Mom?"

"I need for you to trust me, sweetie. I have never lied to you and I'm not lying now." I rested my hand on his arm. "But your daddy and I need to tell you something."

He huffed and puffed, but he picked up the book again and then held it in his large hands. Tenderly, as if he would break it. He furrowed his brow, leaned back in the chair and then took in several deep breaths. Just like I'd taught him how to relax many years ago when we first found out about Kenya's disappearance. He used the back of his hand to wipe away a lone tear that managed to slip through his closed eyelids.

"Okay," he whispered. "I'm listening..."

Chapter Eleven

For the next hour or so, I relayed the entire story of what transpired since it first began. I started with my missing a day after a meteor shower—briefly mentioning that Malcolm did too. I told them about Kenya showing up in the beam of light and my visit to the spacecraft. I tentatively told them of my encounter of meeting a black alien who she called, 'The Teacher'. That she had been with him all that time because he was teaching her who she was. Explained that the pages of her story magically appeared by means of an 'inanimate object' the size and shape of a computer mouse. I shared Gerald's and my experience the day of the tornado, explaining how Kenya had shown us visions of ancestors who used to freely roam the open land. Gerald only interrupted to include details I had inadvertently omitted. We finally shared the plan to publish the book and freely distribute it to everyone we knew. When I was interrupted by someone's question, Gerald gently reminded them to hold off until I was finished.

Stokely sat there the entire time mesmerized by what he was hearing. When I said something that seemed too incredulous—which was practically every word that came from my mouth—he looked over at Gerald, gauging his dad's reaction. Satisfied that we were both on the same page, he remained quiet and continued listening until the last word was uttered.

"Have you both lost your minds?!" Sharleen shouted.

Neither Gerald nor I spoke a word because her reaction was anticipated and entirely appropriate.

"That story is so incredibly unbelievable!" Sharleen stated, shaking her head from side-to-side. "You honestly want us to believe that Kenya is living on some distant planet?! With black aliens?!"

Ricky sat back in his chair with a smug, yet deeply satisfied expression plastered over his face. He now felt wholly justified embracing this particular so-called conspiracy theory. He turned to Sharleen and said, "Told you there are aliens out there!"

"Wow!" Stokely exclaimed, leafing through the book. "Kenya really gave this to you?"

"Yes, son," I said. "These are her exact words. Her story. *Ourstory*. I wasn't allowed to change anything."

"This is nuts! I don't believe any of it," Sharleen whispered, as if she were trying to convince herself that her sanity was still intact.

"It's all true," Gerald said. "Both of you should read the complete novel once we get it published."

"Which will be when we return home," I added. "And we'll send books to both of you. Free of charge."

"Can I read this copy?" Stokely asked.

"Of course you can." I was surprised by how low key he seemed now, especially considering his initial reaction to learning of Kenya's reemergence had been so emotional. I hoped he wasn't experiencing some kind of shock. Or that he would have a delayed reaction and come undone. "Honey, do you have any questions?"

"Not right now. I just need to read this," he said, scooping up a large serving of banana pudding into a plastic cup.

"I thought you gave up sugar," Sharleen said to Stokely. By turning her focus to her nephew's eating habits, she hoped this bit of normal conversation would bring her back to a familiar reality.

"Today is my splurge day. Besides, this is a healthier version of traditional banana pudding."

"You made that too?" I asked.

"Yes. The pudding is made with coconut milk and a few other healthy ingredients. The sweetness comes from dates and monk fruit. Bananas are packed with goodness so that's good anytime. The cookies are sugar-free and vegan. And the Dominican vanilla extract I was lucky enough to find in the international section of the grocery store is the key to the unique flavor," he explained hurriedly, trying not to be rude. Their questions only kept him from the contents of the book he couldn't wait to dive into.

"It looks delicious!" I remarked honestly, noting the absence of the mandatory vanilla wafers that everybody knew was needed to make banana pudding the right way. "If it tastes as good as that other dish you made, you just may have a convert."

Stokely understood his mom's concern. She was just trying to feel him out to make sure he was good, but he had things on his mind way more important than food. With dessert in one hand and the book in the other, he headed towards the patio. "Okay, Mom. I'll be out here if anyone needs me,"

"He took that much better than I thought he would," I remarked to Gerald.

"Yeah, he sure did," he replied, also wondering what had come over his son.

"Stokely is much more enlightened than either of you realize. That boy has tapped into something," Ricky explained. "He changed once he started cleaning out his body... I guess it did something for his mind, too."

"Yeah, probably corrupted it," Sharleen scoffed. "Honestly though, ever since he started hanging out with that group of kids you invited over here, he started to change. Won't even go to church with me anymore."

"The only reason he was going with you to church in the first place was to meet girls. That boy ain't interested in no manmade religion."

Gerald added, "When it comes to that 'feel good' prosperity gospel they're pushing these days, I'm not surprised he gave it up. Those preachers fleecing their congregations ought to be ashamed of themselves anyway. They know damn well what they're preaching isn't right for us, but they continue to do it."

"Indeed! Misleading our people right over a cliff like a flock of sheep," Ricky added.

Sharleen explained, "Well, just so y'all know, when the pandemic ended in-person services, I realized that pastor wasn't offering me anything more than glimmers of hope while asking us to give more money in 2nd and 3rd 'love offerings'. I even began listening to online sermons. Hearing those men of God teach about topics I'd never heard before... Well, they blew my mind wide open. So I found a church focused on raising our people's consciousness to help us cope with this new world we're living in. Even some of what Ricky has been saying for years started to make sense."

I gently warned her, "Be careful who you listen to, sis. There's a whole lot of folks on the internet who'll say anything just to get followers. They're making money off the ignorance of our people."

Ricky said, "I tried telling her that she can't believe everything she hears on the internet."

"Look who's talking," she snapped back. "All those crackpots you've subscribed to..."

Instead of responding to Sharleen's jab, he lowered his head, releasing a frustrated sigh.

"So what do you think?" I addressed my brother, changing the obviously touchy subject. "Do you believe me?"

"Hell yeah, I believe you! I know there is more to this world than meets the eye." Ricky grinned and continued, "Sis, now that we're all placing our secrets out in the open, I have to tell you what I've been up to."

"Oh lawd, here we go," Sharleen said, rolling her eyes. She scooped out four portions of pudding into individual dessert flutes and handed them out. "Don't nobody want to hear about your lil' group."

Ricky abruptly stopped speaking, turned to his wife and showing tons of restraint, he whispered, "Don't. Do. That."

"You're right," she apologized. "I'm sorry. Go ahead."

"Thank you," Ricky said. "Like I was saying, I've been working for the post office... How many years has it been now?" Ricky pondered, rubbing his bearded scraggly face. "Ten... no, eleven years. And I've come across all kinds of strange people who mostly just cause me to shake my head. Anyway, earlier this year I was delivering mail along my usual mail route to an address just south of the city, not too far off Kingshighway. On this particular day, there was a young brotha sitting on the front stoop reading a book. He reminded me of a young Malcolm X way after he was no longer known as Malcolm Little. Young man was red-boned with reddish hair. Freckles across his face. Even wore similarly styled glasses."

"What was he reading?" I asked.

"That's exactly what I asked him because he was so engrossed in that book, he barely acknowledged me. I had to step over the young brotha just to place the mail in the slot."

"And?" Gerald asked, hurrying him along to get to the point.

"He told me he was reading a survival manual. When I asked why, he said it was because the city had gotten too hot for niggas like him. Told me he needed to learn how to survive in the woods until things cooled down."

I frowned before speaking, "You mean like... camping?"

"Not camping. Survival in the wilderness. Like what he needed to know if he went off grid for a while."

"No black person in their right minds wants to voluntarily live in the forest. Shoot, we don't even like to walk through the woods," I smirked.

Ricky explained, "That's exactly why he was reading about it in a book. He told me he didn't know a single person who had ever camped out, much less hiked the backwoods of the country. Not a one. He had no idea where to begin, what he needed, or even where to safely go."

"Now that you mention it, I don't know anybody who does those things, either. I mean... every now and then I go fishing, but that's usually just for a few hours," Gerald said.

"Same here," Ricky replied. "And as far as fishing goes, I haven't been since the last time we went together about twenty years ago."

"So did he tell you why he wanted to live in the woods?" I asked, nibbling at the banana pudding, which was delicious!

"Since I was ahead on my route, I had a few minutes to spend with the young man. He introduced himself. Told me his name was Quincy and he had just turned twenty-two. He said his mother gave birth to five boys and one girl. He never got the chance to know his father because he'd been imprisoned for most his adult life. Two of his brothers died last year only months apart. The oldest brother was killed by the police; gunned down right in front of the house he shared with his girlfriend and their two kids. Police claimed his brother had committed a robbery, despite the fact he was wearing a work uniform and had just gotten home. His friend and coworker backed up his story. Yet still, they murdered him. Come to find out, it was a case of mistaken identity. Quincy's younger brother, who was only sixteen, was killed over a drug deal gone bad."

"I feel so bad for his mother. I cannot imagine what she must be going through," I sighed.

Ricky continued, "His remaining brother is in prison for selling marijuana—locked up before selling it became legal. And his only sister is strung out, but trying her best to raise six kids by four different men. Quincy was his mother's last hope for at least one of her children to make it to thirty unscathed."

"Damn," Gerald uttered. "These young cats are putting their lives at risk just by leaving their houses."

"Our young people aren't safe anywhere," Sharleen chimed in. "Police are coming to our homes and breaking down doors, killing folks asleep in their beds. We've been shot while doing nothing other than sitting in our living rooms eating a bowl of ice cream. And now I've heard rumors that white boys from the suburbs are coming into our neighborhoods to start mess. They've been spotted doing drive-bys and randomly gunning down innocent black and brown people. This has even been reported to the police, but nobody is ever arrested. The local news has the nerve to report these shootings as 'black-on-black crime'."

"That's right," Ricky said glancing around the room. "That's why *we* should never feel that it can't happen to us, too. I'm telling y'all... 45 emboldened all these knuckle-draggers to notch up their killings of us. Man, it feels like we reverted back to the 1930's instead of progressing forward in the 21st century. What we're experiencing now is almost as bad as what our grandparents went through back then."

"Make America Great Again, my ass," I huffed. The delicious banana pudding did nothing to alleviate the vile taste of racism that our people faced on a daily basis. "They want to take this country back to the days when black people had no rights. When our only purpose was to serve them."

"What that young brotha told me got me to thinking about my baby, Jewel, going to college in D.C.," Ricky said. "Even though she lives in the nation's capital—our *supposed* seat of democracy—she still ain't entirely safe. She says folks are out there protesting all the time. Then I thought about Stokely living here in St. Louis. In the middle of it all. There is no good reason he, nor any other young black person, should have to live their lives being concerned with upsetting the feelings of some self-entitled, white person—juiced up by a false belief of white supremacy. All the damn microaggressions we have to deal with while on the job, going to school, and hell, even when we're out bird watching in the fuckin' park..."

"Girl!" Sharleen interrupted, "So what do you think your brother did? Never mind. I'll tell you what he did. He started a group and called it *Thriving & Existing in Nature*."

Ricky explained, "We're calling the group 'TEN' for short."

Gerald glanced over at me before speaking. "But didn't you say the young dude was already reading a book to learn survival tactics?"

"Learning survival skills is for white people. Black people already know how to *survive*. We use survival tactics every single day just living in America with this dark skin. What *we* need to learn is how to thrive and exist with nature, like the ancestors used to do when food was scarce. They were the original 'preppers'. Hence the name of the group, *Thriving and Existing in Nature*," Ricky further explained. "That young cat started me thinking about what we would do or where we would go when this nation finally collapses."

"I think that's a great concept," I said, thinking about Kenya's last words about spreading the word of the Nigiro. "Tell us more..."

"I researched how our great-grandparents lived— when they were still in the south, raising their own food and living off the land—before they began migrating to the northern cities in search of decent paying jobs. I read accounts of how wealthier blacks pooled their money together to purchase hundreds of acres of land, and then then sold smaller plots to poor black families for next to nothing. Our ancestors weren't playing around back then. Despite the government reneging on the promise of 40 acres and a mule for each freed slave, they pooled their resources and started up black communities on as little as 10 acres of land before increasing the acreage up to hundreds."

"You're right, Ricky. That was how the all-black communities of Robertson and Kinloch began. Back when they were looking to put down roots and raise their families, North St. Louis county was mostly rural farmland. Because those Negro communities were outside the city limits and built on what they considered as 'undesirable land', white folks really didn't care what they did as long as they weren't building homes next to theirs. Our ancestors developed those small-town communities because they wanted safe places to raise their families."

Sharleen added, her voice dripping with sarcasm, "Don't y'all know the purpose of integration was to help the 'poor disadvantaged Negro race' to move forward."

I sighed wearily and stated, "Our ancestors had no idea county officials would arrive decades later under the guise of 'imminent domain' to destroy what they built. The city purchased the land for pennies on the dollar and with the exception of the elementary school used to train military dogs, they totally leveled those towns. It was supposed to be an airport expansion that didn't materialize. Driving through those industrial areas now, you'd never know that thriving black communities once existed there in the 1930's through the 80's."

"Well... At least they didn't touch the churches."

"You're right, Sharleen. But what good is a church without a community of people around it?" I asked, rhetorically. "If it was their intent to wipe both those black towns off the face of the map and totally out of our consciousness, they almost succeeded."

"I agree, Zumira." Ricky explained, "Though it's truly sad that those towns were destroyed, it is important to note that their descendants remain in contact to this day. An annual reunion brings back residents from states far and wide."

"We've even been to a few," Sharleen added. "It's nice to see how everyone is faring, especially these days."

"Good for you," I replied.

"Look, y'all, I've been living in this city my entire life. My point is, if our ancestors could start a city back then with little money and much less education than we have now, what is stopping us from doing something similar?

White folks don't want to live with us, so it might be time for us to start up our own towns again."

"It sounds like a great idea on paper, Ricky. But we all know we ain't never gonna get black people to come together and agree on nuthin'," Sharleen, ever the naysayer, uttered. "Black folks have gotten really good at talking and planning, but when it comes to putting that plan of action in place, we always seem to fall short."

"I don't believe that's true," I said. "I think that narrative of black people being unable to work together is being pushed by the media. Because it is not in this country's best interest for African-Americans to come together, they keep telling us we can't.

"I think we're on the same page, Zumira. I want to spread the word about TEN to the peeps. Offer them a blueprint on how to live harmoniously with nature. We need to get out of these damn cities and return to the country. Build on our own land like our ancestors used to instead of relying upon these people for our very existence."

"I think you have a great idea, Ricky!" I proudly proclaimed.

"Are you sure about this?" Gerald asked, addressing his brother-in-law who Stokely most favored.

"What do you mean?" Ricky said.

"We all have seen what happens when we try to uplift ourselves as a people. Although most are now long deceased, I personally know people who survived the Tulsa massacre. Including some of my relatives. They were doing nothing except living their best lives. Wasn't bothering nobody. So what do you think happened when whites saw black people doing well? They got jealous, formed into a hateful angry mob, then went in and started killing folks. Then they torched the city to prevent the survivors from having a town to return to. It's been over 100 years since it happened. To this day, none of the victims has received proper restitution for what was done to them. Nor were their survivors ever compensated for the accumulated wealth that was lost."

"Look man, I never said this was going to be easy. Those devils are counting on us being afraid and continuing to do nothing. But we've got to start somewhere. If not for us, then for our children. And our children's children."

"Dang," I sighed. "This government really did a number on us. They made us scared of terrorists from other countries, but turned a blind eye on the terrorism they inflicted on our ancestors back in the day."

"That's right!" Ricky exclaimed. "The United States is best in class for terrorism because they've been practicing it on black and brown folks from the moment this country was formed. As a matter of fact, the CIA taught other countries how to use terrorism to keep their black people in check. And how do you think they got so good at it?"

"Well, if you ask me, we're still being terrorized," Sharleen said. "We can be randomly stopped by the police, just because. But what really pisses me off is we can't even walk down the goddamn street without somebody calling the cops on us for absolutely nothing!"

"What's your plan?" Gerald sat back, perplexed.

Ricky pulled out a stack of pamphlets promoting his newly found group and placed the pile on the table. "I hand these out when I'm delivering mail. But only to the people I think will be receptive. They get in touch with me and let me know they're interested." He then pulled out a yellow legal pad. "So far, I have over eighty people signed up."

Sharleen joked, "Most of 'em probably signed up for the free hot meals we provide at the meetings."

"I don't care what gets them here, just as long as they show up."

"Is this why you were arrested? Because you're forming a group to help blacks learn how to survive outside the system?" Gerald said, eyes scanning over the documents.

"Had to be this," Ricky replied. "There is no other reason for them to arrest me. I figure they must have gotten wind of what we're doing. I wasn't charged with anything other than disturbing the peace, but I believe they were trying to send me a message."

"They get an inkling that we're trying to help our sisters and brothers and they want to shut us down! Just what kinds of damn devils are we dealing with?!"

I glanced over at Sharleen, surprised to hear her swearing. I supposed that even the most religious, loving, and peaceful of us eventually get tired of the non-stop madness.

"What?!" she asked laughing. "I'm more aware of what's happening in this country than you think I am."

"Alright, sis," I joined in her laughter. "I hear ya!"

"Check this out, man. Up until a few years ago, I thought the Black Panther Party was a terrorist group because that is what I was taught," Ricky explained. "When I actually did my own research, I discovered they wanted to empower black people."

"Really?" Gerald interrupted. "I never heard that about the Panthers. I thought they were a militant organization formed to overthrow the government."

"Man, back in the 60's, this government was telling us all kinds of lies about our people. Those young cats— men and women—were only trying to protect the black community because no one else would. I gotta hand it to the man, though... He made us question our own people to believe they were not only unpatriotic, but were terrorists."

As I watched my brother speak, the words from Kenya's account bounced around in my thoughts. If I were to believe what she had written was factual, that meant Ricky was never the kook we made him out to be. He was far beyond the rest of us when it came to seeing the world as it truly is.

"Like I was saying... That Saturday afternoon—the day I was arrested—I had introduced about ten new students to the group. Thanks to Stokely, I was able to reach the college kids. They clearly see what's happening in these streets. This is their future and they want to protect it. However, because I know we got some nosey ass neighbors, we first met inside the house so I could privately share my vision with them. Then we discussed a few strategies. After business was taken care of, we took the meeting outside. When the police busted into the backyard, Sharleen was in the kitchen fixing the side dishes while I was grilling the burgers. Stokely was outside too with the rest of the kids acting as the DJ. It was all very low key."

"Stokely is involved in this?" I asked, surprised.

"You should ask him about it. After the first meeting, he wanted to get involved. He spread the word around the university. I was surprised by the interest in TEN. Even had to restrict the number attending because of the possibility of arousing suspicion with too many of us gathered in one spot."

"Lot of difference that made. You limited how many could come and we still got the po-po called on us," Sharleen said, shaking her head.

Ricky replied forcibly, "That don't have nuthin' to do with nuthin'! We shouldn't need these white folks permission to have a little get-together! We pay taxes. This is our home!"

"I agree, love. We shouldn't need their permission, but these people are so full of entitlement, they think they have a say-so in our every coming and going. If we get too out of hand, they call their personal security detail—the police," Sharleen said.

"Well, we can't worry about them. This country is going downhill fast and if we don't get our asses in gear to do something, we are all headed back into slavery."

"Do you really think it will come to that?" I asked.

"If it happened before, it can happen again," Ricky said.

I allowed their words to sink in. The history lesson that my child presented to me within the pages of her story opened my eyes to many harsh realities. While I was happily going through life with blinders on, this country was slowly changing. White people in fear of losing everything they owned—including ill-gotten generational wealth passed down from their forefathers, which was built upon the backs of our enslaved ancestors'—were gradually losing their minds. Not realizing they too were being played by the system, many blamed black people for what went wrong in their privileged lives. Kenya's metaphor about the frog gradually boiling to death because it didn't recognize the hot water it was in, came to mind. That's where we were in this country. Not just black and brown people, but anyone who wasn't exceedingly wealthy.

Ricky handed the stack to Gerald, saying, "Take those pamphlets home. You can both read through them when you get a chance. Stokely can fill you in on any questions you might have. Then, if you don't agree with me that we need to make a move quickly, no harm... no foul."

Gerald perused through the stack before handing it over to me. As I tucked the pamphlets securely inside my tote bag, in the back of my mind, I secretly wondered if my brother would play a part in the rise of the Nigiro. Kenya told me I would receive messages and people would be sent to help us. I was supposed to keep my eyes open. *Is Ricky one of those sent to help?* His desire to start a group to teach people how to thrive in nature couldn't be a coincidence. Was this a synchronicity described in her book?

"One more thing... Keep this quiet. We don't want them cracka's in charge finding out what we're doing because as soon as they do, they'll try to shut it down."

"Hey man, you don't have to worry about us saying a thing!" Gerald replied, "Between you starting TEN and Zumira publishing Kenya's book, I'm starting to feel we just might be making a difference in our community."

I squeezed my husband's hand, grateful that he was by my side.

Sharleen's focus shifted to me. She asked, "So what's this about publishing a book? You ever do something like that before?"

"Drive me to that bakery on the southside and I'll tell you all about it. Malcolm asked me to pick up an Ooey-Gooey Butter cake while I'm here."

Ricky offered, "You want me to drive you?"

"Naw, we'll be fine. This'll give me and Zumira more time to catch up."

"Girl, I just checked the bakery's hours," I told Sharleen. "It closes soon so we should get going."

"It's also getting dark so y'all be careful driving down there," Ricky said, pouring two shots of brown liquor and offering one to Gerald. "While you ladies are gone, I'll fill Gerald in on what else is going on in the city."

"Don't drink too much," I cautioned my husband. "We have to be on the road bright and early tomorrow."

"No need to worry about me. The last thing I want is to have liquor on my breath when we drive through those damn random checkpoints on the way back home."

Chapter Twelve

The next morning, Ricky and Sharleen were understandably saddened to see Stokely go. In fact, she fussed over him, making sure he had safely packed up his artwork—consisting of paintings of which I had no idea he was even interested—in a large leather portfolio she'd given to him for his birthday. Rather than considering him as only a nephew, during those two years spent together, the relationship with his aunt and uncle had evolved into their becoming more like surrogate parents. Since Jewel was their only child, Ricky eagerly accepted having a young man around the house. The day I asked if Stokely could live with them when we were moving to Oklahoma, he never hesitated for a moment to say yes. On the contrary, he was thrilled.

For the love and support they showered over my youngest child during that time, I would forever be grateful. I still wasn't over Kenya's disappearance so the very thought of leaving my son behind almost kept me from moving. But over much deliberation, Gerald convinced me he'd be fine as long as he was with family. And he was right.

After checking our room to make certain we hadn't left anything behind, I filled our travel mugs with freshly brewed coffee sweetened with agave. Sharleen was also gracious enough to have prepared bacon and egg breakfast sandwiches to take with us—although I would remove the pork before digging in.

We hadn't gotten much sleep because we were all up until the wee hours of the morning discussing Ricky's plan to 'change the world'. By the time Stokely came inside the house from being totally immersed in reading *Out Of Nigiro*, it was well after midnight. Without saying much more than goodnight, he trudged up the stairs to catch a few hours of sleep. We all decided we'd better do the same.

We piled in the car early the next day as the darkness of the night slowly gave way to a beautiful Sunday morning. Stokely had the foresight to load up the car the night before, leaving only the task of gathering his remaining toiletries. From the look of how tightly the SUV's cargo space was crammed with his things, he had no intention of returning to school. Or for that matter, to St. Louis.

"You two ready to hit the road?" Gerald asked, settling back in the driver's seat. He took a long sip of hot coffee before placing the travel cup in its holder.

"Ready as I'll ever be," I said, hunkering down in the passenger seat.

"I'll be ready in just a minute. I have to say good-bye first," Stokely uttered, standing outside the car. With a newly discovered hardening of his heart, he glared at the neighbor's house across the street, surmising they were the ones who had called the police on them. Ever since he started parking his car on the street overnight instead of in their driveway, he had unwittingly become the neighbor's focus of attention and misdirected rage. Apparently, they felt the need to leave several passive-aggressive notes on his windshield reminding him that it was illegal to park in the street after a certain hour. The troubled expression he now wore could be a result of all sorts of causes, considering how and why he decided to leave. It was for the best, though. Had he stayed, he'd probably wind up in jail as he would act on the thoughts taking root in his mind.

"Don't forget your Gooey Butter cake!" Sharleen shouted, running to the car with the bright pink box in her outstretched hands. "I don't want you leaving this here because I swear I'll eat the entire thing."

"Thanks, sis. Malcolm would be so upset if I left his cake. Me too, especially since we had to go out of our way to get it yesterday."

Sharleen carefully handed the box to Stokely who set it on the backseat. She then gently gripped him by his broad shoulders. Placing a motherly kiss on his cheek, she told him, "If you ever want to come back. You are always welcome here. Consider us your home-away-from-home."

"That means a lot to hear you say that. I know it was difficult having me around, especially when you and Uncle Ricky finally got the house back to yourself. I can't even begin to thank you for letting me stay with you."

"Yeah, once your cousin moved out we thought we'd finally have an opportunity to do whatever we wanted..." she released a hearty laugh that had probably woken her nosey neighbors. As she spied the blinds of the house across the street part enough to allow a set of prying eyes to peak through, she sighed. She was not about to allow anything to ruin her saying good-bye, so she quickly added, "... still I wouldn't have had it any other way."

Ricky joined the trio at the passenger's rear side of the car. He pushed an old dusty box into Stokely's reluctant hands. "Take this with you. It may be old, but it works just fine."

"What's this, Uncle Ricky?" he asked, studying the package, wiping away the dust. "I wasn't expecting a going away present."

"It's an old hand-held CB radio I used when I was in the military. I got a larger one hooked up in the garage. If ever the cell phones go down, and they will, you can reach me on that. I printed out a page of instructions for you too. My handle is, 'Morpheus'."

"Morpheus?!" Stokely grinned and gave his uncle a quick hug. "Thank you! I hope I never need to use this thing, but if I ever do, it's nice to know you'll be on the other end."

"Also, don't worry about your car. It'll be safe parked in the garage. When you're ready to come get it... or, if you'd rather have it shipped down there, just let me know." Ricky hugged Sharleen by the waist as he noticed her eyes were misting up.

"Thanks Unc. Thanks Auntie," he said getting into the back seat of the SUV. "I love you both."

"We love you, too!" they replied in unison.

I rolled down the window and whispered, "Thanks again for taking care of Stokely. I know he's going to miss you both something terribly. But I'm glad to have my baby back."

Sharleen waved me off. "Girl, don't worry about it. That boy wasn't no bother. In fact, I think we're going to miss him more than he's gonna miss us. Tell you the truth... it was nice having a young man around the house for a change."

"He fit right in from the start. Good having him here," Ricky said with a nod, working to contain his emotion. "All right sis, yaw'd better get goin'. We don't know how long this weather is going to hold up. They're predicting rain later this morning. In fact, I can smell it in the air."

"You're right. We'd better head on out, but we'll be in touch," I replied. "And as soon as we get the final novel in hand, I'll send you both a copy."

Stokely piped up from the backseat. "Mom, they can have this one if it's okay with you."

"Are you sure?" I asked. "Did you read the entire book? It's very important that you read everything."

"I read every single word of it last night. So if it's okay with you, I really think Uncle Ricky and Aunt Sharleen should read it now instead of waiting."

"Um... Ok. I guess," I said turning to Gerald. "What do you think?"

He shrugged. "Either give it to them now or later. They need to read it eventually."

"I really wanted you to have a final version," I told Ricky. "This copy is all marked up with my comments in the margins. But if you can overlook that, I guess it'll be alright."

Stokely retrieved the paperback novel from his backpack and handed it to his Uncle Ricky. "I think you should read Kenya's story first. There's a lot of information in there that coincides with everything you've been teaching me. What's in that book can't be a coincidence."

Ricky accepted the novel, admiring the celestial art on the smooth matte cover. "So you think there's something to this?" he asked in all seriousness.

"Yes, I do," Stokely replied. "I believe this story came from Kenya. I believe everything in the book is true. You need to hear what she's telling us now... Not later. As incredible as it sounds, we all need to be prepared for what's coming. Like you've been saying for the longest time, we've got to get ready."

Hearing that declaration from my son, I was slightly taken aback. He had only read the book once and it had made a profound impact on him. If those words were that powerful to move my son to take action, I reconsidered what I was about to unleash on the world. What if it *were* just a fantastical science-fiction tale? Would I be starting a panic in those who believed it might be some strange kind of new prophecy? In spite of Kenya's last visit where she reassured me to keep going, once again I became fearful of what we were about to embark upon.

"Why do you say that?" Sharleen gently asked Stokely.

"Auntie, don't you see what's going on in this city? In this state? What this country perpetrated and is still doing to our people? Things are about to get real ugly and I want us to be prepared. I think Uncle Ricky's plan to teach people how to thrive and exist in nature is right on time."

She did not respond, but merely nodded.

"I'll start reading it today," Ricky promised. He opened the book, his eyes scanning over the first page.

"Cool," Stokely uttered. "I'm ready now, Pops."

"Let's go, my love," I said.

Gerald placed the gear in reverse and slowly backed from the driveway to the street. He softly tooted his horn and gave a quick wave as he carefully maneuvered around a dew-covered car which ironically had been left parked on the street overnight.

Stokely shook his head in disgust when he noticed there were no notes on the windshield of the car. What he had taken notice of was that car belonged to a visitor of a white neighbor and it had been parked there for days. In the quiet recesses of his mind, he pushed away the hateful thoughts threatening to surface about all those folks.

"Drive safely!" Sharleen shouted and waved.

Each lost in our own thoughts, we remained silent during the ten-mile drive to the interstate. In the span of the time it took to leave my brother's house, the sky had now become pregnant with heavy grey clouds. A light mist settled upon the vehicle's windshield, initiating the automatic intermittent wipers. Gerald's attention was on driving and not missing his turn. We merged into the I-44 traffic flow heading west. My mind was occupied with worrisome thoughts about completing the book, but more so about Stokely hunched down in the backseat. He had turned sullen shortly after we left, placing headphones over his ears to block out the world with some extremely loud music.

Stokely suddenly broke the silence previously interrupted only by the swooshing sound of the windshield wipers fighting to push the rain away. He removed his headphones and quietly uttered, "Mom, Pops... I have somethin' to tell you."

Gerald glanced in the rearview mirror as I turned in my seat to face my son. In the gentlest way possible, I asked, "What is it, Stokely?"

While staring forlornly out the window at the rain now pelting the car with heavy droplets, he murmured, "I think Kenya tried to make contact with me."

"When?" I asked. "How?"

My husband didn't say a word, but instead elected to place his attention on the increasingly treacherous road conditions with traffic zipping by at incredible speeds for the slick surface. Because we were only miles into the 500-mile drive home, he couldn't afford to be overly stressed or distracted. We were in very real danger of some idiot driver hydroplaning out of control.

Stokely uttered, "After readin' Kenya's story, now I know what I saw was real. At first I thought I was just trippin'."

"What are you talking about?" I asked.

"One night... About a month ago, I was at the university library with three of my boys. It's one of the few places left that we can still get together and not be harassed. Even though we could've finished our project online, it's nice to get together in person. Anyway, we were puttin' the finishin' touches on our assignment..."

As I listened to my son's rich, baritone voice that had somehow deepened even more over the last several months to the point he now sounded like his grandfather, my mind drifted to the day he told us he wanted to remain in St. Louis. I set my foot down and proclaimed he was moving to Oklahoma with us no matter what he wanted. I was not about to give up another child to this hellacious world, even if he was going to college. I knew how badly the world treated young black men. I wasn't about to move to another state and leave him behind. But somehow he convinced his aunt and uncle to take him in. And because he would be with my brother and his wife, I agreed to allow him to remain in Missouri. Looking at how the situation had turned out, I knew I had made the right choice. He would have resented both me and his daddy had I made him move with us.

Stokely continued, "...the library was about to close. Since it was gettin' late, we all packed up our stuff. Once we got to the parkin' lot, I remembered I left my earbuds in the library. The other two guys split as soon as they found their cars because none of us likes to be out drivin' after dark. My friend Draynon had parked his car in the overflow lot next to mine so he offered to walk back with me. I told him I was cool, so he left. I couldn't have been gone more than a few minutes, but when I got to the library, the security guard had already turned off the lights and locked the doors. When I returned to the parkin' lot, except for me and my car, it was empty. I was alone. But this particular night, I saw somethin' that tripped me out."

"What did you see?" Gerald asked him.

"At first I thought my eyes were playin' tricks on me."

"Why?" I asked.

"Because I saw *some-thing* in the sky above the parkin' lot. It had the brightness of one of those meteors streakin' across the night sky, but it didn't move. It hovered right over my car. I didn't want to admit it 'til now, but I think it might've been a UFO," he stared out the window and released a chuckle. "To be totally honest, while I was on the way back to the parkin' lot, I lit up a joint that Draynon had given me earlier. I had only taken a couple of puffs so I thought it had to be laced with somethin' for me to be seein' somethin' like that."

I heard Gerald clearing his throat, catching him giving me the side-eye. I knew he was most likely thinking the apple didn't fall far from the tree. I gave him the side-eye right back because if it wasn't for drug restrictions on his job, he'd be smoking cannabis too.

Stokely continued, "I looked around, hopin' there was somebody else out there to confirm I wasn't hallucinatin'. But I was alone. I didn't want to make any sudden moves until I was inside my car. Then this beam of light came down from it and started movin' in my direction! I was freaked because it was blockin' my way to the car!"

As I listened to Stokely describe what amounted to a 'close encounter of the third kind'—and under normal circumstances this information would have caused a totally different reaction in me had I not also had a similar experience—I was intrigued more than surprised. What *did* surprise me was finding out that—my straight-laced nerdy son—imbibed cannabis. But I wasn't about to make it a big deal at this point.

"Sweetie, I know how you must have felt. When I first saw that orb in the backyard that night, my feet refused to listen to my brain when it told them to run!" I snickered.

"Mom, for real though... I ain't never been that scared! When the beam of light retracted, I jumped in my car, put it in drive, and peeled outta that parkin' lot as fast as I could. I didn't slow down until I reached Uncle Ricky's driveway."

"I'm glad you didn't get pulled over for speeding," I added.

"Me too," he replied.

"So, Stokely, you didn't actually *see* your sister?" Gerald asked. Though his focus was on driving, he was thoroughly captivated by his son's experience.

"Not exactly. When I got home, I was still kinda freaked out so I went straight to my bedroom. Tried to come down by drinkin' lots of water."

"That doesn't work," I interrupted. "Try sweets next time."

Gerald threw another disapproving look my way.

"What?" I shrugged. "If he's going to smoke marijuana, he should know this."

"You're right, mom." He dropped his head, shaking it from side to side. He sighed when he said, "If only I hadn't been so high that night, I might have actually seen Kenya. She may have even taken me up for a ride like she did with you. I guess I blew my chance."

"There was no way you could have known it was your sister. Shoot, I think if I'd been anywhere else except in our backyard, I might have run too."

"I finally fell asleep after checkin' outside my window to make sure that thing hadn't followed me home." He sat back in his seat, releasing a weary sigh. "That same night, I think Kenya reached out to me through my dreams. I think she was tryin' to tell me somethin'. At the time I thought it was a coincidence considerin' what happened in the parkin' lot. Now I know it wasn't."

"What did she tell you?" Gerald asked, prepared to hear an amazing tale.

"It's not exactly what she told me... It's what I saw." He closed his eyes to retrieve the elusive fragments of his dream. "It was a warm moonless night and the sky was filled with stars. Thousands of tiny lights scattered in every direction. Seemed like hundreds of people were outside just havin' a good time. Maybe after a concert or just hangin' out because it had cooled off from the heat of the day. At first, I remember feelin' at peace. Then it all changed."

"Go on..." I encouraged him.

"I watched the 'stars' slowly began movin' around in the sky. Hundreds appeared to be lining up in formation. They moved like they weren't really celestial objects, but more like military fighter jets—but without the loud noise or jerky movements. I got scared when the formation started descendin' to the ground. At some point, I must've figured out that the bright objects weren't stars at all, but were really spaceships. UFO's. Then a section of the night sky suddenly opened and revealed another world that looked nuthin' like this one. But it was like lookin' at a city in the sky..."

"That's very interesting," his father whispered. "What else do you remember?"

"Dad, I usually don't pay attention to my dreams, but this one was too real not to. Everybody was runnin' around like ants tryin' to find a place to hide. My dream reminded me of a movie about an alien invasion! I ducked inside a house and hid in an upstairs bedroom. I searched for a weapon. Anything to defend myself, but I all I found was a belt with a big buckle. I heard a noise outside the window that sounded like a loud buzzsaw cuttin' through wood. Then it got quiet. A few moments passed before I heard a knock at the bedroom door. I was scared, but I opened it anyway. There was this half human, half android thing with no legs. Its torso sat on what looked like a hoverboard. It had light brown skin, slanted black eyes, and a thick braid hangin' halfway down its back."

"Sounds like you were having a nightmare," I interrupted. "You didn't wake up?"

"Naw, I guess I didn't. I was cool because this thing wasn't tryin' to hurt me. But it communicated with me some kind of way and asked if I was Stokely. When I said, 'yeah', it told me that *they want to see me*'."

"That's quite a vivid dream, you had son," Gerald said, wondering who the 'they' was.

"Then that thing handed me a small takeout box like we used to get from the Chinese food restaurants. When I opened it, it was filled with fortune cookies. It wanted me to follow it outside. That's when Malcolm showed up out of nowhere and said that thing was tryin' to trick me."

"Malcolm was also in your dream, too?" I asked, perplexed.

"Yeah, he was tellin' me not to trust it. That I was being tricked. But I felt no threat because I followed the thing down the stairs. It took me outside and showed me its spacecraft. Malcolm kept yellin' at me to hide. Then I woke up."

"Why do you believe it was Kenya trying to contact you? It could have only been a dream," Gerald explained.

"After readin' that book and hearin' what happened to you and Mom. It's just a feelin' I have that it was Kenya trying to reach me." Stokely opened his eyes and leaned towards the front seat. "Mom, remember when you used to get Chinese takeout for dinner and sometimes they'd put extra fortune cookies in the bag?"

I nodded.

He explained, thoughtfully, "Me and Kenya used to arm wrestle for the extras. She always let me win.

"I never knew you two did that," I remarked.

"That's how I know it was her tryin' to contact me because nobody else knew about the fortune cookies."

"Did you tell your aunt and uncle what happened that night at the school?" Gerald asked with concern. "But more importantly, why are you just now telling us?"

"I never told nobody about that night in the parkin' lot because I didn't want y'all to think I was crazy. Plus, that dream always bothered me because it seemed so real. Like I was starrin' in a scene from a movie. Or kinda like rememberin' somethin' that I'd forgotten..." he confessed. "For real though, until last night when I read that book... I didn't know what to think."

"Stokely. You are not losing your mind. Trust me on this because your father and I had a similar conversation when it first happened to me," I explained, looking to Gerald for confirmation.

"That's right," he agreed. "Your mother and I have experienced many strange occurrences lately that also caused us to question our sanity. I gotta admit, at first I thought your mother had snapped when she said she saw Kenya. Then we both experienced an amazing event that changed my mind about everything."

"You're talkin' about the incident with the tornado?" Stokely asked.

"Exactly!" Gerald had finally reached the outskirts of town where traffic became sparse. He took a long swig of coffee, visibly relaxing, before engaging the cruise control. "What I've come to realize is this phenomena we're now experiencing is all new to us. This *awakening* we're going through."

As I listened to my husband and son converse, I said, "I think this is more than an awakening. I think a shift has taken place in the atmosphere."

"Possibly," Stokely added thoughtfully, taking in the beautiful rock formations situated alongside the highway. "I just hope Unc and Auntie are goin' ta be alright on their own up there."

"I just hope he knows what he's getting himself into by starting that group, especially now that he's on the police's radar."

"I'm sure Ricky knows the risks," Gerald replied, glancing back at Stokely. "Besides, we need more folks like him who are willing to stick their necks out to help our people."

"Uncle Ricky is more woke than either of you guys think."

"That's funny," I chuckled. "He said the same thing about you."

"Unc is actually really smart, mom. He's always readin' books about black empowerment. At least once a week, he'd give me a book to read and then we'd sit and discuss what we believed the author was trying to convey."

"You and Ricky did that?" Gerald asked, feeling a certain kind of way because the deepest conversations he had with his son often revolved around sports. Or his education, to make sure he maintained his grades and stayed out of trouble because he couldn't afford to lose his partial scholarship. To learn that his brother-in-law had engaged his son in intense conversations brought out strange and uncomfortable emotions. Feelings he was not aware he possessed.

"Yeah. He is definitely not a conspiracy theorist. He was always doin' little stuff within the community that y'all don't know about."

I cleared my throat, ashamed of how I had referred to my own brother. Especially since I often called him that in front of my children. "You're right. Ricky is a very intelligent man who only wants to help his people. I was ignorant for believing he was anything else."

"It's okay, Mom. He used to say that you and Dad were, *bougie*."

"*Bougie*?!" Gerald and I exclaimed simultaneously.

"What makes Ricky think we're bougie?" I asked.

"Actually, both Aunt Sharleen and Uncle Ricky used to think that until recently. They understood you guys wantin' to move out of the house because of what happened to Kenya, but they were surprised when you left the hood and then relocated to one of the whitest states you could find. Oklahoma?! Really?!"

Gerald gently corrected Stokely, "Now that is where you are wrong, son. You should know your history before you start dissing our families' home state. I'm surprised Ricky didn't tell you this, but on second thought, maybe he wanted you to hear it from me."

"Go on. I'm listening," he replied, showing more interest in what his dad had to say than normal.

Gerald continued, "During the early 1900's, Oklahoma had the distinction of being the only state to have over 50 all-black towns. Thousands of black people migrated to the Oklahoma Indian Territory in the late 1800's when they learned it was initially intended to become an all-black state. Both the recently freed enslaved Africans, as well as tribes of indigenous people from the Southeastern states, forcibly displaced during the Trail of Tears, settled in the territory. As expected, the white settlers pushed back on the idea of a black state, but that didn't stop our ancestors from building up towns including the city of Greenwood near Tulsa that they fondly called the 'Black Wall Street'."

I added, "We all know what happened to Greenwood and all the other black towns when whites discovered that not only could we live without them, but do extremely well on our own."

"That may have been true back then, but look who represents the state today. I don't see very many black or brown faces representin' us," Stokely replied.

"Unfortunately, most of the state's representatives are ultra conservative white men who have been voted back into office for way too long. Because of them, outsiders view the entire state as being populated by backwards thinking ignorant poor rednecks. But our numbers are increasing."

Gerald outright stated, "Well, you know my thoughts about voting Republican or Democrat... In all actuality, I don't care much for government involvement in our daily lives because inevitably, it always brings about strife. And if that makes me labeled 'conservative', then so be it."

"Liberal. Conservative. Progressive. Blah, blah, blah… it's just more labels to further divide us," I added.

"That's right, Zumi! Since when did being 'conservative' become a political tag. It used to mean holding to traditional family values, which is what our ancestors did."

"Not to worry, my love. All that is about to change. I can feel it in the air."

"What do you mean by that, mom?" Stokely asked.

"This country is slowly devolving," I explained. "Maybe the fact that you and your uncle started that group to help our people get out of the cities is part of some master plan."

"That's right, Zumira. We're about to join the revolution when we publish *Out of Nigiro*."

"Honestly, I never thought I'd be involved in something so… radical."

"What's that old saying?" Gerald recalled something he often heard his parent's generation proclaim, *"The white man stole this country from the red man, the black man built it, and the brown man maintains it."*

I heard quiet bursts of laughter coming from the backseat. I glanced in the passenger mirror I was using to refresh my lipstick. "What's so funny?"

"I didn't know my parents were so woke," Stokely remarked. "I think it's cool that you guys are keepin' an open-mind."

"Sharleen has got some nerve calling us bougie," I replied, slightly offended. "Look at where they moved. Nothing but always-searching-for-a-cause liberal white people in their neighborhood. People with too much money and time on their hands trying to meddle in other people's business!"

"In all fairness, Ricky and Sharleen were there first," Gerald reminded me. "Way before those gentrifiers showed up."

"It's cool. They don't think that way anymore. I straightened them out," Stokely explained. "They thought you had abandoned your peeps back home when you moved to Okieville."

"Well, good for you for taking up for us," I replied. "But back to your dream..."

"Yeah, back to that... Now that I read Kenya's story, I really believe she was tryin' to contact me." He pondered out loud, "I can't help but to wonder, *why*? I know she wants you and Dad to help publish her story, but what could she possibly need me for?"

"Maybe she just wanted to see you. To personally tell you that she's alright and not to worry anymore," I told him. "You two were very close... Maybe she saw something in you. Who knows?"

"Yeah, maybe..." Stokely replaced his headphones on his head and settled back to enjoy the ride. Out of nowhere he whispered, "But I still can't shake the feelin' that somethin' big is about to happen. I feel like we're headin' towards an event so spectacular, most of us won't believe our senses when it does happen."

I took in what Stokely was saying, also contemplating the message behind Kenya's words. From out of nowhere, I whispered a thought that swirled inside my mind, *"An indescribable supernatural occurrence is on the horizon. The only way to properly explain it would be to make a proclamation that the event will be a miracle from The Almighty God. Paraphrasing James Baldwin, the 'Last time the world was destroyed, it was by floods. The next time, it will be by fire.' There will be nowhere to run and nowhere to hide, not even underground. The disobedient ones will be severely punished for their treatment of The Almighty's Children. None will be spared, especially those who pretend they are of Him, but are not."* When I snapped out of whatever spell I was under, I saw my husband looking at me strangely.

"Uh... While you two are predicting the end of the world, let's try and get home first," Gerald offered. "I just hope we're ready for whatever comes our way."

The rain had finally let up. In the distance, I spied the faintest blue of the sky peeking through the dark storm clouds. As we passed through the westernmost city limits of suburbia, I was quite surprised by how far the westward expansion had gone. The outskirts of St. Louis county were practically butting up against the county of St. Charles. Used to be there was nothing but farmland out that way.

"Do you notice all this new development? Banking, insurance, investment firms, healthcare... Not to mention those exclusive gated communities. It's disgusting how much money they're investing out here when areas of the actual city they've piggy-backed on for recognition are falling apart," I whispered, sadly.

"Hmmm? What did you say?" Gerald asked absentmindedly while fiddling with the windshield wipers. Seemed like they swished across the windshield either too fast or too slow.

"Nothing. Just thinking...," I replied, sinking down in the seat, pressing my head against the headrest. *'Here I am, making monumental life altering decisions that will not only change my life, but my families' lives, too. I must take into consideration how my actions will impact them. What will happen after I publish the book? Will our lives change for the better? Or, for the worse?'* Yet, even as I pondered over those concerns, I knew I could never doubt what my daughter had written was true. Now she needed *me* to help spread the word about the pending liberation to the others.

As we drove through the gorgeous countryside in southwest Missouri, I was hit with the following epiphany. "Gerald, I just thought of something!"

"What's that?" he asked.

"Kenya's story was filled with so many historical facts that its believable enough to be entirely true. In my humble opinion, when it comes to our daughter, the truth *is* indeed stranger than fiction."

My husband briefly glanced over, long enough for me to see the smile forming at the corners of his mouth. And then, he laughed out loud.

Chapter Thirteen

Seven hours after saying good-bye to Ricky and Sharleen, I caught my first glimpse of the Oklahoma City skyline in the distance. The Devon Energy building towered over all other downtown structures, looking out of place in a city that had been rocked too often by destructive tornadoes. For the longest time, I believed the builders who had designed the spectacular 50-story tower had intentionally mocked mother nature, especially because it was built with 30 stories covered in glass. But so far, so good. Other than the economic depression that had befallen the entire country, no natural disasters had yet occurred to take down the mighty structure.

I steadied myself with my hands on the dashboard as Gerald drove over numerous potholes in another construction zone that never seemed to reach completion. As the car bumped around, I felt anxious to get home. I had things to do! But the most important reason was, I loved returning home from a long road trip. In my mind, there was no place like it. I loved our house and neighborhood. Birds of all species also seemed to love it. In the skies above our backyard, I have spotted blue jays, cardinals, turtle doves, crows and blackbirds, the scissortail, mighty hawks and elusive barn owls, ducks and geese, and so many other species of birds who call Oklahoma home. Living so close to the country had spoiled me from ever wanting to live in the city again. There was something so special about being outside in nature, I chose to experience it as frequently as possible.

"We're almost home, son!" Gerald happily exclaimed. "The house is just around the corner," he added, taking a left turn into our subdivision.

"Cool," Stokely replied, realizing his father had apparently forgotten he'd visited for a few days just last year.

"Honey," I said gently touching my husband's arm, "... he was here for the baby's birth, remember?"

"You're right, so much has happened in the past couple of months that it slipped my mind," he replied, before looking in the rearview mirror to address Stokely. "In that case, welcome home!"

Stokely did not acknowledge his father's mistake, but continued staring out the window. Lost within the boundaries of his own private thoughts.

I tried to imagine with my eyes what he was seeing through his. When we first discovered this lovely neighborhood tucked away from the hustle and bustle of the city, the stately custom-built homes, situated on beautifully landscaped acre lots, separated by tree-lined streets, I was immediately pulled in. At the time the realtor showed us the home, we didn't know it was in a predominantly white neighborhood, nor did I care now. The house was beautiful and perfect for me and Gerald, so I figured, if anyone had a problem with us moving here, they'd just have to get over it. Some might say the neighborhood was over the top, yet still, it was a nice enough place to live. Several neighbors out for their noon-day stroll, were quick to throw up their hands in a friendly wave as we drove by. We caught the occasional 'what-are-you-doing-in-this-neighborhood' vibe, but so what. The neighbors weren't overly friendly, but neither were they not.

Regardless of how I once believed it to be our good fortune in discovering our beautiful home, thanks to Kenya's recently shared vision, I now understood serendipity played no role in it. Our moving to Oklahoma, to this neighborhood, and buying this specific house was all part of The Almighty's plan.

Malcolm's car was parked in the driveway when we pulled up. Once again, he had used the key designated for emergencies to let himself in. I grinned when I saw him sitting on the couch eating a sandwich. A bottle of his father's favorite beer was situated on the coffee table.

Drena and the baby were nowhere in sight which meant she had probably taken the day to visit her parents. Malcolm rarely went with his wife when she visited her family. He said it was because they didn't particularly care for him, but that is a story for another day.

"See your brother is already here waiting for us," I said, turning towards him with a huge smile on my face. "Welcome home, Stokely."

~ ~ ~

At that very moment, as he listened to his parent's conversation, Stokely realized, past his family, he didn't know anyone here. He had only briefly set foot in Oklahoma City. Twice, in fact. The last time was when his niece was born nine months earlier. Gratefully, within his short existence on this planet, he understood that home was not a physical place. It is where the heart is. So in essence, even though his experience with Oklahoma twice left him feeling as if he had regressed twenty-five years back in time, he supposed he was home.

"Boy, get your butt up and help me with these bags!" Gerald said to Malcolm.

"What's up, lil' bro?" Malcolm asked, greeting Stokely in a warm embrace. "It's about time you came home to visit your family."

Stokely glanced around the living room of the house in which he'd never lived. He didn't recognize the furniture because his parents had left most of their old stuff behind, giving it away to family and friends before they moved. Something about not wanting to be bogged down with memories of the past. Told everyone that they wanted a new and fresh beginning away from the grit and grime of St. Louis. He ran his hand along the back of the fine leather sofa, feeling the buttery softness of Italian leather underneath his touch. It was the kind of furniture his mother would never have purchased with three teens in the house. Beautiful artwork graced the beige walls to offer a touch of color to an otherwise drab décor.

"Man, I've been busy. School... Helpin' Uncle Ricky get his project up and goin'..." he replied, embracing his older brother. "But hey, I'm here now."

"Right on!" Malcolm replied, enthusiastically. "After you get settled in, I'll take you around town. Show you what's going on... the places to stay away from... where it's safe to shop for food to avoid the idiots who refuse to mask up."

"Lotta dumbasses live here too, huh?"

Malcolm walked behind Stokely to help unload the car. He uttered, "Brotha, I don't know what's happening in St. Louis, but they can't seem to get this pandemic under control. With the exception of essential businesses—hospitals, grocery stores, government offices and the military base—most of Oklahoma City has shut down."

"Things aren't much better back home. Probably worse because they—black and white—still won't be vaccinated. And what gets me are the supposedly 'woke' ones pushin' the narrative that because they believe it was man-made, they honestly think they can't catch it." Stokely maneuvered a heavy box from the trunk and set it down on the driveway. "Well, I say even if it was made in a lab, it's out in the world now. Can't nobody stop this virus, or keep it from mutatin' like it has."

Malcolm replied, "I can't understand how anyone still believes this virus is a hoax. I mean, thousands of people across this country are dying every day."

Stokely glanced at the neighbor across the street out tending his yard. "Man... For real, I think it's the media creatin' the havoc around the pandemic. They're manipulatin' statistics to make it seem worse than it really is to keep up their news ratings. One day they report it's controlled, then the next day they say the numbers are way up. I do believe that people are dyin' from the virus, but not at the high rate they're tellin' us."

"If what you're saying is true, I'm fine with them getting what they deserve. But you do realize it was the media who first reported it was Russian bots behind the spread of false news stories. These bots targeted young black people to go out and protest in support of *Black Lives Matter.*" Malcolm naively wondered aloud, "I'd hate to think it's our own people who are the true terrorists."

Stokely wanted to shake his brother by the shoulders and tell him to 'Wake up!' But it wasn't Malcolm's fault that he wasn't able to see the world as it truly was. If it hadn't been for valuable time spent with his uncle, he himself would still be under the illusion that this system is the only one that exists. He barely contained his composure when he replied more harshly than intended, "Dude, are you serious?! The United States of America is the number one terrorist in the world! The U.S. government sold guns, bombs, and weapons of mass destruction to practically every so-called third world country—which by-the-way—is now using those weapons against their own citizens!"

"Nations have to protect themselves and if they cannot, then another nation should step up to do it. That's why they have coalitions with other nations. But, I agree that the United States military shouldn't be used as the world's police force."

"Listen... it was the U.S. government who created the problem by sellin' weapons to all those little countries. The only ones to benefit from the military industrial complex are the defense companies."

"Dang, lil' bro. You're really starting to sound like Uncle Ricky. Him and his crazy-ass conspiracy theories."

"I wouldn't write Unc off so fast. Look what happened durin' the last election. Special interest groups specifically targeted *us* through social media, tryin' to influence us on who to vote for. When brother Floyd was murdered, white people were out in the streets protestin' for the rights of black people to live safely and peacefully. But now, most white people are focused on anything but black lives. They're no longer tryin' to hide their assumptions that blacks have no power." Stokely helped his brother lift the large box from the ground.

As Malcolm struggled walking backwards towards the house, he grunted out, "You got me there. The Black Lives Matter struggle has been taken over mostly by young white people. They say they're marching for equality, but I think they're really trying to regain their own freedom so they can return to their 'normal' lives."

"If this country were really serious about equality for all, they could put an end to systematic racism in a heartbeat. *If* they were serious... But real talk big bro, the government and its alphabet agencies know who the real terrorists are in this country."

Malcolm chuckled, "One good thing that's come out of this pandemic.... Since we can no longer gather in large crowds, the mass shootings have stopped."

"Yeah, they quit for now. But just wait until the mandatory restrictions are lifted and people try to go back to normal. Watch 'em start shootin' again." Stokely took the brunt of the weight on his end, to keep his brother from stumbling and losing his balance as he struggled through the entrance into the house. The box overflowed with historical and pertinent books that Uncle Ricky suggested he read to expand his knowledge of the black American experience.

Malcolm guided them into the guest room, lowered the heavy box to the floor, and took a seat on the bed to rest his aching back. "So, you quit school. Moved in with Mom and Dad... Now what? What are you going to do now that you're here?"

Stokely took a seat on the bed beside his older brother. He stared off into space listening to his brother's questions.

Malcolm asked again. "What are you going to do now? What's your plan?"

"Man, fuck school! All they're teachin' me is how to become a better worker to keep this jacked up system runnin'."

"Unfortunately you need a degree just to get a job that pays above minimum wage. Especially here in Oklahoma. If I hadn't gotten my degree, I wouldn't have this good-paying job. So while you're enjoying living back home, I hope you're thinking about your future."

"I guess I'll just have to wait and see. What I do know is Kenya's book has to be published."

When Malcolm did not immediately respond, Stokely tilted his head and asked, "You did read her story, didn't you?"

"Yeah, I read it."

"Well?"

"Well, what?" Malcolm replied. "It's a really good read. Lots of interesting historical nuggets about the black struggle are addressed."

"Man, I believe everything she wrote in that book is gonna happen. I think Nigiro is real."

Malcolm shot his brother a look that vacillated between fear and disbelief.

Stokely continued, "I don't think *we* have anything to worry about. If Kenya's abduction was part of some bigger plan, there is nuthin' we can do to change anything anyway."

"Why not?" Malcolm's fear of the unknown was more powerful than the idea of the existence of black extraterrestrials.

"I don't know. It's just a feelin' I have."

"Well, Mom is intent on getting that book completed." He added with a little snort, "But what bothers me is, she actually believes that Kenya came down from a UFO and *gave* her the book."

"Who says she didn't?"

"I should have known you'd accept what was written as the truth. You've always been a bit more open-minded than me when it came to that kind of thing," Malcolm said with no intended malice.

"I'm just sayin' that Kenya never lied to me. Even when it hurt, she told me the truth," Stokely's voice became clouded with emotion. "There was a section in her book that only me and God would know about. I don't know how she knew that unless she is who she says she is."

Malcolm stood to his full height, prepared to end their uncomfortable conversation about, as far as he was concerned, their *still* missing sister. He said, "How about we talk more later."

"That's cool," Stokely said. "As to your earlier question about me movin' home.... I'll just have to play it by ear. But in regards to the book, we both know that neither Mom or Dad know the first thing about marketin'. Or promotion. Or how to distribute. So, maybe that's why I moved back home. To help."

"Okay, little brother. You'll have plenty of time to think about your future." Malcolm backed out of the bedroom. "But for now, grab what you need and be out in the driveway in five minutes. We're going for a ride."

~ ~ ~

Stokely got into Malcolm's Jeep that inside resembled more of soccer mom van than it did a vehicle built for the rugged outdoors. As he tossed his backpack in the backseat, he noted the baby's car seat, an umbrella stroller, and baby bag packed with extra diapers. It was a reminder that his brother was now a full-grown man with a wife and child. Responsible for the safety and welfare of the two women placed in his charge.

Malcolm's intent that afternoon was to familiarize his younger brother with the general north-south, east-west grid layout of Oklahoma City's county roads. After he provided a quick tour pointing out places of interest between his parent's neighborhood and his own, he jumped on the nearest entrance ramp to I-35, drove a few miles and then headed east to I-40. To the northeast side, an area of the city that was once considered the 'black' section of town, that is up until a few years ago. Ever since his family had relocated to OKC, he began to notice a subtle shift of the demographics in that part of the city. It was slowly changing. He brushed off the nagging suspicion of something more sinister happening, choosing to believe the significant shift in the residents' ethnicity was an unfortunate side effect of the pandemic and not due to greedy out-of-state investors taking advantage of people losing their homes.

"Oklahoma City looks way different than I thought. It's not at all what I expected."

"Better or worse?"

"Neither. Just different," Stokely said as he observed a family of three on the street corner begging for money. The little girl's wispy blonde hair was pulled back into a ponytail with a colorful scrunchy. She couldn't have been more than six.

After Malcolm felt he had depressed his brother long enough by driving through neighborhoods with boarded up houses and overgrown vacant lots with 'For Sale' signs dominating the landscape, he headed west to the gentrified Arts District. "I'll take you to a nicer part of the city."

"You mean a whiter part of the city?" he joked.

"Naw man, that's not what I mean. Lots of different people are moving here. Africans, Asians, Indians, Mexicans, Central Americans... You'd be surprised how diverse the state is becoming."

"Wow!" Stokely exclaimed, taking in the trendy shops and restaurants. "I sure didn't expect to see this many black people in Oklahoma City."

"More of us have moved to Oklahoma over the last few years, but there's still not enough to make a difference in the politics. But there are several well-qualified black people running for state and local office. They're trying to improve the lives of black and brown people so they'll have decent neighborhoods to live in and good schools to send their kids to."

"That's what I'm talkin' about! Those are the kind of people I want to meet," Stokely replied with a new hope building.

"Where to now?" Malcolm asked, not knowing how to respond to something he'd never given a second thought to. "You ready to head back home?"

"I'm hungry," Stokely said. "Let's find somewhere to eat."

Malcolm glanced at his brother sideways before responding. Tried to gauge how to ask a question without sounding like a complete asshole. "Mom tells me you stopped eating meat. You used to love cheeseburgers and had them at least five days a week. We practically lived at *White Castle*. So what is this about you going vegan? Is this about some girl?"

"Man, the way these companies raise the animals they sell to the public for 'food' is disgustin'. When I discovered the truth on how they process animals in the food supply, I had to stop eatin' meat. Cow, pig, chicken, and even most fish. They're all mostly bad for you."

"Considering that everything we eat is processed, how do you know what's good anymore?" He made sure the center lane was clear before signaling to change. "I hear organic is better for the environment. Couldn't you have just switched to that?"

"It's still dead animal flesh. So, yeah even organic meat isn't great. But not just the meat. Most of the fruit and vegetables are genetically modified or the produce is so full of E.coli that it's not safe to eat."

"Damn, pretty soon we won't be able to eat anything," Malcolm remarked.

Stokely swiped through several screens reading rave reviews of a local vegan restaurant. "How about this Indian restaurant. Most of the reviews says it's supposed to have the best vegan food in the city."

Malcolm punched the address into the jeep's Global Positioning System (GPS). Noting where the directions would take them, he paused. "Can't you find something closer to home? I didn't plan on driving all the way north of the city. Besides, I heard they're starting to harass us up there."

"Man, I don't care who lives in the damn neighborhood. I'm not tryin' to buy a house up there. All I want to do is get something to eat," Stokely sucked his teeth."

"I told Drena I'd be gone just a couple hours," he replied, following the GPS female's soothing voice. "We should pickup the food and then head back."

Stokely pointed to a billboard advertising an upcoming football game between Oklahoma State University and the University of Oklahoma. It was supposed to be a really big deal as most states had recently banned games with teams coming from out-of-state. "Did you know that OSU's mascot is a pistol-packin' white cowboy? What's up with that?"

"I never thought about it until now," Malcolm said. "But what I do know is Langston University's mascot is one bad-ass Lion!"

"Fo' sho!" Stokely agreed, "And even though I'm over goin' back to school, I think it's cool that Oklahoma still has an HBCU."

"Me too!"

"Hey Malcolm... Did you know that most of the cowboys back in the day were black?"

"Where did you hear that?"

"I first heard about it in a documentary. Watchin' it reminded me of Grandpa Williams," Stokely reminisced as he spoke, "Remember how much he loved Westerns? He always wanted us to watch them with him when we were kids. Now I wish I would've spent more time with him instead of blowin' him off like that." Stokely shook his head sadly. "For real though... I wonder if he even knew who the true cowboys were."

"Maybe. But what *I* saw in those few westerns starring John Wayne was him trying to act tough."

"Yeah right. He was a fuckin' actor who didn't do shit in real life! Hollywood made him into a so-called hero when all he did was kill the 'savages'—red, black and brown skinned people. I'ma tell you the truth, that man was never a hero to me even though Grandpa idolized him."

Malcolm tossed in his own observations, now that Stokely had opened the door. "You know, when you stop and think about it, it's pathetic that white people have so few heroes in real life that they place celebrities—actors, singers, athletes…"

"Don't forget the military generals…"

"Yep," Malcolm agreed. "…and crooked-assed billionaires they put on a pedestal. Just because those people have money, power, or both."

Stokely asked, rhetorically, "Can you believe that 'Bozo' actually became a trillionaire when people started orderin' everything online instead of goin' out shoppin'?"

"That's crazy," Malcolm uttered, impressed by how much Stokely had matured. He signaled to exit the highway, aptly listening to the gentle authoritative female GPS voice giving directions. And as the gentle soothing voice calmly guided them into an unfamiliar section of the city, he realized that although he was driving, he had not been paying attention. He knew they were heading towards trouble the very moment he eyed the artistically unique hand-painted shingles displaying the street names. Old-fashioned, black novelty lampposts graced the extra wide sidewalks of palatial estates that were purposely set back from the street by their professionally manicured lawns.

The Neighborhood Watch's welcome sign advertising the small enclave's community name, also included a not-so friendly notice to visitors. The consent to monitoring should have been a warning sign for them to turn around. Yet, they continued on.

"How much farther?" Stokely asked, staring at the stately homes. He wondered how the people who lived inside those houses had gotten so comfortable in their own skin that they felt no need to curtain the windows. The familiar, yet uncomfortable first inklings of nervousness that comes from being a black man driving through a white part of town, began to surface. "Malcolm man, my spidey senses are beginning to tingle."

"Chill. We're almost there," he said, making sure he came to a complete stop before proceeding through the stop sign.

"How about I order the food online? We can get it to go. I don't like the vibes I'm getting' from them," he explained, referencing two young white women who had stopped pushing their baby strollers in order to watch them.

Malcolm's eyes trailed Stokely's. "Yeah, why don't you do that." He observed the less attractive woman shouting into her cell phone, while gesturing wildly with her free hand in the direction of their vehicle.

Stokely punched in their order for an immediate pickup. He didn't want to spend any more time up there than necessary.

"What the fuck is she doing?!" Malcolm shouted, swearing uncharacteristically.

"Now this is some bullshit if that bitch is callin' the cops on us! We're not doin' nuthin' wrong. Even the racist police in St. Louis stopped rollin' up on us over calls from the 'Karen's'.

"Well, you're not in St. Louis anymore." Malcolm slowly drove the remaining half mile to the restaurant. He parked in a spot marked 15-minute pickup.

Almost immediately, two police cars pulled in behind them, minus sirens but with their lights flashing. Both vehicles effectively blocked any exit Malcolm might foolishly attempt to use as an escape. The scene would have been comical if they lived in a different time and place. But they were living in an increasingly segregated country where white nationalist racists felt it their responsibility, their civic duty, to call the police and report any person who looked out of the ordinary. In this case, two young black men driving much too slowly. However, in Malcolm's defense, he believed the slower he drove, the less attention he would garner from the residents.

"Ain't this some shit?!" Malcolm exclaimed.

Stokely dropped his head, clenched his jaws tightly, and struggled to control his growing anger. "Those muthafuckin' bitches called the cops on us?! For what?! Drivin' down a city street and mindin' our own damn business?! Unfuckin' believable! Not even in this city 24 hours and we get pulled over."

"Stay cool... We didn't do anything. My papers are good. They'll see this is just a misunderstanding."

"Misunderstandin', my ass!" Stokely took in several deep breaths to calm his growing anger.

"Chill, man! These white boys aren't afraid to shoot us first and then ask questions later."

"I'm good. Let's just make sure we both survive this stop and make it back home safely."

Malcolm lowered both driver and passenger windows and then turned off the engine. He placed his key fob on the dashboard, both hands on the dashboard, and with a nod of his head motioned for Stokely to do the same.

"You got that right! Mom and Dad won't be receivin' that damn call anytime soon," Stokely whispered through clenched teeth.

Two policemen approached the vehicle. One on either side. Neither wore the facial coverings mandated by the city ordinance. The older officer looked first at Malcolm, then over to Stokely, before finally glancing in the backseat. His eyes rolled across the baby's car seat before returning his gaze to Malcolm. "License and registration, please."

Malcolm nodded towards a small pocket secured to the dashboard. "Officer, my documents are inside that pouch. I'm going to slowly reach in and get it for you. Okay?"

The officer nodded his agreement to proceed as he kept one hand firmly planted on the handle of his holstered weapon.

"Do you mind if my brother and I put on our protective face masks?" Stokely chimed in sarcastically. "Seein' that y'all ain't wearin' one."

"No need to worry about us. We've both been vaccinated," explained the older officer. "And we both tested negative just a few weeks ago."

Stokely doubted the man's words held any credence. Although he preferred to take his chances with the latest virulent strain of the virus over the trigger-happy finger of a potentially racist cop, he didn't want to add any more fuel to an already potentially combustible situation.

"Where you guys headed to?" asked the younger cop standing on the passenger side.

While Malcolm calmly handed the older policeman his documents, he fought against the urge to respond in a manner—righteous indignation—that would have been appropriate in this type of situation. But he understood that in those cops eyes, they were just two niggers traveling in a part of the city where they were not welcomed. With a slight smirk on his face that only his brother recognized, he told them, "We heard they had a good vegan restaurant up here. Just thought I'd bring my brother and let him be the judge... for a change of pace."

"Keep an eye on them," the older police told his partner. "I'll go run their info."

The cop who remained at the passenger's side, joked, "Vegan?! You guys don't eat meat?"

"No. I'm plant-based," Stokely said, trying his best to not allow the man's friendly conversation to put him at ease. He was all too familiar with the good-cop, bad-cop routine.

"My wife is a vegetarian and she is a complete pain in the ass." The younger cop studied Stokely intensely before saying, "You look familiar. You famous?"

Stokely turned his head slightly to see the man's crooked yellowed teeth smiling back at him. "No," he said, "I'm not famous." *Yet.*

"You look very familiar," the young cop continued. "Did you go to high school here?"

"No," Stokely replied.

"You remind me of a guy who used to be on our high school football team," the young cop recollected. "He took us to the championship! That boy sure could run!"

Stokely remained quiet, not wanting to engage with the police any more than necessary. He knew that all it took was one misunderstood word for this situation to rapidly go south.

The older officer returned after a few minutes and returned the documents to Malcolm. He said to his partner, "They check out. Let 'em go."

"Um, officer, if you don't mind... Why did you stop me?" Malcolm asked, returning his license and registration to the dashboard pocket for the next time the cops pulled him over.

"We received a call about a vehicle with two men behaving suspiciously. Driving very slowly and looking into windows. Casing the homes, more than likely... You guys fit the description."

In the rearview mirror, Malcolm saw the back-up squad car pull away. He boldly stated, "Well, officer, the speed limit *is* 18."

Although the officer agreed with him, he wasn't about to let on that he did. It was his job to keep the elitist wealthy residents safe. So what if harassing a couple of young black men is what it took. "I'll let you go with a word of advice. Be careful where you're driving nowadays."

Malcolm accepted his words with a grain of salt. As far as he was concerned, he should be able to drive wherever he pleased. This was supposed to be a free country.

"You boys get your food and head on back home," he said, authoritatively, before turning to speak into his radio.

"Will do," Malcom replied, cognizant of how easily the situation could have turned tragic. He waited until both cops were inside their vehicle before moving an inch. Looking over at Stokely, he calmly asked, "You ready to get your food?"

"Man, fuck that food and this damn restaurant! If this is how these people gonna treat us, I'll be damned if I spend my good money up in here."

"Well, we still have to eat," Malcolm declared. "Thankfully, I know a really good soul food restaurant over on NE 23rd street. Me and Drena go there all the time because the food is down-home delicious!"

"Fine with me. I just hope they have at least one healthy option on the menu that I can eat."

"Wait a minute..." Malcolm whispered, glancing in his rearview mirror. "Oh shit! One of those cops is coming back."

"Damn... Now what?" Stokely said, leaning forward and resting both hands on the dashboard.

Malcolm sat up in his seat and this time followed his brother's lead by replacing both hands on the steering wheel.

The younger cop approached the driver's side. He was alone. He motioned for Malcolm to roll down his window. Malcolm complied while Stokely seethed over in the passenger seat.

"Sir," he said, clearing his throat. "I just want to let you guys know, this is my first time patrolling this part of town. I can certainly understand why you'd be driving so slowly past these houses with those big picture windows. I don't live up here so I cannot for the life of me understand why anybody wants to live in a house with no curtains. Even at night you can look straight through these houses. It's like these rich people are showing off all the riches they've accumulated."

"What can I do for you, officer?" Malcolm exclaimed, showing tons of restraint. "We'd like to get going, if you don't mind."

The young officer tucked both thumbs into his belt loops, turning his gaze towards the customers in the restaurant. Many were jockeying with each other for the best position with their cell phones poised and ready to hit 'record' for what they secretly hoped would be another national display of racist police brutality. Something interesting to post on their social media sites to generate comments and likes. He was not about to be in the next viral video.

"I felt bad about stopping you guys today," the officer said, handing Malcolm a small white envelope.

Stokely's ears immediately pricked up. He had never heard a cop apologize.

"What's this?" Malcolm asked, eyeing the envelope suspiciously.

"We're giving away tickets to the *National Cowboy and Western Heritage* museum. They're showing a marathon of John Wayne movies. I don't know if you guys like westerns, but there's four complimentary tickets in there for today," he said with just a hint of a smile. "Think of this as a goodwill gesture."

"What's the catch? Do we have to make a donation or somethin'? Cuz as long as I've been livin' I learned that nuthin' is for free."

The cop suddenly took a step back from the driver's window. He shook his head back-and-forth a few times, as if he were trying to snap back into himself. He not only appeared confused, but also tortured—a man experiencing his own private internal battle between good and evil.

"Are you all right, officer?" Malcolm asked, wondering if the cop was on drugs. *Or about to pass out, which would not be a good thing to happen.*

"Uh... yeah, I'm fine. There's no catch. No donation required. We've been handing these tickets out for the last several days. Apparently, since the pandemic, people have stopped visiting the museum. If they don't drum up some business soon, they'll have to shut the doors. I'm offering this to you guys. I'm hoping it will make up for the harassment."

"Thanks," Malcolm replied guardedly, handing the envelope to his brother. Although the young cop was being extremely 'nice', his experience with police taught him to always proceed with caution.

"You guys really should get out of here before dark. Of course, this is just between you and me," the cop checked to make sure no one was eavesdropping before continuing. He lowered his voice and stated, "Unofficially... this little part of town has once again gone 'sun-down'. We pull you over after dark, this situation would turn out way different for you. Know what I mean, bro," he said with a wink of the eye. "Now get going."

Malcolm replied, hesitantly, "Uh, thank you."

"Have a good evening."

Neither brother spoke another word until the police car drove away.

"What the fuck just happened?!" Stokely exclaimed.

"Which part? Us talking about Grandpa Williams and how much he loved westerns? Or 'Officer Friendly' handing us free tickets to a western marathon? Or how weird that cop was acting."

Stokely added, "Or the fact that a cop treated us decently?"

"Synchronicity!" they uttered at the same time, before breaking into nervous laughter, relieved that they had both survived yet another unwarranted encounter with the police.

"What are we waitin' for? I thought you couldn't wait to get out of here," asked Stokely, studying his older brother.

"It's been years since I was pulled over. I need a few minutes to get my head back right after that bullshit."

"I hear ya." Stokely carefully opened the envelope and pulled out two of the four tickets. He was tempted to toss them both out the window until his brother asked the question he'd been waiting for since they'd gotten in the car.

"So do you really believe Kenya came back?"

"Yeah, don't you?"

"What about her story? You think it's true?"

"It must be true. There's no other explanation that makes any sense," Stokely replied. "But what I really want to know is, why now?"

Malcolm quickly regretted engaging in another conversation with Stokely challenging a simplistic view of the world as 'this' or 'that'. There must be other explanations for what happened, but none he could immediately put his finger on. He quietly uttered, "Honestly, I don't know whether to believe it or not, but I read the entire book."

"There was a passage that alluded to a string of unrelated events comin' together to provide a message. I think she called them, 'breadcrumbs'. Maybe that cop givin' us those tickets is one of those events." Stokely used his phone to pull up the museum's address. "That was too coincidental for it not to be."

"The cowboy museum, huh? Well, no disrespect to the memory of Grandpa Williams, but I still hate westerns!" Malcolm exclaimed with a chuckle. He plucked one ticket from his brother's hand, reading through the information at least three times to make sure it was correct. "These tickets are for this evening's show."

"Cool! We should go!" Stokely continued scrolling through the information about the museum. He stopped when he reached the information about the movie marathon. "Tonight's movie is *Hatari!*, starrin' none other than John Wayne."

"That doesn't sound like the name of a Western."

"It's not. The description says it's an 'action-adventure romance movie that was shot on location in East Africa'."

Malcolm furrowed his brow trying to retrieve a memory that refused to be dislodged. But he persisted until he captured the tidbit held together by a miniscule wrinkle in time. His little sister was always going on and on about Africa. About how one day she wanted to visit the lands of her namesake. "Kenya had a map of Africa on her bedroom wall!"

"That's right! I remember she had highlighted all those different African countries—Kenya, Mali, Gambia, Ghana, Nigeria, Ethiopia, Tanzania, Democratic Republic of Congo, Zaire, and Egypt because she said when she grew up, she wanted to see as much of the continent as possible," Stokely turned to face his brother. His eyes lit up with excitement when he spoke, "Oh shit! You're not gonna to believe this!"

"What?" Malcolm asked.

"That movie *Hatari* was filmed on location in Tanzania!"

Malcolm whispered, "that's one of the countries that borders Kenya."

Stokely grinned. "Kenya sent us a breadcrumb to go to the museum."

"I don't know how you made that leap, but okay," Malcolm whispered quietly, allowing the realization to sink in. He didn't want to admit it, but his interest was piqued.

"Movie starts in an hour. If we get our food now, we can drive over there and eat in the parkin' lot."

"I thought you changed your mind about buying food from up here," Malcolm said.

"Man, I believe we were destined to be at this restaurant. Look, since I already ordered the food, and we're right here, we might as well pick it up. Plus, it smells delicious and I'm starvin'!"

"All right. If you say so."

Stokely retrieved a face covering and pair of disposable gloves from his backpack. He pulled one debit card from his wallet and placed it in a small sandwich bag. "Honestly, I don't know what the fuck is goin' on. But somehow Kenya reached out to us through that dumbass cop. And since that movie is almost three hours long, I figure we'd better eat before we go in. Popcorn and water won't be enough to fill me up since I haven't eaten at all today."

"So this is how it works, huh?"

"I think so. Remember what Mom and Dad used to do on Christmas morning?" Stokely smiled warmly. "They used to give each of us half of a clue, like riddles written on cardboard. We had to place both halves together before we could find our gifts."

"That's right. We had to work together before we could find the present. If we didn't, we only had half of a clue."

"Accordin' to Kenya, the universe, God, is always sendin' us signs. We just have to open our eyes to see what they are. Uncover what the hidden meanin' is and discover how it applies in our lives."

"Like putting pieces of a puzzle together?"

"Somethin' like that..."

"Wait a minute. I thought you didn't believe in God," Malcolm uttered.

Stokely scoffed, "Man, I never said I didn't believe in God. I said I didn't believe in the white man's religion. There is a huge difference." He opened the car door. "Stay here. I'll be right back."

Malcolm felt weary after the tense run-in with those cops. His plan was to give Stokely a simple tour of the city, not go on some wild goose chase all over town. He sat back in his seat and watched his younger brother enter the restaurant. In many ways, Lil' Stok had matured way above his nineteen years. Attending college and living with Uncle Ricky probably helped him in that area.

First the book, then his parents seemingly going off the deep-end, and now he was getting spiritual messages from his sister through a white cop of all people! Humoring his mother was one thing, but this thing with Kenya contacting them directly threatened to push him over the edge. His perfect little applecart of life was slowly being overturned. Why *his* sister? Why *his* family? Things were fine the way they were. Life was simple, not perfect, but everything used to make sense. Even with this pandemic going on and people dying daily by the thousands, he had become accustomed to living in the 'new normal'—which was actually 'the abnormal'.

And with that realization, Malcolm had an epiphany! Life was no longer normal and never would be. Like the passage he read this morning on his NLT Bible App, Revelation 3:15-17, he was living his life 'lukewarm', neither 'hot' nor 'cold'. Over the past several years, he had adapted to living in what the world called the 'new normal'. He had gotten way too comfortable in accepting the 'anything goes' mentality by following the crowd. *He* was the frog in Kenya's parable. If his younger brother could uproot himself from college and move home to help-out his parents, he knew there was more that he should also be doing. If not for himself, then for his daughter, Mali Zambia.

Malcolm watched Stokely pay for the food and then make his way towards the restaurant's exit. He took the opportunity to make a quick call home. Drena answered immediately.

"Hey... It's just me checking in."

"Hey love, you've been gone awhile. Everything okay?" she asked, picking up on something in her husband's voice that something wasn't quite right.

"You know anytime my brother and I venture out into the world, we're going to run into a few bumps along the way. But we're good. I should be home in few hours."

"What happened?" she asked. "I thought you were just doing a quick tour of the city. It's not *that* much to see here."

"You're not going to believe this, but when we stopped for food, the police pulled up on us."

Drena sat up in bed with her heart pounding heavily with dread when she asked, "What?! You got arrested?! Are you okay? Where is Stokely?"

"We're both fine. He's picking up his food. Some stupid women called the cops on us because we were in *their* neighborhood."

"Damn... driving while black?"

"You know it. But what I wanted to tell you is, one of the cops who pulled us over gave us free tickets to a western marathon at the Cowboy Museum. And the crazy part is, we're actually going!"

"You don't even like westerns... Or museums!" Drena stated, staring at her cellphone as if the voice on the other end didn't belong to her husband.

"I know what you're thinking. Never in a million years have I ever expressed a desire to see the cowboy museum. But Stokely wants to go," he said, intentionally leaving out the part about the 'breadcrumb' theory.

"That's fine, sweetheart. The baby and I are settled down watching old episodes of *The Bernie Mac* show. That man and his television family are always good for a few laughs. Takes my mind off what's going on in the world for just a moment."

"Enjoy Bernie Mac." Malcolm smiled, relieved to hear his wife's voice after his strange encounter with the police. He understood that stop could have gone an entirely different way, which still left him shook. "I'll see you in a few hours."

"You guys have fun!" she chirped on the other end, between bursts of laughter. "We'll be here when you get home."

Chapter Fourteen

Malcolm dropped Stokely off at the museum entrance remaining alert for anything out of the ordinary to happen. Stokely stood in the ticket line while his brother parked the car. After confirming the theater tickets were indeed legit, he patiently waited for his brother to join him. Within thirty minutes of taking their seats, they walked out disappointed.

"Man, that movie sucked!" Stokely shouted, leaving behind dozens of older white men who had very different ideas about his review of *Hatari!*. For those old dudes, it was like watching their favorite actor of all time give his greatest performance. "Good thing those tickets were free or I'd have demanded a full refund."

"Why would Hollyweird make a movie like that?" Malcolm asked as he clicked his fob, listening for the 'chirp-chirp' unlocking his vehicle from a distance.

Stokely responded sarcastically, "For the so-called upper-class white folks. You know they love to kill animals for sport so they can mount the heads on the wall as trophies."

"Malcolm shook his head in disbelief. "I tried to get into the storyline, but twenty minutes in, I realized there wasn't one. That was the worst movie I've seen in a while!"

"Man, I was ready to leave after the first five minutes. But since we were supposed to be receivin' a message from Kenya, I wanted to wait it out. See if there was somethin' significant hidden within the movie."

"Did you get anything from watching it?" Malcolm asked.

"Only that rich white men with big guns enjoy huntin' down defenseless animals for sport," Stokely shrugged, then sarcastically replied, "Maybe if we had stayed to watch the end of *Hatari,* we'd have found out what it was really about."

"Well, if you can suffer through it, you can come back and tell me what, if any, hidden messages it held. But for now, all I know is some wealthy Caucasians killed a bunch of rhinoceros' with the help of African guides who led the way, which made it easy for those men to kill as many rhinos as they wanted." Malcolm surprised even himself when he uttered, "Think about it. Europeans stole *human beings* from Africa, brought them to this country, and then enslaved them. So why wouldn't they kill the most ferocious beasts on earth for bragging rights and souvenirs?"

"Where did that come from?" Stokely replied with a grin. "Forget about it, man. Where did we park?"

"We're all the way over there," Malcolm explained, pointing towards the back row of the parking lot. "I didn't want to risk looking suspicious if we have to sit here and wait for something to happen."

"So you don't think two young black men sittin' in their car in a dark parkin' lot look suspicious?" Stokely guffawed. "In some people's minds *we* are the definition of suspicious."

"We're customers so we should be able to park wherever we want to park, but I get what you're saying. Thankfully, the sun is beginning to set, so they won't see us when they leave the museum."

"If you say so," Stokely replied. "I just hope you have some decent music to listen to while we wait."

"Man, I've got satellite radio. We can listen to whatever you want," Malcolm said, as he tried tuning in his favorite soul station. "That's weird..."

"What's up?" asked Stokely, digging into his food.

"The satellite radio is out. When the signal drops, it usually only lasts a second, but now I can't seem to get a signal at all. I paid my bill, so that's not it."

"Considerin' everything else that's happened today, I am not surprised," Stokely uttered between bites of falafel.

"I'm not sure what we're waiting for or how long we're supposed to sit here. But in the meantime, I found something to listen to besides the local radio station."

"Cool," Stokely uttered while stuffing the last morsel of food into his mouth.

Malcolm popped in a CD that Drena had purchased in support of a very talented local Oklahoma City band, the *Merry Walkers*.

Stokely sat back in his seat, fully satisfied with his meal.

"Dang man, you ate that food like you were starving!"

"Told you I was hungry."

After several minutes of listening to what amounted to going on an uplifting musical journey, Stokely recalled the night he spotted the UFO; in hindsight, that was when his world changed. As mind-blowing as that experience was, tonight, in spite of Malcolm's nervousness, he silently hoped that whatever they were about to experience would overshadow even that.

~ ~ ~

"How long are we supposed to wait?" Malcolm asked. "The last car left twenty minutes ago. I'm starting to feel exposed sitting out here."

Stokely scanned the now empty parking lot. He too was tired of waiting, but he wasn't about to miss another opportunity to interact with his sister. "Let's wait just awhile longer. If nuthin' happens, at least we tried."

"At some point, some 'concerned citizen' is going to report a suspicious looking vehicle parked in the museum parking lot. We're black, so I don't plan on getting arrested this evening."

"Well, if the cops show up, just remember to be cool like you were earlier," Stokely advised.

"I'll stay cool as long as you do," he replied.

The last remnants of the sun disappeared in the western sky. It was now twilight, the moment that day officially turns into night.

"Left is right and right is wrong," Stokely quietly repeated to himself. "Left is right. Right is wrong."

"What did you say?"

"I was just thinkin'... That sayin' is something old heads used to take seriously back in the day. I heard it in a movie and it got me to thinkin'."

Malcolm's eyes continued to scan the parking lot.

Stokely looked out at the darkening sky. Speaking in hushed tones, he said, "Yo, man. It was just a random thought. I started thinkin' 'bout how this world sometime feel like its rotatin' in the opposite direction."

"What are you talking about? And why do you suddenly sound like you're from the streets?" he teased.

Stokely sighed, lowering his head. When he looked up, he had excitement in his eyes. "Dude, some days when I wake up, I be feelin' like I'm livin' a different version of my own life. I don't feel the same way I used to. It's trippy."

"Why do you say that?" Malcolm asked, puzzled by the noticeable St. Louis accent now coloring his brother's speech.

Stokely exhaled long and slow, taking his time searching for the right words, before responding, "It ain't nuthin' I can put my finger on. It's just a feelin' I got. Like I be gettin' lost inside a dream. When I come out of it, I'm a different version of myself. Stronger, confident, more powerful. Like I am slowly evolvin' into a higher version of me. Like the old me is slowly dying, and a new me is being born."

"You seem the same to me."

"Naw, man. I ain't the same." He shook his head. "I had to get hard 'cuz the streets of St. Louis ain't no joke!"

"Sorry you had to deal with that on your own," Malcolm said, thinking *'But it was you who chose to stay.'*

"When y'all first moved, I was depressed. Seemed like nuthin' in my life was goin' right. Two of my homeboys was murdered over some stupid shit. Way too many of my partners and they family got sick or died from that virus. It felt like there was nuthin' 'cept death, despair, and hopelessness in everybody I was around. These past couple years done changed me."

"Like how?" Malcolm asked with growing concern.

"Ever since movin' to Unc's house, I think this weird shit started happenin' to wake me up."

"Are you high?" He teased.

"Naw bro. My eyes were opened to see the world as it really is. Fucked up!" he chuckled, before returning to being serious. "Then I started havin' some real 'deep' dreams most every night. That was cool. I like lucid dreamin'. But when I started to hear voices inside my head, I wondered if I was losin' my mind."

"What were the voices saying?" Malcolm joked, nervously. "Maybe you've been smoking too much *cheeba cheeba.*"

"Man... shut up! Cannabis ain't got nuthin' to do with it. Plus, I don't actually *hear* their voices audibly." Stokely wiped the extra tzatziki sauce from his fingers with an old napkin he found stuffed underneath the passenger seat. "It all happens inside my mind. Like when I'm talkin' to certain people, it's like I'm havin' two different conversations at once. One's out loud, at the physical level. External."

"I'm tracking..." Malcolm replied.

Stokely continued, "The other conversation is at a higher level—the supernatural level. Instead of us speakin' words out loud, my spirit connects with the other person's spirit. Sometimes, if they're really cool, I can feel their 'vibe'."

"Really?"

"Half of the time, I don't know if the other person is even aware of what's happenin'. I know... Weird, right?"

Malcolm remained quiet. Uncertain if his entire family was slowly going crazy, he didn't want to interrupt his brother. On some level, he was glad to know that his younger brother hadn't been left out of the family's nuttiness. By each one having undergone their individual unexplained events, it had somehow strengthened their family bond.

"Honestly, I think my spirit is communicatin' with yours right now." Stokely said back in his seat, pleased by this realization.

"So let me get this straight... Even though we're speaking out loud right now, we're having an entirely different conversation, but on a spiritual level?" Malcolm added, unable to stop himself, "What are our spirits saying to each other now?"

"You don't believe me, but that's okay. I know what I'm talkin' about."

"I hope you're not going around talking to yourself out loud. That'll get you labeled a kook in a heartbeat."

"Man, I have complete control of what comes out of my mouth. Besides, I learned the less I say, the easier it is to avoid sayin' the wrong thing."

Malcolm leaned back in his seat trying to not become overwhelmed. He struggled for some profound words to offer his younger brother, but none came. Times like this, he regretted having a job that prohibited his smoking marijuana, because he sure could use a hit right now. He rolled down all four windows. The warm evening air flooded into the car bringing with it the scent of freshly cut grass. He uttered, "I don't understand what's happening with our family. First Kenya went missing. Me and Mom mysteriously lose an entire day. She and Dad think they saw Kenya coming down from a UFO. And now Mom's working on publishing a book that she believes Kenya gave to her. Now you're telling me that you've gone *spiritual*? What in the world is going on?"

"I don't know. But whatever is happenin', I feel at peace with it," Stokely explained. Suddenly, a movement outside the car caught his attention. He shushed his brother.

"What's wrong?"

"Did you feel that?"

"Feel what?"

"Wait a minute," Stokely whispered. He steadied himself with both hands on the dashboard. Sporting a big grin, he exclaimed, "Wow! Here it comes again! It feels like the vibration that comes outta those humongous concert speakers when a mad bass beat is playin', but *without* the sound!"

"Yeah, I feel it," Malcolm replied. "Maybe it's an earthquake."

"Naw, man. That didn't come from no earthquake!" Stokely pointed toward the side of the museum. Barely able to contain his excitement, he shouted, "What the fuck is that?!"

Malcolm looked in the direction from where his brother pointed.

"Over there!" Stokely shouted, gesturing excitedly. "Did you see that?!"

"What the...!?"

"Wait a minute! There it is again!!!" Stokely shouted in a voice two octaves above normal.

Malcolm's alarm increased when he spied successive rapid bursts of bright lights that seemingly came from the clear night sky above the museum. He scanned the parking lot, confirming they remained alone, before turning the key in the ignition. The engine quietly turned over.

"Wait a minute!" Stokely shouted, gripping his hand over Malcolm's to prevent him from shifting into gear. "That might be Kenya. Maybe she's tryin' to get our attention!"

"It might also be two fools shooting at each other."

"You and I both know that was not gunfire."

"Not if they were using silencers."

"Oh shit! That vibration is comin' back again! Hold on!"

"What the fuck is going on?!" Malcolm yelled, clutching the steering wheel. "Do you feel that?!

"Whoa! Maybe we're being scanned!" Stokely shouted unable to contain his excitement. "I feel lighter already!"

"That was weird," Malcolm uttered, feeling as if his head were swimming.

"Man, stop being a pussy. Drive over there," Stokely pointed towards the side of the museum from where the lights had originated.

Still trying to process what he'd just experienced, Malcolm took his time before speaking. Staring at a picture of himself, Drena, and Mali that he kept on his dashboard, he responded almost apologetically, "Look Stokely, I know you had to get used to living in a crime infested city... I'm sorry you had to deal with all that after we moved, but I don't live that way anymore. We don't know who—or what—is over there. And I'm not trying to get us in the middle of something that we can't get out of."

"I'm tellin' you, that's not gunfire. I think Kenya is signalin' to us," Stokely massaged his temples. "I can feel her vibe. It's very powerful. I think she wants us to drive over there."

Malcolm stared at his brother, each of them determining what their next move should be. As if on a timer, the lights in the parking lot went off one-by-one. The bright security lights, meant to deter burglars from breaking into the museum, dimmed like someone had flipped a switch. Without benefit of the parking lot lighting, the area became enveloped in the kind of darkness one only finds deep in the country on a moonless night. He weighed his options. In his mind, there were only two. *Leave or stay.* Before he changed his mind, he switched on the headlights and slowly drove through the vacant parking lot towards the side of the museum. He parked, dimmed the headlights, but left the engine running—just in case, and said, "You notice how quiet it is over here?"

"Yeah, this must be what it's like inside a sound vacuum," Stokely surmised. "The vibes are stronger. And they're comin' closer together."

"You're right," Malcolm replied, glancing around nervously. His breathing remained labored as a result of the last adrenaline rush brought on by the lightshow. "What now?"

"We wait." Stokely leaned forward to scan the sky above. He vowed that this time he was not going to miss his sister's appearance. No matter how long it took for her to show up, he was in for the long haul.

"What's that?" Malcolm whispered, focused on the rustling sounds coming from a cluster of overgrown bushes.

"Chill out, man." Stokely glanced in that direction, explaining, "It's just a stray cat. You gonna make yourself have a heart attack if you keep jumpin' like that."

"Listen, I know you believe that Kenya is going to somehow magically appear, but I have a family now. I'm not trying to get myself killed because you think that our sister is trying to make contact with us."

"You're right, I don't have a wife and kids, but I got y'all." Stokely opened the car door and bravely stepped outside, into the hot humid air of the summer night. No longer was he afraid.

"What are you doing?! Get back inside the car!"

"I know you're not too sure about this whole scene. The last thing I wanna do is get you into some shit you can't get out of. But I'm gonna hang out here until she shows up," he replied, confidently.

"Stokely, man. Get back in the car! Mom would kill me if she found out I left you here alone!"

"Don't worry about me. I got this!" Stokely shouted over his shoulder. He used the light from his cell phone to further check out his surroundings.

"Stop playing and get in the damn car!" Malcolm shouted in frustration.

A loud whooshing noise caused a sudden break in their conversation. A strong blast of air seemingly came out of nowhere, nearly knocking Stokely down. He easily regained his footing and then backed up slowly until he had returned to the front of the jeep. With his heart beating wildly with excitement, he latched onto the hood and looked through the windshield to make sure Malcolm was watching. And then, ever so slowly, after taking a moment to prepare himself mentally to see whatever it was that had caused the unusual disturbance, he slowly looked up.

In that very same moment, Malcolm also felt the first blast of hot air. He stuck his head out the driver's window, turning every which way trying to gauge from where the air had come. He looked through his windshield to see his brother clutching the front of the jeep. Then he saw Stokely's face. He watched as the expression on his brother's face change from uncertainty to pure joy, right before his eyes. Because he too wanted to see whatever it was that put that smile on Stokely's face, he too looked up.

Chapter Fifteen (Sistah Kenya's Second return)

Three Earth days after The Teacher's last visit, I left Nigiro to reunite with the others in an area unknown to man—a lunah waystation on the dark side of the Moon. I had not meant to tell you this, but the Moon is incredible! It is its own light source! Every surface luminates light, though not as brilliant as the Sun's. The moon's glow is more diffused, the type of lighting that you may use to light your way at night.

The lunah station is also a wondrous sight to behold! Just the sheer enormity of the area, which is basically the size of a small city, puts me in awe. The climate-controlled hangers are joined together by brightly-lit hallways, similar to how an airport is connected by various concourses. The hanger where the motherships are docked is massive! The ceilings are so high I cannot see the top. Yet the building seems to be flooded with what appears to be natural sunlight. Everything is so clean! Living spaces, in a beautiful resort-like setting, are made available for all those who maintain this particular waystation. I even once came across several telescopes set-up in an area for celestial viewing. When I looked through the lens, it was pointed towards the Earth! All those nights I spent staring up at the Moon, I had no idea there might be someone staring back at me.

Now for the truly amazing detail of the sight that practically left me speechless. The lunahstation was staffed entirely by very tall, physically fit, highly melanated blue-black people wearing spacesuits made of a shiny metallic-type material! The color of spacesuit was determined by one's position.

The Teacher is pleased because I am diligent with my studies, learning my lessons much quicker than expected. I passed the course on orbital flight, so I can now pilot one of the smaller Nigiro spacecraft without an instructor present. At first I was extremely intimidated by the thought of solo-piloting a vessel that runs on solar power and radiates heat like the corona of the sun. The interior cubic feet is probably equivalent to a Boeing 747 is size— but the vehicle itself is shaped like an isosceles triangle.

With the excellent flight instruction and training I received from the Elders, I am more than ready to do this! Instead of the gold jumpsuit, I wear a custom-made spacesuit constructed of some incredibly advanced material which allows me to become as stealth as the vessels in which I travel! Not only can I make my entire body invisible, but I am also one hundred percent undetectable!

As I prepared the spacecraft for my solo trip to earth, I felt the Teacher's powerful magnetic presence long before I saw his face.

"Braveheart!" he called out telepathically.

"Teacher!" I shouted in excitement, turning to watch him fully materialize in his ten-foot splendor. The gold collar of his emerald green spacesuit shimmered alive with energy. "I am so happy you came to see me off."

"You forgot this," he said aloud, his baritone voice reverberating throughout the enclosed space. He placed the miniaturized teleportation-object in my hand. As a special treat, he had it designed exactly like the rings my parents wore.

"Thank you, Teacher. I thought I had it with me," I said accepting the tob, placing it securely on my left index finger where the chance of me misplacing it were greatly reduced.

"While you are on the earth, always remember, 'A wildflower is a flower that has yet to be named; it is considered a weed to those who cannot appreciate untamed beauty'."

"What do you mean, Teacher?" I asked telepathically.

"Every seed-bearing plant was placed on the earth for hue-man consumption. I caution you to not allow man's laws to prevent consumption of what is naturally provided from The Creator."

"Are you referring to cannabis?"

The Teacher smiled.

I nodded, taking note of his profound words, as I focused on completing the preflight checklist. This would be my first solo flight. I couldn't afford to mess it up.

"The Creator has given signs and wonders to your family. They will be at the proper place for you to reach them."

"Where is that, Teacher?"

"It will be a safe place. For you all."

"It's been several years since I last saw my brothers. How will I recognize them?"

"You will know, when you know," he said, wholly fully confident in my piloting skills. *I shall see you upon your return. Peace be with you, Braveheart!*

"Thank you, Teacher. I will do what is required," I replied.

The Teacher left me standing alone inside the spacepod. I was not saddened because I knew I would see him and all the others in good time.

Upon completion of the last pre-flight checklist item, I powered up the spacepod with a touch of my fingertip. The machinery made a barely audible whirring sound. With a practiced swipe of my hand, a colorful small-scale 3-D map of the solar system magically appeared. I was immediately enveloped in a virtual outer space reality. Real time holographic images of actual planets, stars, asteroids, meteorites, satellites and various other manmade space junk orbiting around the earth, soared past me at incredible rates of speed.

The last item before 'taking off' was to familiarize myself with the pod's navigational system for I had no intention of becoming lost in outer space. Using the center of the familiar Milky Way galaxy as my starting point, I did a virtual practice run—soaring past an infinite number of unknown solar systems—just to see how far as I could go in the expanse of space. If you are curious, I have yet to reach the universe's outer limits.

I felt my heartbeat quickening in nervous anticipation of seeing my brothers again. And in that moment, an ethereal playlist that automatically selects and plays music according to my mood incredibly synched itself to the orb's sound system. The mesmerizing voice of Philip Bailey singing one of my mother's favorite EWF songs—one she often hummed while she was cleaning the house—played softly in the background through 'invisible' surround-sound speakers.

With practiced precision, I disengaged the spacepod from the mothership and expertly piloted it away from its base. As I was thinking about how to find my brothers, an incoming thought transmission from the Teacher, something I had become accustomed to receiving, placed an image of my long deceased great-great-grandfather—one from a familiar picture displayed on the fireplace mantel—in my mind. In the sepia photo, he was sitting atop a beautiful horse. A cowboy-style hat with a long eagle's feather in the hat band, was perched atop his two shoulder-length braids. Another image of a large building filled with antiques and historical relics replaced the first one. Because I knew my family had moved to Oklahoma City, and from my experiences of 'connecting the dots', I surmised the location provided to my brothers had something to do with Native Americans, Oklahoma, cowboys, and 'history'. I'd never lived in Oklahoma, so I was not familiar with how it all tied together. So I did what I learned when I was only eight years old. I plugged those words into a search engine of the earth's worldwide web. Out of all the various sites that came up, the *National Cowboy & Western Heritage Museum* in Oklahoma City seemed to be the most likely choice.

I entered the coordinates into the spacepod's outer space version of a GPS. When a green light appeared on the console, confirming my destination was the museum, I knew I had deciphered the message correctly. I placed the system on auto, and then I sat back and relaxed for the short duration of the ride. This was not my first trip to earth in one of these spacecrafts. Just my first solo without an instructor. Using my newfound ability to receive high vibrational frequencies, I scoured the Earth's lower atmosphere for my brothers' unique signatures. I was only searching for their vibrations to see if I could find them that way. And I did!

Although the spacecraft was cloaked invisible thanks to the Nigiro's superior stealth technology—undetectable from all known radar tracking systems—it still made enough noise to draw attention when it reached the lower atmosphere. I don't completely understand the physics behind how the spacepod works, but it runs on solar power. It emits powerful bursts of energy that results in waves of strong vibrations through the air, similar to how heatwaves look as they bounce off the street surface on a hot summer day. Or how a pebble causes ripples upon the water's surface after its tossed into a pond of still water.

Thus, making my arrival appear as nothing more than an unexpected downward burst of wind was critical. I had to be very cautious. I could not chance scaring off my brothers.

Malcolm and Stokely were exactly where the Teacher projected they'd be, parked under a cluster of evergreen trees bordering the perimeter of the cowboy museum's parking lot. I maneuvered the spacepod about 500 feet above the museum. When I first spotted my brothers, I was slightly taken aback. Each had aged more than either should. I suppose it was because of me. The heartache my family must have experienced because of my disappearance had taken a tremendous toll on everyone. But on the bright side, I was now returning to deliver good news.

Maintaining stealth mode, I hovered above the building that housed the museum until the sun had completely set. I waited until the first star shone brightly in the night sky before initiating contact. One wrong move could make my attempt to contact them go entirely wrong. As eager as I was to see my brothers again, I had to be patient. At the right moment, after confirming the coast was clear, I made my presence known with three more successive flashes of light.

I watched from above as my oldest brother drove to the side of the building. Stokely got out of the car. Cognizant of the energy output from the spacecraft, I was amused watching Stokely wander about, trying to determine from which direction the disturbance had suddenly come.

When I received a transmission from the Teacher with the command, 'Now!', I knew it was time for me to make my move. I placed the controls to 'auto hover', initiated the transport beam, and then I stepped into the protective light and descended to the parking lot.

Chapter Sixteen

Malcolm remained in the car afraid to move. He had no idea how to react as he watched a figure appear, courtesy of a beam of light that mysteriously came down from what appeared to be a low-hanging cloud. Had someone told him that he had accidently wandered on to the set of a movie production scene, that would have been more believable than what was taking place right before his eyes. He took a good look at the figure shrouded within a luminous radiation of light. "That's impossible," he whispered to himself. "It can't be her..."

Moving in slow-motion, as if in a dreamscape, Kenya turned to face the jeep. A halo of light, like the glowsticks they used to play with as children, surrounded her body. He fought the urge to place the car in gear and speed off. Had his little brother not been standing outside the vehicle, that is exactly what he would have done. One thing was for certain, the world he once recognized had forever disappeared.

"Stokely! Get away from it!" Malcolm shouted, snapping back to reality. "You don't know what that thing is! It might all be a trick!"

Stokely was the first one to make a move. He waved off Malcolm's dire warning, instead he crept towards what he hoped was his sister. Engulfed within that hazy light, she appeared ethereal.

"Is it really you, Kenya?" he whispered.

"Hi Stokely. Yes, it is really me," Kenya said, standing face-to-face with her younger brother.

"Wow!" he said, staring at her luminous face. "You look like an angel from above!"

Giggling in delight, she replied, "And you look just like a younger version of father!"

"Yeah, I've grown-up." He resisted the urge to reach out and touch her, to make sure she was real. He whispered in amazement, "But you... You look exactly the same. Well, except you changed your hair from braids to locs." He thought, '...*and your eyes. Something about them looks different.*'

"*Greetings Malcolm!*" she relayed to her older brother, who remained in the vehicle. She was not surprised when he did not respond.

"Kenya! I read your book!" Stokely announced, before posing the one question burning in his mind from the very moment he read the last word on the last page. "Is it true?"

With a nod of the head, she answered, "*Yes. I was rescued.*"

"Not that part," he retorted, inhaling to calm his wildly beating heart. Watching his sister's fluid movements, just a touch under full-speed, made the situation seem even more surreal. "The part about us bein' 'aliens'... I mean, God's children."

"*We are not of this world,*" she relayed to Stokely. "*Yes, it is true.*"

Stokely took a step backwards when he heard Kenya's thought inside his own. Staring deeply into her eyes, he relayed, '*Hold on... Did you just answer me... telepathically?*'

Kenya smiled so broadly, her gumline showed.

And upon Stokely seeing hers, so did his.

Malcolm killed the ignition. He slowly opened the car door. And then one at a time, he placed both feet on the ground, simultaneously checking the area to see if anyone else had arrived to witness this otherworldly phenomena. He confirmed they remained alone. If his younger brother wasn't afraid of this 'alien', neither should he be. He joined Stokely by his side, staring at whatever this thing was.

"Who are you?" he called out, tentatively at what appeared to be an apparition of his sister.

"*Hi Malcolm. I am Kenya,*" she gently explained. "*Your sistah*".

"I-I-I d-d-don't understand," he stuttered, trying his best to put on a brave front. He rubbed his chin and asked suspiciously, "How do *I* know you're who you say you are?"

"Who else would I be?"

"She does have a point," Stokely agreed.

"But who are you, *really*?" Malcolm narrowed his eyes at the apparition who claimed to be his sixteen-year-old missing sister. An expression he heard from his late great-grandmother drifted into his mind. *'That chile moves slower than molasses on a cold winter's day.'*

Kenya whispered in a throaty voice, no longer used to speaking out loud, "You ask, 'Who am I?', really? Let me tell you, I am a beautiful child of The Creator! A heavenly spirit having an earthly experience. I am Love. I am Loved."

"Wow!" was all Stokely could manage to say.

"If love was the air, I would be breathing it into my lungs, as it is the essence of my eternal being. It is such a wonderful delightful feeling! Like a cloud of purple love dust sprinkled down on me from angels above, it surrounds me, blowing in and over me like the currents of the mighty Mississippi river overflowing the bank when the rain has filled it to capacity. Love is a feeling! Love is an action! Love should be experienced by everyone! Love is all there is when you know who you are."

Stokely thought, *'She looks like Kenya, but she sure don't sound like her. And what's with that moving in slow-motion?'*

"Trust me. I am your sistah." She declared to Stokely before further explaining, "My movements appear strange to you because my physical body is no longer accustomed to this low-vibrational atmosphere. The protective light source restricts my motion."

Stokely remained still, afraid to move lest he upset this perfect encounter with something he had no words for. So instead of talking and asking a million questions like he normally would, he listened.

"My brothahs," Kenya continued, "if everyone understood how splendid it is to experience a perfect Love—free of expectations and judgement—there would be no hatred in this world. Love is the highest of the high! Breathing it in charges the soul. Fuels the spirit. But sadly, too many within this generation do not know how to *Love*. They are lost. Pursuing only what they can see with their natural sight—material wealth created by living in this vulgar world. If only they knew, they are merely chasing the wind."

Stokely thought, *Dang! the only time I've ever come close to reachin' the 'high' you're talkin' about is when I smoked ganja. If I can get where you are without usin' marijuana, I'm all in!*

Kenya replied to Stokely's thought, *"What I have obtained can only come from intimately knowing The Creator."*

"My bad," he apologized. "I got overly excited."

Malcolm inched backwards until he connected with the solid brick surface of the museum. He was terrified, but didn't want to release his true feelings in front of Stokely. He also didn't want to faint, but if he did, at least the wall would break his fall.

Stokely regained his voice and asked, "Where have you been all this time?"

"On Nigiro," Kenya explained, straightforwardly. "I have been with the Teacher. The layers are being unfurled one at a time."

Stokely exhaled his nervousness so he could continue speaking to the sister he no longer understood. "I don't understand why you've come back. Why now?"

"My dear brothahs, the deception you're living under goes deep. Make no mistake about it. Our people must throw off hundreds of years of 'white' oppression before we can move forward. I am the bridge gapping the space between the Nigiro and The Almighty's children on Earth. Your awakenings will not happen all at once. When you are ready to accept the magnificence of what is awaiting you on the other side, that is when it will occur. Just know that once your senses are 'heightened', you will see, hear, feel, touch, taste, and discern what others cannot. You must know you are not who they say you are! You are one of us! The Nigiro! The original children of The Most High God! I am here because The Teacher has tasked me to help others find the way."

"Kenya?" asked Stokely.

"Yes."

"Is it possible that I can get a hug from you?" Stokely asked, courageously stepping forward.

"Of course, you can! But, I must warn you, I cannot leave my protective aura. It blocks the environmental toxins that not only harm earth's atmosphere, but also damages cells in my human body."

"What did they do to you?" Malcolm asked with concern. "Are you still... human?"

"I am a spiritual being having a human experience. Living in Nigiro has cleansed my body of all ailments I suffered from living a life in America. Unfortunately, your physical bodies are full of environmental toxins, which makes it difficult for me to bear being in your presence for long. Therefore, in order for us to really enjoy our precious little time together, you are both invited to my spacepod. There your bodies will be 'cleansed'."

"Cool! I can't wait to get inside a real live UFO!" The joy beaming from Stokely's huge smile could have lit up the night sky with its sheer brilliance. He sprang towards Kenya, and called out, "I'm ready! Let's go!"

Still unconvinced, Malcolm jumped between 'Kenya' and Stokely to stop him. He didn't know with any certainty *what* this extraterrestrial was who stood in front of him. His voice shook when he uttered, "Stokely! I know you think this is Kenya, but look at her! She looks the same as the day she disappeared! Whatever it is, it's trying to trick you!"

"Why would I need to trick either of you?" Kenya replied, disappointed by Malcolm's non-wavering stance of disbelief.

Stokely shook his head a couple of times. The nagging question of, *'What am I forgetting?'* continued to bother him. A déjà vu fragment trickled through his mind, triggered by something Malcolm said.

"Look, I don't know what's happening here, but I'm not going to play mind games with whoever—or whatever—that thing is!" Malcolm admitted. He grabbed

Stokely by the arm and shouted, "Get in the car! We need to go! Now!"

No longer smiling, Stokely pulled free from Malcolm's grip, he cried out in desperation, "This has to be Kenya! I can feel her."

"You don't know what you're feeling. Neither do I!"

As Kenya's brothers struggled with trying to come to terms with their little 'situation', she watched Malcolm's disbelief slowly drain into Stokely when he turned his head from her. Witnessing the rapid disappearance of her younger brother's innocence, that is when she understood she needed to prove that she was indeed their sister. And always right on time, the Teacher relayed the message *'sweet tooth'*. that's when she knew what she had to say.

"Fortune cookies!" she shouted out to Stokely.

"What about 'em?" he replied with hesitation.

"Your dream! Mother never knew you and I used to arm wrestle to see who got the extra fortune cookies when we got Chinese food takeout."

Stokely dropped his head, chuckling with disbelief. He wasn't just having a déjà vu moment, he felt as if he were reliving remnants from the dream itself. He paused momentarily before saying, "Mom and Dad are the only ones I told about my dream. There's no way you could have known. So how did you?"

"The Teacher told me what to say," Kenya relayed telepathically to Stokely.

"For real?!" he replied aloud. "That's dope!"

"Yes, it is."

Since he no longer questioned Kenya's authenticity, he took the opportunity to ask a question that continued to nag at him, "Since you know about my dream, was that you in the parkin' lot that night?"

She cocked her head to the side, unsure as to what he was referring.

Malcolm frowned, looking at his younger brother, wondering what he had missed in the conversation.

"I thought I saw a UFO one night in the library parkin' lot at school," he explained to him. "I'm just tryin' to find out if it was her or not."

"Yes, Stokely. I did attempt to contact you. The Teacher was with me the night I tried to reach you. However, due to your reaction, he encouraged me to wait for another time."

"Like now?" he snickered, relieved that the mystery had been solved.

She nodded.

"Do you think I'll get a chance to meet the Teacher?" he relayed back, enjoying their newfound ability to communicate.

"That is entirely up to The Teacher," Kenya replied, reveling in the knowledge that Stokely already possessed the gift of telepathy. What he needed now was to learn how to use it effectively.

"I have another question. Why did you want to see me and Malcolm back here? All clandestine like."

"That was also the Teacher's doing. Consider it a lesson to see how well you two work together when given clues. Like how our parents used to send us on scavenger hunts to locate gifts."

"L-l-like putting the pieces of a puzzle together?" Malcolm asked, guardedly.

"Something like that," Kenya responded.

"Children. Children…" relayed an incoming thought.

"Shhhh…" Stokely interrupted abruptly, "I think I 'hear' something… Like that voice I told you about." He massaged his temples like he was trying to fine tune the reception. "It's coming in real faint."

"Listen carefully…" Kenya relayed, "It is The Teacher."

His message continued, "Those with eyes shall see, those with ears will hear."

"Are you getting this, too?" Stokely asked, grinning at his sister.

She nodded, pleased that the message was getting through.

"The moment has arrived for you to take your place. All The Creator's children, from the four corners of the earth, shall gather together as one in preparation for that which is yet to

come. The one who holds the key (ankh) shall show you the way. Come now, my dear children, the time is nigh."

"Wow! That was amazing!" Stokely exclaimed, and then asked, "Was that meant for me?"

"Yes," Kenya relayed. *"Because you received the message, it was intended for you to hear."*

"That's cool!" Stokely cheered. "I just received a message directly from the real H-N-I-C! The Head-Nigiro-In-Charge!"

She cocked her head to the side, responding in kind, *"Then, we must go."*

"What just happened?" Malcolm asked. "I didn't hear anything."

"I always believed, and The Teacher's message has just confirmed, that Stokely has proven he has the ability to 'hear'. To receive."

"What in the world are you two talking about?"

"Malcolm, that voice in my head that I told you about... Well, I just heard it again. So did Kenya." Stokely said, "I think I figured it out. I think they want to see me."

"*Who* wants to see you?"

"I don't know, but I think I'm supposed to go with Kenya. Up to her spaceship," he said hopefully, staring at the moonless sky. "Maybe I'll even get to meet a real live *Nigiro*. I can't wait!"

When what Malcolm said no longer seemed to matter, he tried appealing to his brother's sensibilities. He gripped Stokely's arm and shouted, "What if you don't come back?! What am I going to tell mom and dad?"

"C'mon, man. Don't do this, now!" he begged. "This might be my only chance to learn who I really am. Ya feel me?"

"Malcolm, he is protected," Kenya said.

Shifting his focus from his brother to sister, he pleaded, "If you're really Kenya, please help me understand what's going on."

She peered right into Malcolm's eyes in that peculiar slow-motion movement that made her look as if she were moving underwater. She raised her right hand and flashed the peace sign; 'V' for victory. "Stokely is safe. The Nigiro will protect him. As well as you. And yours. Forever."

"I still don't understand..."

"You read my story?"

"Yes," he answered. "Every single word."

"Please read it again," she advised. "But this time, do so with an *open* mind."

"I promise I will. But first tell me... Did you have anything to do with me and mom losing an entire day?"

"Our arrival that night caused you both great distress. It was the Teacher's decision to clear your troubled minds, if even for a day. Twenty-four hours of restful sleep is good for the body, mind, and soul. It was something badly needed."

Malcolm sighed in relief, uttering, "Wow... I thought I was abducted by aliens and had my memory erased. But missing a day because I slept twenty-four hours sounds much better."

"My brothah, my hope is that you too will remember and recognize the truth about who you are. Before it is too late."

"Ok, sis! I'm ready!" Stokely said, jumping around like an eager puppy. "You cool, Malcolm?"

With her outstretched hand, Kenya motioned for Stokely to join her.

Stokely hugged Malcolm tightly and Malcolm clutched unto his little brother afraid that this would be the last time he'd see him. Neither wanted to be the first to let go, but Stokely gave in. When he gave pulled back, that big goofy smile had returned.

"Don't worry, big bro. It's all good! When I return, I'll tell you all about it."

"Be careful!" Malcolm said in return, because that's the only thing that came to mind.

"No worries!" Stokely turned and walked confidently into the light. When he reached out to touch his sister's hand, he was immediately transformed.

"I am who I say I am!" Kenya shouted, one last time.

Malcolm opened his mouth to respond, but thought better of it. Instead, he remained silent and took in the amazing sight.

Kenya stretched out her left hand, energizing the ankh tob. With her free arm, she held tightly unto Stokely. They waved excitedly to Malcolm as if they were going on vacation. He watched as they slowly ascended upwards, disappearing into a spacecraft disguised as a 'cloud' in the sky. For the briefest of moments, the space vessel revealed itself. And then poof! In the time it takes to blink an eye they were gone.

Malcolm stood in the museum parking lot, staring up at the night sky, wondering what in the world just happened. One minute he was sitting in the car enjoying good conversation and cold falafel with Stokely, five minutes later, he found himself watching his brother and sister disappear into a UFO.

It was late. He was drained. Feeling more alone than he'd felt in his entire life, Malcolm slumped into his jeep, disheartened—not only by what just happened, but more so by how he'd break the news to his parents. He fiddled with the radio trying to find some relaxing music. He needed a distraction to take his mind off wondering if he could have done anything differently to alter the string of events that led up to Stokely leaving with Kenya. Finding nothing suitable, he opted for driving in silence with the windows down.

One thing about driving with the windows down, listening to the white noise provided by the rushing air, is it gives one time to think. Before telling his parents about tonight, he needed to talk it over with his wife. That time of night, traffic on all highways was pretty much non-existent, so he arrived home much sooner than expected. When Malcolm finally staggered into the bedroom, it was well past midnight. Drena stirred in her sleep.

Malcolm wearily removed his shoes, his clothing, and leaned over to plant a tender kiss on his wife's cheek.

"Hey baby, you made it home," she greeted him, groggily. "Did you guys have a good time?"

He didn't know how to break the news, so he simply blurted out, "Drena... Stokely's gone. And I don't know how to tell Mom."

"What do you mean, Stokely's gone? Where is he?" she asked, sitting up in the bed, alarmed.

"This is all going to sound kind of 'out there', so please bear with me."

Taking in her distraught husband's face, Drena pushed herself upright in bed. "Sit down love. Tell me what happened."

"I don't even know where to begin," Malcolm replied dropping his head, shaking it from side to side.

"Start anywhere... How about from the beginning?" she encouraged him. "Go on. I'm listening...."

With a weary sigh, he began, "We were just out driving around. I wanted him to have a feel for the lay of the city. Stokely was hungry so we went looking for a place to eat. Once we drove to that Indian Restaurant, things got really weird."

"You're talking about when the police rolled up on you?" she asked, trying to make sense of what was going on with her husband. "Is that what you mean?"

"Yeah... But for real though, Drena... The moment Stokely and I drove off from Mom and Dad's house, I think that's when our world once again turned upside down. Just like when Kenya disappeared..."

~ ~ ~

Malcolm and Drena got very little rest that night. While he lamented over how he was going to tell his parents, especially his mom, that he was responsible for losing Stokely, Drena spent the night trying to soothe a fussy baby. Apparently little Mali was quite perceptive to the slightest change in her father's moods, thus, her heartbreaking cries reflected the anguish he suffered within.

After a very long night, hyped up on caffeine and not enough sleep, they all piled into the jeep for the twenty-minute drive to his parent's house to deliver the news. It was the crack of dawn, those few precious minutes between darkness and light, when night gives way to day. Slow moving clouds bringing in humidity from the south, became noticeably tinted orange and pink as the sun made its way over the horizon to brighten the morning sky.

When Malcolm was only a few minutes from the house, he quickly changed directions and headed towards the nearest bakery. A dozen donuts might help soften the blow. Lord knows, he needed all the help he could get over the next several hours.

Chapter Seventeen (Lunah)

Kenya understood the risk of making contact with her brothers in a fairly populated area of the city, were great. From what she remembered about living in the world, two young black men out alone at night, sitting in a parked vehicle outside of a closed venue, were sitting ducks. But thankfully, the Teacher had cloaked their visit from any interference from outsiders. The chance of her spacepod being spotted by anyone was virtually nil because it was in stealth mode, disguised as a fluffy cloud, indistinguishable from the others that lazily floated by in the night sky.

The moment she received the incoming transmission from the Teacher, she understand that it was time to leave. It was imperative her departure from the mothership was performed expeditiously. Since the Nigiro visits to the earth had become more frequent—due to others like her making contact with their loved ones—sightings of UFO's around the world had increased exponentially. Thus, various countries' militaries had been placed on high alert for any 'unusual' extraterrestrial activity.

Their ascent to the spacepod, shrouded within the lightbeam, went rather smoothly considering Stokely could barely contain his excitement. After he securely strapped himself into a seat on the bridge, he became so overwhelmed by the entire experience, he literally passed out. Kenya took that opportunity to boost his sympathetic nervous system so he'd have an easier time traveling through outer space. Because of the relative short distance to the moon, she attached a high-tech version of an IV, inserting a painless 'needle' into Stokely's arm to provide the serum directly into his bloodstream, instead of a 'patch' that would've slowly administered the serum. By the time they reached the moon, the serum would have taken effect.

It was tricky business piloting the spaceorb from earth, especially since she was transporting precious cargo. At the high rate of speed she normally traveled, it should only have taken less than an hour to make the 383,797-kilometer journey. Yet because of the negative effects flying supersonic speeds would have on Stokely's still fragile human body, the trip would take four times as long to make. In time, he would become accustomed to outer space travel with no long-lasting ill effects.

When Kenya heard her brother coming to, she was thrilled that he'd be awake to actually experience portions of their magnificent flight to the moon. She knew he was watching her, but she wasn't able to respond because she had to focus on safely piloting the spaceorb.

Since this was her first solo spaceflight, she preferred to rely upon the technologically advanced instruments to descend far enough down in order to make a visual approach for landing. Through the vessel's cosmicshield, Kenya had an unobstructed view of the lunahstation runways, brightly illuminated in the distance of the black sky.

When Stokely finally awakened, he was slightly disoriented having no idea of how long he'd been out. Last thing he remembered was holding onto Kenya inside that magnificent light and waving good-bye to Malcolm. He now found himself securely strapped to a chair courtesy of a safety harness holding him upright while his sister piloted at the controls. As he took it all in, he didn't know what pleased him more... The return of Kenya, or watching his big sister do her thing.

"Hey sis," he called out excitedly. "I can't believe you're actually piloting a spaceship! This is so cool!"

Standing at the center console totally immersed within a section of a very realistic looking space-sky, Kenya skillfully zipped past asteroids as large as skyscrapers, avoiding debris from old satellites, rockets, and various other unidentifiable stuff. Dexterous hands and fingers danced around the celestial images as if she were performing a sign language symphony for the universe.

Momentarily breaking her concentration, Kenya offered her brother a quick smile before shushing him with a finger poised to her mouth. She had to maintain focus. One missed movement and they both might end up orbiting the earth with the rest of all that debris.

Stokely held off asking the zillion questions that swirled within, opting instead to take this opportunity to study his surroundings. The flight bridge of the spaceship was nothing like what he imagined, nor did it resemble what was depicted in the hundreds of space movies he'd seen in his lifetime. What did surprise him was how sleek and modern this... vessel, was. He expected to see hundreds of exposed buttons, knobs, and circuit breakers inside the compartment. But there were none. Every surface was luminescent, emitting filtered light, as if the vessel itself was powered by the beams of the rising sun. The spacious "window" offered a spectacular panoramic view of the vast night sky. He could tell they must be traveling very fast, as the image of the earth grew further and further away, whereas the moon loomed large in the distance. He recollected the first time he saw the moon up close. It was through the lens of Kenya's beloved telescope, the one her parents bought when she declared she wanted to become an astronaut. From the age of seven, he had considered those craters to be nothing more than 'blemishes' on the face of the moon.

"Wow!" Stokely exclaimed looking through the window. "We're so close, it looks like I can reach out and touch it." But when he tried to raise his arms, he saw that both were securely strapped to the armrests of the chair.

Unfortunately, the very second she disconnected the autopilot and went visual is when she heard Stokely's distress. Sensing his burgeoning fear, she regretted not adequately explaining the detoxification process before injecting the toxicity removal serum into his arm. But mostly she regretted not telling him that they'd be landing on the moon. At the high rate of speed she was flying, she couldn't afford to take her focus off the controls even for a second.

"Teacher!" Kenya called out telepathically. *"My brother is in distress. Please send help!"*

Though Kenya had called out for assistance, there really was no need. What she failed to realize was, for as long as she was on God's green Earth, she would always be under the Teacher's watchful eye. With the concern of a father for a daughter flying solo for the first time, he never stopped monitoring her status. Thus, he had already dispatched two brothahs who would—within moments of each other's arrival—get the situation under control.

The Teacher relayed, "It is done."

"Thank you," she replied, with a mixture of gratitude and relief.

Kenya began their initial descent using a practiced sequence of hand movements, zooming past meteorites that appeared like streaks of light passing by. Her dancing fingers reminded Stokely of the fluttering of a hummingbird's wings.

Before Stokely realized it, they were skirting the lunar surface. That's when the moon's 'blemishes' revealed themselves as greyish craggy mountain ranges, bordering hundreds-miles wide valleys. With the realization that they were actually going to land on the moon, he felt as if he had gotten sucker-punched in the throat. He struggled against the safety harness and arm restraints that refused to budge. Even more worrisome than being unable to free himself from the seat was discovering the small contraption attached to his wrist, pumping a clear fluid through a tube into his veins.

"Oh shit!" he whispered to himself, "What the fuck have I gotten myself into?"

Fear is a funny thing. It can sneak up and grab you before you even realize it's there. One moment Stokely was proudly watching Kenya pilot the spacevessel, excited to be sharing an amazing adventure with his long-lost sister. Then, the very moment when he realized they were no longer on earth, he allowed the fear of the unknown to take over. Hollywood movies featuring horrific alien monsters that wanted to inhabit his body and take over his mind flooded his thoughts. In a matter of moments, all of Malcolm's fear became his.

~ ~ ~

Stokely struggled unsuccessfully to free himself from the seat harness. Yet the more he struggled, the tighter the restraints became, causing him to panic even more. As his breathing become shallow, he realized he was starting to hyperventilate, so he focused on the tube in his forearm. Using his teeth, he tried to wiggle it free.

There was a sudden increase in temperature within the cabin. All of a sudden, a Nigiro brothah materialized in the compartment. Within seconds of the first, another brothah appeared by Stokely's side. In a silky-smooth bass baritone voice that even the likes of Barry White might envy, the first brothah warmed Stokely calmly, "I wouldn't do that if I were you."

"Who the fuck are you?!" Stokely shouted.

The second brothah raised his large hand holding that ankh object towards Stokely and projected a calming thought into his mind. He visibly relaxed as if he were given a sedative rather than a mere suggestion.

Kenya overheard the commotion. However, since it was the Teacher who'd sent the brothahs in response to her request for help, she had no reason to believe Stokely was in any danger. So she proceeded with making the final preparations for landing, vowing to provide her brother with a more complete explanation at a later time.

"W-w-who are you?" Stokely asked again, trying his best to not be frightened. The men had a 'familiar' quality, as if he should somehow know them. He guessed their heights to be between 9 and 10 feet, even taller than the tallest people on the planet, Africa's South Sudanese *Dinka Tribe*. The skin on their bearded faces was so melanin rich, it almost didn't appear real. Each wore his shoulder-length hair in free-formed locs that skirted the collars of their still energized spacesuits. Mirrored goggles that protected their eyes from the bright lights they were exposed to when 'transmissioning', shaded their faces. Each one held a footlong golden ankh in his hand.

"Do not fear," the first one said. "We have come to assist in removing your distress."

"Where did you come from?" Stokely asked, suddenly feeling less afraid.

"We are Nigiro," explained the taller one with the deeper voice.

"You guys are real *Nigiro*?!" Stokely said excitedly, noticing that Kenya was totally engrossed in doing that cool fluttering thing with her hands.

Both nodded.

"Wait! You guys speak English?!"

"We communicate in the language you understand," explained the first brothah.

"Cool! My name is Stokely. Of course, I don't know my *real* name. I'm Kenya's little brother," he chattered uncharacteristically. "I'd offer to shake your hands, but as you can see... I'm a little tied up."

The brothahs were listening but chose not to respond.

"Know what? After reading my sister's book, I think I might be Nigiro too," he proudly declared.

The second brothah replied, "After all this is over, you will once again remember to whom you belong."

"Cool!" Stokely addressed the taller one because he seemed to be in charge. "By the way, what's this stuff goin' into my arm?"

"It is a 'detoxification' serum to remove impurities from your body," he explained. "It will permit your human lungs to adapt to breathing in the lunah atmosphere which has different ratios of nitrogen, oxygen, argon, carbon-dioxide, and water vapor than what you're used to breathing on earth.

"Kenya cool with this?"

The first brothah cocked his head to the side inquisitively at Stokely's continued reference to temperature. However, the second one didn't miss a beat when he replied, "Considering it was the sistah who initiated the serum, I would say, yes, she is *cool* with this."

"Where are we?" Stokely asked, looking past them through the cosmicshield.

The first brothah explained, "We are about to land on what you know to be, *the Earth's moon*. In actuality it is one of an infinite number of lunah waypoint stations located throughout the galaxy. This is the place where we have gathered."

"What are you talking about?" Stokely's eyes suddenly darted towards Kenya.

"The sistah is busy," explained the second brothah placing another calming thought towards Stokely. "She will explain more to you later."

"I gotcha. I'm cool," he uttered.

Monitoring the situation while maintaining control of the spacepod, Kenya relayed, *"My brothahs, thank you for your help. Now, please prepare yourselves for landing."*

Stokely sat back in his seat, this time with visible relief. He watched the brothahs physically strap into chairs that seemingly magically appeared on either side of him. He figured they would remain to prevent him from freaking out and possibly distracting Kenya from making a safe landing. But they need not have been concerned. Stokely was fascinated by what he saw through that cosmicshield! He never knew there were so many stars out there in the sky.

Zipping through softy-lit valleys with luminous rocky mountain ranges bordering on either side, he imagined the entire moon was illuminated within by one humongous LED lightbulb located far beneath the surface. Despite his 'understanding' that the moon was illuminated as a result of the direct reflection of the sun, what he saw with his own two eyes was every bit of the moon's surface was 'glow-in-the-dark'! Further out in the distance, he spotted what he thought was a spaceport due to multiple runways outlined by brightly-lit florescent blue lights.

Stokely chuckled. As much as the thought of ancient black people living on the moon fascinated him, the pride he felt watching his sister flying that UFO all by herself, surpassed even that. For the first time in his life, he dropped his guard. He thought to himself, *'If this is a dream, I don't ever want to wake up.'*

Chapter Eighteen

Early the next morning, as I sat at the kitchen table making final adjustments to the book cover's design, the doorbell rang. I shrugged into my robe, went to the foyer, and opened the front door fully expecting to see Stokely standing on the other side with an apologetic grin on his face. Not only didn't he come home last night, but he hadn't bothered to text me that he'd be out overnight. But as Gerald reminded me throughout the evening when I checked my cell phone for a message or missed call, Stokely was a grown man who was spending time with his very responsible brother. Thus, I wasn't overly concerned when I hadn't heard from him by the time we went to bed.

"Well, good morning, you two. You're out early," I greeted Malcolm and Drena, who carried a still sleeping Mali on her shoulder.

"Good morning Mama Zumira. I hope we didn't wake you."

"You didn't. I've been up for a while. C'mon in," I said, with hugs for all.

"Good morning, Mom. I brought donuts," Malcolm said, thrusting the box towards me. "Is Dad up yet?"

"He's in the back getting dressed," I explained, accepting the box. I strained my neck towards the jeep parked in the driveway and asked, "Where's Stokely?"

"Um... Mama Zumira, let's go inside first," Drena jumped in, closing the door behind us. "I'll make a strong pot of coffee to go with the donuts."

"What's wrong?" I asked, immediately sensing something was off.

Malcolm gently lifted Mali from Drena's shoulder. He strolled to the living room where he laid the baby on the leather sofa, remembering to place her blanket down first, before going off to find his father.

Drena's normally sunny disposition was gone, and it had nothing to do with the time of the day. I sensed they weren't telling me something. I turned to her and slowly asked, "Where is Stokely?"

"All I can say, Mama Zumira, is Malcolm has something to tell you and Pops," she said, taking the donuts. "I'll go start the coffee."

Standing there in the foyer, my mind went in all different directions. First I imagined Stokely was hurt. Or in jail. Or worse. Then I became angry with myself for imaging the most horrific scenarios and allowing fear to take ahold of me. I shook it off. From the past several months, I learned that all it takes is a small crack in your faith to allow evil inside. From out of nowhere, I heard a tiny voice inside my thoughts, quietly whispering, *'Be good, or be gone! Love will win in the end.'* And all of a sudden, I not only captured a glimpse of Kenya's face, but Stokely's smiling face, too. I felt our spirits connect. I don't know how I knew this, but I did. That's when I instinctively knew both my children were alive and well.

"Mama Zumira? Are you all right?"

When I snapped back, I was sitting at the kitchen table with my daughter-in-law knelt down by my side, holding my hand. A look of concern was plastered all over her face.

"Yeah... I think so. What just happened?" I asked, still feeling confused. "For a second there, it felt like I was somewhere else."

"Are you alright? Should I get Malcolm?"

Drena's concern was endearing. I shook my head and instead asked, "How did I get in the kitchen?"

"You walked in here, sat down, and rested your head on the table. I thought you had fainted. Are you okay?"

After allowing the realization of what had occurred in that moment to sink in, I exclaimed, genuinely surprised, "Oh my goodness! I believe I might have connected with Stokely's spirit! Just like that time when I *felt* Kenya's. I received a message to let me know that he's, *'Cool'*."

"Stay there. I'll get you a cup of coffee," Drena said, wanting to busy her mind on something else. As she listened to her mother-in-law, and with Malcolm's mumblings from last night about his brother and Kenya being carried off in a UFO fresh on her mind, she silently prayed that whatever 'special gene' the Williams family seemed to carry, that it would skip her child.

"I don't know what just happened, but I'm going to be fine." I whispered a familiar aspiration to calm my wildly beating heart, "God doesn't give me what I can *handle*. God helps me *handle* what I am *given*."

Drena arranged the donuts on a platter. Extra cream and sugar on the counter next to them. She added sweet cream and an extra shot of agave to her mother-in-law's coffee—just the way Mama Zumira liked it—before placing the steaming cup in front of her. Malcolm chose that moment to stroll into the kitchen on the heels of his father. From the look on her father-in-law's face, she determined Gerald had already received the news about Stokely. Now it was time for Malcolm to break it to his mother. She took a deep breath and joined Malcolm, standing by his side to provide moral support.

Malcolm too took a deep breath, exhaling strongly. He said, "Mom, I'm glad you're sitting down. I have something to tell you."

"What is it, my love?" I asked gently.

"I don't know how to say this," he said, looking to his father for reassurance.

Gerald, standing behind me, placing his hands on my shoulders, I heard him sigh, "Go on, son. Tell her."

"It's about Stokely, isn't it?" I blurted out.

All eyes were now on me when I calmly said, "He's not coming home, is he?"

"No, he's not. But how did you know?"

"I just know. That's all," I replied, noting the growing look of concern on my son's face. "Look, son. There's nothing to worry about, okay. Stokely is fine. Now how about you pass me one of those decadent donuts."

Malcolm went to pour himself and his father a cup of coffee. This was going to be more difficult that he thought. His mother had the appearance of someone whose mind had finally snapped.

"Sweetheart," Gerald said with his hand rested on my shoulder. "Give Malcolm a chance to explain. I think you'll want to hear this."

We heard Mali beginning to stir in the living room. Drena went to see about her while Malcolm took a seat at the kitchen table. Gerald followed suit taking the opposite chair.

"I'll listen to what you have to say, but I just want you both to know that I'm fine. In my heart, I know that Stokely is safe."

"Well, I'm glad *you* feel that way, because I'm not so sure..."

"Alright. Tell me what happened. I'm listening."

Malcolm went on to explain the events from last night, from the moment he and Stokely left their house, up to the point when he watched both younger siblings disappear in a UFO camouflaged by the clouds.

I hung on Malcolm's every word, watching him struggle with explaining the inexplicable. By the time he had finished, my untouched cup of coffee had gone cold. Despite his earlier declaration that he was onboard with publishing Kenya's book, I could only imagine how difficult it must have been for my even-keeled son to process what he'd seen last night.

"So let me get this straight. You're telling us you actually saw Stokely leave with Kenya?" Gerald asked. "In a UFO?"

"That's right, Dad. I'm telling you the truth. He joined her in that beam of light. They waved goodbye to me and then I watched them ascend into a cloud. I only saw the spaceship for a brief moment before it zoomed off."

Gerald rubbed the 3-day old stubble sprouting from his chin, what he affectionately called his 'whiskers'. He was convinced now more than ever that something amazing was happening to his family. For him, his wife, and every single one of his children to have experienced powerful encounters with the unknown couldn't have been a mere coincidence.

I recalled an earlier conversation I had with Kenya. Lowering my voice to barely above a whisper, I said, "Malcolm... This isn't your fault. I asked Kenya to take Stokely back with her."

"You did what?!" Gerald shouted. "When did this happen?"

"The same night she introduced me to the Teacher. She made Nigiro sound so wonderful, I asked if she would consider taking Stokely with her."

Gerald said dismayed. "You must have forgotten to tell me that part."

"Sweetheart, everything has been moving so fast lately. I guess I'm still getting my memory back of that night in bits and pieces."

"First Kenya, now Stokely..." Gerald stated, "I don't know whether to be depressed or elated!" Ever since that fateful night when he found Zumira, fully dressed and asleep in bed during the middle of the day, he silently wondered if others were also experiencing this spiritual 'shift' within the atmosphere. He actually started to believe that God really was working miracles in their lives.

"He's safe. I know it deep down in my soul." I exhaled all my worries away when I declared, "Now I no longer have to worry about Stokely being out there in the streets. He's with his sister, and his sister is with the Teacher. Which means, he is also with the Teacher."

"Dad, you're okay with all of this?" Malcolm asked, shocked.

Gerald nodded.

"Mama Zumira, I thought you'd be more upset..." Drena added, as she returned with a hungry Mali squirming in her arms.

Gerald lowered his eyes, resigned to the fact that there was so much more to life than he could see. He had witnessed far too many astonishing events for his child not to have been who she said she was. And just like that, he knew. Kenya *was* a beautiful child of The Most High God. So was Zumira. So was Malcolm. So was Stokely. As was he. And with that revelation, he became awash in a sea of peace.

"What now?" Malcolm asked, feeling spent.

I explained, "Well son, after the book is published, I will gift it to as many of our family and friends as possible. Hopefully, they'll read it."

"Mom, what do you mean?" Malcolm's sensibilities on financial irresponsibility kicked in when he uttered, "You're *giving* the book away?! Why?!"

"The point isn't to make money. We're here to deliver an important message to God's children. They must recognize the time we are in. Obviously, since they came for Stokely, the Nigiro rescue mission must be closer at hand than we thought. Those who have discernment will understand."

My phone chimed with an incoming text, distracting everyone from our excited conversation.

"Who in the world is texting me this early?" I asked, aloud, checking my cell phone, feeling slightly annoyed that I didn't have the foresight to store it away in the lead-lined box before we began talking. *Oh well. What was said, was said. If anyone or anything dared to eavesdrop on our conversation, they got an earful.*

"Who's that?" Gerald asked, noting the surprised expression on my face.

"Oh my goodness! It's from Sharleen," I said. Momentarily putting our discussion about Stokely aside, I allowed the cryptic words from her text to sink it.

"Is she okay?" Gerald asked, leaning forward.

"Yeah," I replied.

"What did she say?"

"She says, 'We red NIGIRO! Wow! R. putting 10 in action. More l8r'." I leaned back in my seat taking a deep breath. "Since they're moving forward with TEN, they must believe Kenya's story is true."

"Here we go..." Gerald replied, glancing at the survival pamphlets sticking out of my canvas tote bag sitting next to the door.

Drena asked, "What is *TEN*?"

"*Thriving & Existing in Nature*," I explained, not wanting to say more. "I'll get in touch with them later."

"I gotta agree with Ricky, this time," Gerald stated, forlornly. "All one has to do is turn on the news to see the state of this world. Wars. Racism. Global pandemics. Death and destruction. Poverty. Climate change. World hunger. It's the song that never ends..."

"Well, this sucks!" Drena whispered, snuggling Mali a tad closer to her chest.

"Sure does..." Malcolm co-signed. "First my sister disappears, now my little brother. What next?"

I looked at my husband, my son, and his wife. They didn't get it. They were looking outwardly, seeing only the worldly view of life. Which was not the right way. They needed only to look inward to get the big picture. I had to set the record straight.

"Hey you guys! Cheer up!" I stood at the table, proclaiming, "Kenya and Stokely are alive and well! This isn't a time to be feeling depressed. There is nothing to be scared of. Don't you see!" I explained, "Nothing bad is going to happen to us. You must understand that!"

"How do you know that, mom?"

"Because I know we come from greatness!"

Gerald snapped out of whatever funk that had overtaken him. He stood, draping his arm across my shoulder and lightheartedly said, "That's right, you two! Listen to your mother. She must be getting some of those downloads of wisdom that Kenya talked so much about."

"Well, I don't know if I am any wiser than I was when this all started, but I sure do feel like a powerful force is guiding me," I explained. They all appeared to be struggling with my explanation, so I continued, trying to help them understand, "I feel like I'm getting extra help, not only with this book, but with life in general. Like all I have to do is get my 'self' out of the way..."

"Baby, I don't know what any of this means. Or where it's going to take us. All I know is nothing bad has happened to us..."

I looked at my husband, finishing the sentence for him "... and I expect it never will."

Suddenly, a series of vibrations—similar to what I felt both times Kenya was near—'flowed' over the room like gentle waves coming ashore. I started to feel a little shaky, so I retook my seat at the table. This strange feeling I became awash in was something new, yet totally pleasant at the same time. I looked to my husband hoping he too was experiencing the sensation. I tilted my head towards him with an unspoken question, *Do you feel that?*

He nodded gingerly in my direction. Upon realizing we were somehow sharing thoughts, Gerald and I broke out into nervous laughter.

The frightened looks on Malcolm and Drena's faces made our laughter pause. Whether or not they experienced the vibrations Gerald and I felt remained a mystery. I did not want to add to their distress in case they didn't.

"C'mon guys, relax," I said. "Whatever that's about to happen will bring in a glorious new day for the oppressed. The down-trodden will stand up! The last will be first and the first will be last!"

"But what about Stokely?" Malcolm asked.

"Stokely will be fine because he is where he belongs. Safe with *our* people," I stated confidently. "The Nigiro!"

"Dang! That must be one heck of a book!"

"Believe me, Drena. It is," Gerald remarked.

"After everything that Malcolm told me about last night," she exclaimed excitedly, "I really cannot wait to read it now!"

"Well, all right!" I said, hi-fiving her.

Gerald and I watched a palpable expression of relief replace Drena's previous one of dread. Our beautiful daughter-in-law gradually released any remaining reservations she had about our family and joined my husband and I in gleeful laughter.

"What's so funny?" Malcolm asked, suddenly feeling left out.

Gerald advised, "Son, go back and re-read Kenya's story."

"I don't see how that's going to change anything, but fine. I'll read it again," he replied, recalling how his sister offered him the same advice.

"My love," I explained. "We are not trying to be cruel. But that is the only way you will understand what is truly going on. After you do that, then we'll have another conversation."

Chapter Nineteen

Stokely and I still had adequate time remaining before we would be requested to return to the hanger for his introduction to the brothahs. After we landed, he was thoroughly checked over by a healer who was happy to report that Stokely had no ill effects from either the detoxification serum or the space travel. After he got over the initial shock that we had actually landed on the moon, learning how to breathe the lighter moon air was critical. After several episodes where he couldn't catch his breath, he eventually relaxed enough to not think about breathing at all. I'd actually forgotten how excited I was the first time I realized people—especially black people—lived on the moon, but I got to experience it all over again through my brother's eyes.

After getting Stokely settled into his sleeping quarters, I returned to one of the 'classrooms' to debrief my instructor with details of the flight. I was excited because I know The Teacher would be there waiting for me.

"*Braveheart, you did very well,*" relayed the Teacher, catching his first glimpse at me.

"*Thank you, Teacher,*" I replied, excitedly.

"*Your brother? How is he?*"

"*Stokely is very happy. He is looking forward to meeting with you,*" I said, gratefully, looking up at The Teacher's full height. "*But of course, you already know that.*"

"All will be revealed in good time, Braveheart," he replied, his deep voice bouncing off the high ceiling of the classroom. "For now, attend to your family."

"Thank you," I replied.

"*I will see you again soon,*" the Teacher relayed. He raised the gold ankh, motioned to take a step forward, and then dematerialized as quickly as he came.

My debriefing to the post-flight training crew only took minutes because my first solo mission had gone very well. I returned to Stokely's quarters. When he opened the door, he was fully dressed, wearing his very first spacesuit.

"Why are you up? You're supposed to be resting."

"I'm too excited to sleep. When I saw this cool looking spacesuit was for me, I couldn't wait to put it on," Stokely said, amazed at how well it fit. "What's it made of?"

"I am unsure of the material. But this specially designed exoskeleton spacesuit synchs up with your biological system to protect you from the harsh outerspace atmosphere. It also naturally cools you down or warms you up."

"I feel like a superhero!" Stokely laughed admiring his reflection in the floor to ceiling metallic wall covering.

"Space flight can be tough on the body the first few times out. You should take it easy."

"I'm good. This is my first time on the moon. And I don't know if I'm ever gonna return, so I want to see as much of it as I possibly can."

"In that case, we shall go sight-seeing."

"Right on, sis! Let's do this thing!"

I wanted my brothah to experience what I felt the first time I landed on the moon, so with permission from the elders I borrowed a lunahcraft (a high-tech flying version of a jetski) and after a quick tour of the lunah facility, I gave him a safety briefing on what to expect when we ventured outside the perimeter. I showed him how to properly attach the required lunahband to his wrist. As it was explained to me, the lunahband operates similar to how the nicotine patch works. It distributes a steady dose of specially developed nutrients into the bloodstream which allows humans, new to the moon, the ability to breath in the lunah air with no ill effects to their bodies.

Stokely and I walked through spacious climate-controlled corridors to reach the 'hanger' where thousands of lunahcrafts vertically arranged along the walls, hovered in their assigned parking stall. I waved my hand over the control center; the 'artificial intelligence' immediately recognized me by my vibrational signature, selecting the vehicle best suited for my sightseeing tour with Stokely. Within moments, we watched our assigned lunahcraft disengage from its stall located six stories high. It gradually descended, automatically making minor directional adjustments until it stopped an arm lengths away from me.

"Is this what we're riding?! Stokely slid his hand over the smooth metallic exterior.

I nodded.

"Sweet!" he said, climbing behind the driver's seat.

"Not yet," I helped him get down. "For now, you are the passenger. And remember the safety briefing. We will be flying at extremely high rates of speed, so make sure you are securely fastened in."

"Don't worry about me!" Stokely said, climbing on the rear seat. "I got this."

The best part about being on the moon is seeing the bluish-grey lunahscape up close. With the exception of the color, others have told me it looks similar to the landscape within the Zion National Park located in the state of Utah.

"Are you ready?" I asked, getting a feel for how this particular unit flew.

"Ready as I'll ever be!" he replied.

Just as soon as I began to accelerate, I heard a shout of surprise come from Stokely. I immediately stopped. He told me he'd almost fallen off the lunahcraft! Upon my determining there was no equipment malfunction, he finally admitted he hadn't properly secured the safety harness because he'd forgotten how. After I made sure he knew how to properly 'lock-in', we were on our way.

Twenty minutes and hundreds of miles later, we stopped for a break. I pulled into an area known for the best celestial viewing. We hovered the lunahcraft and I helped him dismount.

"Welcome to Lunah!" I threw my arms open, gesturing to the vast openness.

"Wow!" he said, removing his protective helmet, confident in his newfound ability to breath in the cool lunar air.

"What do you think?" I asked, watching him take it in.

"It's beautiful up here. Maybe a little too quiet, but I could get used to this if it wasn't so dark."

"Not all of Lunah is shrouded in darkness; only the land where the sunshine never reaches. If you were to travel to where the sun is able to fully reach the surface, you would find it resembles the desert during the hottest part of the day. Unfortunately, that trip requires a much different lunah vessel for our safe transportation than what we're using today."

"So the lunah station is located on the 'dark side of the moon'?" he asked looking confused.

"We do receive some sunlight, but, yes, an entire Nigiro waypoint station is located on the dark side. If it was operating on the sunny side of the 'moon', it would then be possible for man to see our movement."

Wow, everything I thought I knew about the moon was a lie! Just like practically else I've been taught. "Hey sis, can I ask you somethin' that's been botherin' me?"

"Of course."

"Why did you bring me back with you?"

"The Teacher told me to."

"I read your story so I know you know what your gift is. But why am I here?"

"I did not ask the Teacher 'why' he requested you, Stokely. That was not for me to know."

"Do you always do what the Teacher says?" He laughed. "Mom and Dad would be surprised to find that out because they said you always questioned everything they had to say."

"When it comes to following the Teacher's instructions, yes, I always do as I am told. Without question."

"So you've changed. That's cool." Stokely sighed in frustration, "I don't have any special gifts or talents that I know of. Maybe I'll become a writer. Like you."

"My purpose might be completely different than yours. I discovered my gift. In time, you will discover why and what you have been called to do."

Searching the clear dark skies above, observing constellations he had never known existed, he contemplated, "Hey sis, I have another question."

"Please, go on."

"Is… Is that… Is that *Earth*?"

"It's beautiful, isn't it?" I said, remembering how I too was fascinated the first time I saw Earth from a distance, awash in a sea of darkness. It appeared so… *Fragile.*

"Yeah, it *is* beautiful, but it looks much *smaller* than I thought it would. If I didn't know what I was lookin' at, I might have thought it was the *Moon's* moon," Stokely said, before adding, "I'll tell you what… Bein' up here with you puts my life down there on earth in the proper perspective. All my troubles seem insignificant."

I made the gentle waving motion with my hand to signify, 'bye-bye' to his troubles. I then received another incoming transmission from an elder, thanks to my newly developed ability to communicate within the spirits realm. I pinched my middle finger to my thumbs and fluttered my response that we'd be there shortly. I needed a few more minutes with my younger brother.

Stokely's mind was flooded with colliding questions. Picking one randomly he asked, "What's that thing you do with your hands?"

"One moment, please." I went through a series of practiced hand movements to tap into a virtual universal database of every inspirational song every created by Nigiro. I thought it would be easier to demonstrate than explain. As the first notes of Stevie Wonder's 'Rocket Love' blasted from the lunah-mobiles speakers, I 'fluttered' the first couple of stanzas while Stokely sat back and watched.

After a round of applause, he said, "That was a really cool dance, Kenya. But what does it mean?"

"It is a form of vibrational communication. The elders taught me how to 'flutter' with my hands so I'd have the ability to communicate within the spiritual realm. Because music is the universal language, the elders used music created by the Nigiro as a way to reach me."

"Huh?" Stokely said, obviously confused. "What does that have to do with your cool hand dance?"

"Music is composed of rhythmic vibrations that create sound notes. With every precise movement of my body, I am manipulating the air, moving it here and there, creating a vibration in the unseen world that travels throughout the universe. I have the ability to interpret musical notes and use my body movements to create vibrations in the spiritual realm. It's like throwing a handful of pebbles in a still pond, but what most fail to realize is that tiny pebble moves the water below as well as the surface. I am a bridge between the seen and the unseen. This is how I communicate." As an afterthought, I said, "It's possible my hand and finger flutters may have been a precursor to modern-day sign language."

"Sis, I can't tell you how cool this is!" he gushed, taking in the magnificent view experienced by only a handful of lucky men. "You know, I was surprised when I read about black and brown people bein' abducted and brought to the moon to build an international lunar colony. That sounds very similar to how Africans were stolen from African and then enslaved in America to build their colonies. But who would've thought Nigiro built somethin' this amazin' on the moon!"

"The earth's international space exploration community abandoned their plan for a secretive moon base when astronauts reported back that it was being used as a galactic waypoint."

"Dang sis! I don't know whether to be excited or scared to death. This is all happenin' so fast."

"You are safe here. No one will harm you ever again."

"That's good to know!" he exclaimed, dropping his glance to his feet. "Whoa! What's this we're standin' in? Is it poisonous?"

"No, it isn't. This plant life is similar to the flora that grows in the earth's desert."

"Is it alive?" Stokely asked, gently nudging the footlong blades with the toe of his spaceboots. "It looks like dead grass."

"Very little sunlight reaches this side of the moon. The plant-life does not receive sufficient light to allow the chlorophyl to turn green."

"And yet, they live," Stokely whispered, running his hand across the plant matter. He was amazed by the silky thick texture that reminded him of a bath mat at home.

An incoming telepathic transmission caught their attention. "Children, children..."

Stokely's facial expression suddenly changed from curiosity to astonishment. He turned to me and asked, "Did you hear that?"

"Yes, it is the Teacher."

"Wherever you are in the universe, first search within. There is much more to learn."

"The Teacher has requested our immediate return to the station."

"That's not what *I* heard!" he looked at me strangely. "How do you know the Teacher wants us back right now?"

"I learned how to discern incoming messages. I cannot explain how I knew what the Teacher's message meant, I just did," I answered, climbing into the pilot's seat of the lunahcraft.

"Somehow that makes perfect sense," he said with a thoughtful smile.

Another incoming transmission to me interrupted our conversation.

"He is ready?" relayed the Teacher.

I alone had received the Teacher's incoming message. With a full understanding of what The Teacher was asking, I replied, "Yes, Teacher. We are ready to return."

Unaware of the private conversation I was having with the Teacher, Stokely's attention was focused elsewhere. "Hey sis!" he called out, pointing towards the dark sky. "What is that?!"

"I'm not sure what you are asking," I feigned. Though I didn't answer directly, I suspected he knew that I knew to what he was referring.

"Over there! I've never seen anythin' like that! What is it?"

"It's a planet. I can't tell you much more."

"What?! There's an entire other planet out here that I didn't know about?! For real?!" He scratched his head and wondered, *"How can you keep an entire planet hidden? Why would they keep it a secret?"*

"Stokely, you will have time to ask me all the questions you'd like. For now, we need to return to the lunahstation. Please make sure your straps are tightened. I do not want you almost falling off again."

"Sorry about that," he said, unable to take his eyes off the massive reddish-orange celestial body nearly eclipsing the earth.

I waited for him to settle down. Once the lunahcraft was in flight, even though we could communicate via the earphones in our headgear, my primary focus would be on flying us back safely.

Stokely was barely able to contain his excitement at his newly found discovery. Continuing with his version of 'connect the breadcrumbs', he blurted out, "Sis! I know what it is! That must be the 'so-called' hidden planet Uncle Ricky told me about!"

As I plugged in the GPS coordinates to return to base, I recalled the first time the Teacher tried to inform me that our ancestors had originated elsewhere in the universe, on the planet Nigiro. Back then, I must have momentarily lost my mind when I foolishly dismissed what he was trying to tell me.

Without answering directly, I replied, "The Teacher will explain more later."

"Hey sis, do you remember us havin' a family reunion in Forest Park when I was about five or six? Dad was grillin' ribs. Lots of family from out of town was there. When it started to get dark, I saw somethin' weird in the sky. I asked everybody what that big red thing that looked like a balloon was. Smarty pants Malcolm said it was the last full moon of the summer. He called it the 'Harvest Moon'. He explained it was that color because it was hangin' low on the horizon. But I always liked great-Nana's explanation much better."

"I remember what she said. Do you?"

"Yeah, I do because it didn't make sense until now. She told us *'a harvest moon provides a special kinda light to guide the way for the angels yet to come.'*"

"That's exactly what I remember. Very good."

Stokely's mouth gaped open in surprise by the thought taking form in his mind. He sputtered, "Is... is that... is that planet... is that planet *Nigiro*?!"

The Teacher advised me to not speak about Nigiro just yet to Stokely. So, I merely nodded.

"What?! For real?!" he shouted, with his eyes widened in fascination. "Wait 'til I tell Malcolm that there is another planet out there! That is really gonna blow his mind!"

"Come now, brothah. We must be going."

"Awesome! You just called me, 'brothah'!" Picking up on my train-of-thought, Stokely shouted out elatedly, "I got it! Now I know why the dream about the fortune cookies stayed on my mind. *'They want to see me'*, is what that thing said. We're going to meet with the others and travel to planet Nigiro?!"

I smiled. He *had* read my story. "That's right, Stokely! You got it."

He sat back in his seat, pleased that he'd made the full-circle connection of discussing the dream with his parents; Kenya knowing that tidbit to prove to him she was his sister; and now, he was standing on the moon looking at the unknown planet of Nigiro, preparing to meet others like him on his journey there.

"Now may we go?" I asked amused, knowing full well the Teacher was listening as well.

"Okay. I'm ready now," he replied, lowering the faceshield of his helmet.

"Hold on tightly, here we go!"

I launched the lunahcraft with a flourish of my hand. We took off and headed in the direction of the lunahbase. I tried flying as closely to the ground as possible because I wanted Stokely to see the amazing luminous lunahscape up close, but he never had the chance to because I was flying too fast. Everything must have looked like a blur to him, but it took less than half the time to return to the waypoint as it took to fly the 100 kilometers out. Before either of us realized it, we were inside the hanger watching the lunahcraft make its way back to its vertical hoverstall.

"Thanks for the sightseeing tour, sistah," he said, using the title for the first time. "I will never forget it."

"You are very welcome. I'll meet you back here after you've had time to cleanup," I told Stokely. "But don't be too long."

"Give me five minutes!" he shouted over his shoulder. "I can't wait to see what's going to happen next."

As I watched my brother's happy gait towards his sleeping quarters, greeting everyone he happened to pass by, I exhaled in relief. I was so happy to finally know that my brother was going to be alright.

~ ~ ~

It didn't take very long for me to explain to Stokely what was about to happen, mostly because I did not know myself. But whatever it was, was going to be impactful!

The floor of the open hanger resembled a summer camp with the Nigiro as the counselors and us hue-mans as the 'children'. I scanned the crowd, easily picking out others who resembled Stokely and myself, not only in height, but also in varying shades of brown. There must have been thousands of 'us'—melanated men and women of all ages—inside that hanger. Each Nigiro stood tall amongst the five or six much shorter 'children' gathered around them. The excitement in the air was palpable.

Auntie Sistah, who I still privately regarded as 'Magnificent Queen', glided into the middle of the crowd gathered inside the hanger. Instead of wearing the usual flowing gowns, today she was dressed in an indigo-colored spacesuit. The gold collar encircling her neck was used to maximize the transfer of energy during teleportation. I hadn't seen her since that day I left the detoxification camp, so I was super excited to hear what she had to say. She waited until we were silent before she spoke.

"Greetings, brothahs and sistahs. Thank you all for being here."

Stokely turned to me and whispered," Is that the lady you wrote about in your book?"

"Yes, that is Auntie Sistah," I replied, overhearing various versions of the same question from the other new brothahs and sistahs gathered nearby.

"Wow! You weren't exaggerating! She *really* is beautiful!" he exclaimed.

"Shhhh..." I shushed him. "It is important that you listen very carefully to every word you receive."

Auntie Sistah quieted the remaining chatter with a flourish of her elegant hands. The crowd grew silent. As if on cue, twelve Nigiro Elders, including Sistah Seshat, suddenly materialized by her sides. Though Auntie was a woman of tall stature, she was dwarfed by the twelve ancient elders. They were dressed in white spacesuits with gold collars that glittered alive with energy. In their hands, they clutched intricately etched silver staffs, designed with the shape of a large ankh at the top. The crowd grew silent with anticipation to hear what each had to say.

"Children, you are Nigiro, from the Almighty God. Your being here is not a mistake," Auntie Sistah relayed telepathically. *"By now many of you already know why we have called you together. For those who don't, I will provide a brief explanation. Because of its proximity to earth, the moon is being used as our gathering place. The Nigiro are in the final stages of the rescue mission."*

Whoops and hollers of cheer came from the recently arrived brothahs and sistahs from earth. Most of them, including Stokely, were still in a state of disbelief at their good fortune to be participating in an event that would become momentous in everyone's lives.

"Look upon the faces of the diaspora represented here! We have come from all four corners of the earth to be gathered today, on the 'Moon'. You children are blessed because you know who you are. Now it is time to wake the others!"

"Are you receiving this?" I relayed to Stokely, who appeared to be distracted by the appearance of the ancient ones. Each Elder, one-at-a-time, telepathically communicated their heartfelt

welcomes to the earth children who were gathered, offering comforting words of encouragement at our coming-to-an-end plight.

Shouts of joy in various languages continued throughout the building as the Elders welcomed us.

Stokely signaled that he was paying attention, but continued talking, "We look a lot like them! Except they're much taller than us. And they're in better shape. And their eyes are different. And they don't say much... Well, I guess we don't *really* look like them. But I'm digging the way they wear their natural hair in locs. Just like mine..."

My brother's nervous reaction made me smile. He hadn't changed that much after all. Whenever he was excited or nervous, he turned into a little chatterbox. By-the-way, although Stokely and I received our telepathic transmissions in English, others received the message in their native tongue.

In a flash of blinding light, the Teacher made a dramatic entrance as he materialized from another realm. The silver collar of his emerald green spacesuit sparkled as if it were still energized by kinetic energy. He gave a brief nod acknowledging the Elders before asking Auntie Sistah to proceed.

"Wow! Is that the Teacher?" Stokely asked, over the roar of the crowd.

I nodded and relayed, *"Please, brothah. Try using your telepathy to communicate."*

And he did, when he replied, *"The Teacher looks nuthin' like I imagined. He could pass for a bass player from the 1970's."*

I giggled because I thought he resembled Verdine White.

Auntie Sistah paused for a moment to allow the joyous commotion to settle down before continuing, *"You all were selected to be here. This is not a competition. There is no test. You will be learning what your specific role is in the liberation of our people. As many of you already know, before you can free a person's body, you must first free their mind. You all are here to help us do that."*

More shouts of excitement came from the crowd.

"Some of you will return to Nigiro to be with the Teacher for more intense instruction, while others will spend 30 days here at the lunahstation, before your return journey to earth. To your communities. To your families."

By now, most of the sistahs and brothahs were well versed in the wonderful stories about Nigiro, but none had actually been there. If this were any other situation, one might expect to hear grumbling coming from the crowd. After all, who didn't want to go to Nigiro? But there were no complaints, only looks of joy beaming from everyone's faces. With the shape of the world today, we all knew someone had to make a change. *If not us, then who?*

"I will now turn you over to The Teacher. He will ensure you receive what you need to complete your mission," Auntie Sistah explained. She took a step back to join the Elders who stood now in a half circle.

"Greetings!" His deep rich, baritone voice boomed over the crowd.

"Greetings, Teacher!" replied a chorus of voices in varying languages.

"Welcome, children. Do not be dismayed by what you have seen on the earth. The time is now. The first will be last and the last will be first."

Shouts of jubilation erupted all over the hanger.

"The Elders you see standing before you represent the twelve tribes. Each tribe specializes in a discipline that is needed to free the minds of the Nigiro children who remain trapped in bondage. You will be under the tutelage of an elder who represents your particular gift." The Teacher paused to allow space for further explanation. **"As many of you have already learned, there are twelve unique Nigiro disciplines: Agriculturists, Teachers, Healers, Engineers, Scientists, Philosophers, Architects, Mathematicians, Carpenters, Technologists, Artists, and Great Warriors."**

I reminded Stokely telepathically, *"My tribe is comprised of Artists; Musicians. Painters. Sculptors. Poets, Writers and Storytellers."*

He acknowledged with a nod of his head.

The Teacher did not directly address anyone in particular, yet everyone understood the words he spoke were directed towards them, individually. **"In this present moment, whether you know it or not, your gift resides within."**

Stokely mentally reviewed the twelve disciplines trying to determine where he might fit in. Not a one came to mind. He whispered, suddenly becoming alarmed, "Kenya, I'm not an artist or any of those other disciplines. Does this mean we might be sent to different places?"

"You will go to where it has been pre-determined. I do not know where that location is. Just know that it does not matter where we physically reside; our spirits are forever joined as one," I replied, hoping he'd accept my explanation without alarm.

"We're gonna be apart?" Stokely's uncertainty of whether he was up to the challenge resurfaced. He started to chew the inside of his jaw, a gesture he did when we was really getting stressed.

One of the brothah's who had so graciously tended to him during the lunar flight there was within earshot of Stokely's question. He replied, *"My brothah, do not despair. We are the children of Almighty Allah. We are blessed with many talents and gifts. With patience, perseverance, and study, the time will come when you will uncover yours. For now, you shall remain with the brothahs. We will teach you all you need to know."*

Relieved by the brothah's explanation, Stokely once again relaxed. After all, his being there was not a mistake. He too belonged.

The Teacher continued, **"Some of you will return to the planet Nigiro with me. For a time there, you will be assigned to an elder who will help you to unlock the mysteries of your past. Others will remain here, where you will undergo intense training for the rescue**

mission on earth. For those who remain here for the great liberation, you too shall see Nigiro. When it is your time."

The roar of the crowd was deafening. I did not get the opportunity to visit with Auntie Sistah as she was busily assigning the children to an elder. One-by-one, without uttering a single word, the Elders raised their staffs, and returned to whichever realm it was they resided. The Teacher was the last to leave, in the same manner as when he arrived.

"I wonder what I'll be doin'..." Stokely whispered to himself, watching the assignments being handed out telepathically.

"Patience," I advised him.

"Hold on," he said, excitedly gripping my forearm. "I think I'm getting something!" When he received his notification that he was indeed going to Nigiro, he jumped for joy!

"Congratulations, my brothah! You are going to be so happy with the Teacher!"

"Are you staying here on lunah?" he asked.

"For now..." I replied.

"But we were just getting to know each other again."

"Do not be sad. We will be soon be together again," I replied.

"Sistah Kenya?" came a telepathic transmission from somewhere in the hanger. *"Girl... Is that really you?"*

I turned to scan the crowd, locking familiar eyes with the Jamaican. She, Sistah Oya, and KC were gathered in a small group away from the noise chattering away. She motioned for me to join them. No longer sullen, they all appeared healthy and filled with content.

"I shall be right back," I replied to Stokely. "I spotted the girls from the camp."

"I'm cool," he said, gravitating towards the two brothahs from earlier. Go hang out with your friends."

We embraced. I watched my younger brother grinning ear-to-ear. Stokely, appeared to be in his element conversing with the Nigiro brothahs. As I turned to make my way towards the old crew I did not know when I would see him again on this journey, but I knew from my own experience, he was in good hands.

Epilogue

Later that evening after Malcolm and Drena had gone home, I decided to take a nice long bath by candlelight to help ease my mind. Smooth jazz playing in the background of my spa-inspired bathroom helped to set the mood for total relaxation. While hot water spewed billowy steam into the bathroom's cooler air above, I sank down into the bathtub with thoughts of my children in mind.

I closed my eyes, resting my head against the fluffy bath pillow, and focused on a pleasant family memory, one when we were all together. With everything that had transpired over the past several years, I'd overlooked how truly blessed I am. I slowly exhaled. Nothing in my life was by happenstance, because it was all part of a larger plan that I had no knowledge of. And with that realization, my stress melted away into the saltwater. In that tiny space where my spirit goes before I fall asleep, a thought as quiet as a whisper slowly crept into the outer confines of my mind.

Ever so gradually, the surrounding darkness morphed into colorful images, becoming more defined until I felt as if I were watching my own private movie. I captured a brief glimpse of Kenya and Stokely together, talking and laughing with several others who I suspected were Nigiro because of their tall stature and dark skin. They all wore the same type of spacesuit, but the colors were different. Then I realized I was seeing a vision! My children are with the Nigiro, because they too are Nigiro! The jubilant expressions on their glowing faces was one of pure joy. They are now free!

I wept happy tears of joy with the knowledge that my children were placed here by The Almighty God to do good in this world. And that is when I finally understood. There *is* a purpose to our lives. We *were* put on this earth to do more than enslave ourselves to others; working for money, a material wealth, that doesn't exist. *Our* wealth is buried deep within. We are like mines filled with 'gold nuggets' that must be discovered before it is too late.

I absolutely do not want the world to end. But then again... perhaps I should. The present world we occupy is nothing more than a great big lie sold to us as 'The American Dream' which was never intended for us to achieve. So, come to think of it, who wants to live in a lie, white or otherwise? The more truth I've come to discover, within the depths of my soul, since I now know the truth of who I am, I can no longer continue to perpetuate the lie. And neither should anyone else. No matter the price I must pay, the truth must be told.

My name is Carmen 'Zumira' Williams, and I am honored to have been entrusted to deliver this very important message.

To Be Continued...

"One day soon we will receive the promise.
Gathered together beneath a blanket of
stars; as One.
Listening to funky music.
Because that is what YHWH has planned."